DARK DISCOVERIES

SUMMER 2013, Issue Number 24, www.DarkDiscoveries.com

Publisher
JournalStone Publishing, LLC

Editor-in-Chief
James R. Beach

Assistant Editors
Aaron J. French
Chuck Caruso
Elizabeth Reuter
Lacey Friedly (Submissions)

**Art Director,
Layout, and Design**
Cyrus Wraith Walker

Contributors
*David Morrell
Eric Red
Gene O'Neill
Stephen Mark Rainey
Jonathan Maberry & David F. Kramer
Cyrus Wraith Walker
William F. Nolan
Brian Sammons
James R. Beach
Mark Seiber
Aaron J. French
Trever Nordgren
Joel B. Kirkpatrick
Robert Morrish
Yvonne Navarro
Michael R. Collings
Amy Shane*

**Contributing
Artists/Photographers**
*Wayne Miller (Cover Image; pg 94)
Cyrus Wraith Walker (Various Inter)
Other Photographers (See Captions)*

DARK DISCOVERIES
(ISSN 1548-6842) is published (Qtrly)
by JournalStone Publications, 1261
Peachwood Court, San Bruno, CA
94066
Copyright ©2012 and beyond by
JournalStone Publications, and where
specified elsewhere in the issue. All rights
revert to the authors/artists upon publication,
with exception of the Logo and images
specifically created for the magazine.
Nothing shown can be reproduced without
obtaining written permission from the
creators. All book/magazine cover images
and author photos remain the copyrighted
property of their respective owners. Direct
all inquiries, address changes,subscription
orders, to:

Christopher C. Payne
JournalStone Publications
1261 Peachwood Court, San Bruno, CA
94066, U.S.A.
christophercpayne@journalstone.com.

Please make check or money order payable
to: JournalStone Publishing and send to the
address above.
Credit/Debit cards via Paypal at:
christophercpayne@journalstone.com.
Advertising rates available. Discounts for
bulk and standing retail orders.

Fiction

Non-Fiction

For Information and More...

Updates
from the Dark Beach

So here we are already with issue #24. Time sure flies when you're having fun. And it's been pretty fun lately. Lots of cool stuff happening on the DD front!

All of you by now should have received your copies of issue #23 and that was a doozy! 112 pages packed full of stuff. Our biggest issue ever (I'm still worn out from that one!). Thanks again to my awesome staff for helping me kick ass on that one – especially our design guy Cyrus Wraith Walker and my assistant editor Aaron French. You guys rock! And everybody who attended the World Horror Convention this last month in New Orleans should have gotten one for free in their goodie bags. (Thanks to our publisher Chris Payne for that one!) Hopefully you liked it and will keep coming back for more. There's going to be a lot more great stuff in upcoming issues. We're on a solid quarterly schedule with issues due out at the end of January, April, July and October. So spread the word!

On a sad note, Richard Matheson passed away on June 23rd, 2013 at 5:22 pm. A major, major legend in the fantasy field. Matheson was a big contributor to the original *Twilight Zone* series, wrote *I Am Legend*, *The Shrinking Man*, *Hell House*, *A Stir of Echoes* and many others (as well as being a huge influence on modern writers like Stephen King, Dean Koontz, Joe Lansdale, etc.). I was extremely honored to have featured Mr. Matheson in *Dark Discoveries* twice as well as talk with him on the phone a couple of times. He will be missed and we are planning some tributes for the next issue of DD. And if you have not read anything by this master, run out and grab anything you can find by him now!!!

So on to this issue. We've got some focus on older Horror and Dark Science Fiction TV with the lovely Kathryn Leigh Scott from *Dark Shadows* talking about what she's up to lately, a great overview article on the series and films by regular Stephen Mark Rainey and even a review of Tim Burton's *Dark Shadows* film. We've also got an article on the short-lived *Darkroom* series with accompanying story by DD regular William F. Nolan and a new intro for it, an article and list for the old ABC movies of the Week, and an article on "The Group" and TV. On the movie front we have interviews with David Morrell (*First Blood*, *Brotherhood of the Rose*); Eric Red (*The Hitcher*, *Near Dark*, *Body Parts*) with a new story by Eric as well; Jeffrey Reddick (*Dawn of the Dead* remake, the *Final Destination* films) and Robert Morrish even pulled Frank De Felitta (*Audrey Rose*, *The Entity*) out of retirement! For additional fiction we have new stories from Gene O'Neill (and we have an interview with him) and regular reviewer Brian Sammons. And lastly, please welcome Jonathan Maberry to our lineup of columnists (along with Mr. Morrish, Yvonne Navarro, Michael Collings and Amy Shane).

Also, we're bumping up our tributes to Rick Hautala for our next issue to coincide with the forthcoming release of a new novel by Rick, *The Devil's Wife*, to be published by our DD publisher, Christopher Payne and his imprint JournalStone. So we'll have tributes for both Richard Matheson and Hautala in our next issue due out in late October.

Lastly, we'd like to offer our apology to photographer Beth Gwinn whose photo of Karl Wagner was not credited in the last issue.

So with that said, let's get on with the show!

- James R. Beach
Editor-in-Chief

DAVID MORRELL:

WRITING AS A FINE ART

By Joel B. Kirkpatrick

In his forty-one years as a published author, David Morrell has used his time very wisely. This is the man who created Rambo. Some authors fortunate enough to create a memorable character—indeed an iconic one—forever stand in that character's shadow. Not Mr. Morrell. He is the illumination behind the presence we all know so well.

The New York Times Sunday Book Review says, "Morrell writes action scenes like nobody's business." Among his more than thirty books, his 1979 horror classic The Totem is in film development, as is Creepers and The Brotherhood of the Rose. His fans are eager for the new experience.

Thrilling readers for decades, Morrell has a devoted following for his darker themes; many of his fans are celebrated horror authors in their own right—some of them will even hit the road for hours to catch him in a personal appearance.

Having just completed a very busy promotion tour for his new novel Murder as a Fine Art, David graciously takes time to visit with JournalStone and Dark Discoveries magazine.

JBK: *Bloody Moon Films* should be in production with their adaptation of *The Totem*. Do film producers constantly seek you out, or do they remain a rare surprise?

DM: More than half my books have been optioned or sold outright to film producers, but only a handful were made, notably *First Blood* and *The Brotherhood of the Rose* (the latter was the only TV miniseries to air after a Super Bowl). Michael Douglas bought *Extreme Denial* but didn't do anything with it. MGM optioned *Burnt Sienna* for Pierce Brosnan, but then Pierce stopped being James Bond, and MGM took the project out of development. There are many reasons for a film to get stalled. One of the most common is that trends change. These days, sequels, remakes, and comic-book characters are the sorts of pictures that are being made. *The Totem* supposedly was going to start production this spring, but to the best of my knowledge, that hasn't happened yet.

JBK: What role do you have in this latest film production? Are you merely spectator, or are you somewhat more active in the project?

DM: The Bloody Moon team has been friendly, but most producers don't want to consult with an author. I once had a meeting with one of the heads of development at Universal Pictures. She explained that they had a corporate policy about not involving novelists in film adaptations of their books. The theory is that authors don't have the objectivity to make the necessary adjustments to convert a 400-page novel into a 110-page film script.

JBK: You were a professor of American literature for sixteen years at the University of Iowa until 1986. Since that time, something extraordinary has happened in the book world—authors have been driven with zombie-like frenzy to take over publishing. Are we witnessing an explosion of talent ... or merely an explosion of reading material?

David Morrell, Photo by Jennifer Esperanza

DM: Everything changed with the e-book revolution in 2009 when readers found a fresh way to acquire books. It's a good news/bad news situation. On the plus side, a skilled author who can't persuade an agent or an editor to accept a book can now make that book available digitally. Usually agents and editors reject a book by saying that it doesn't suit their present needs, which is often the truth. They might not know how to market something that doesn't fit current trends. But now an author can by-pass the gatekeepers and self-publish. On the negative side, some of the self-published digital material is not well written and might make readers hesitate to take a chance on a new author.

JBK: The difference between thrillers and horror is often only a marketing-choice between words. Readers often can't discern any difference at all. Your latest novel *Murder as a Fine Art* is a good example: published as a thriller, but devoting many of its pages to horrific crimes in mid-1800s London. The Horror genre has always had very deep, literary roots, yet publishers seem to disbelieve that or be unaware of it. How do you feel about this?

DM: Douglas E. Winter famously said that genres could be categorized according to the emotions they evoke. Romance is about sentiment. Science fiction is about awe. Thrillers are about excitement. Horror is about

fear. Adding to what Doug said, I feel that horror is also a question of tone. I seldom write fiction with supernatural elements, but I often use an eerie tone, which is one reason why I have three Bram Stoker awards from the Horror Writers Association. *Murder as a Fine Art* is another thriller with an eerie tone—all those fogbound streets in Victorian London.

JBK: You recently praised an author friend for the brilliance of her premise in an historical fiction: M.J. Rose – *Seduction.* When you discovered her project, you were working on your own *Murder as a Fine Art*. How did you come to find Thomas De Quincy, and how did his life speak to you?

DM: I saw a film (*Creation*) that was about Charles Darwin's nervous breakdown. In it, a character tried to explain Darwin's breakdown by telling him, "Charles, there are people such as De Quincey who say that we can be influenced by thoughts and emotions that we don't know we have." That sounded like Freud, but Freud didn't publish until the 1890s and Darwin's breakdown occurred in the mid-1850s. I wondered if the character was talking about Thomas De Quincey, whose work I studied long ago in college. I started researching De Quincey and discovered that he anticipated Freud as early as 1821. In fact, he invented the word "subconscious." Freud might have borrowed it from him. De Quincey even suggested that we have secret chambers in our minds in which alien versions of ourselves can live undetected. I became so fascinated that I decided to feature him in a Victorian mystery/thriller that is based upon his blood-soaked description of the Ratcliffe Highway murders in his sensational essay, "On Murder Consider as One of the Fine Arts." I was also fascinated that De Quincey influenced Edgar Allan Poe, who in turn inspired Sir Arthur Conan Doyle to create Sherlock Holmes. It seemed to me that De Quincey could be placed at the start of the detective tradition.

JBK: You have earned your own praise for *Murder as a Fine Art,* one reviewer even comparing it favorably to Dickens in terms of the realism of its setting. That wasn't just Google research on your part, was it? Did you travel to London to put your hands on the place?

DM: I've been to London many times, but most of 1854 London no longer exists. I needed to become an expert in De Quincey's thousands of pages of prose, seeing London as he described it. Then I accumulated many shelves of history books about London in the 1850s. In addition,

I read every Victorian novel I could find that related to that time and place. I became friends with De Quincey's biographers. The research lasted 2 years. My goal was to persuade readers that they are actually on those fogbound streets.

JBK: You claim on your website to have become your own archivist, working nearly two years to update your entire catalog and website to meet modern readers' demands. With more than thirty works to revisit, I'm sure it was a daunting technological task. It demonstrates that you are a savvy, modern author. How much do you rely on technology and the internet for research on one of your books?

DM: This goes back to my comment about one of the advantages of the e-book revolution. My career has lasted so long that I own the digital rights to most of my work. Some of it inevitably went out of print, especially the short stories and the magazine articles. The e-format allowed me to make them permanently available. As for research, it's usually hands-on, as when I became a private pilot in order to research aircraft sequences in my novel about the mysterious Marfa Lights of west Texas, *The Shimmer*. For the driving sequences in *The Protector*, I spent a week at the Bill Scott Raceway in West Virginia, learning to car-fight and do the spins. For the winter sections of *Testament,* I became a student at the National Outdoor Leadership School in Wyoming and lived in the mountains for 35 days. But sometimes, as with 1854 London, I need to rely on the Internet.

JBK: How has your writing process evolved over the decades? Which was the last book in your career that was written entirely on a typewriter?

DM: The last book I wrote on a typewriter was *Blood Oath* in1982. Thank heaven for computers. I used to be forced to retype each page if I had a spelling mistake on it. My fingers would get sore.

JBK: You have actually embraced the new age by producing e-book projects of your celebrity biographies. You merge your love of music with your love of writing by offering an intimate glimpse at the talents of Frank Sinatra and Nelson Riddle. You also wrote in-depth essays on two other icons: Marilyn Monroe and John Wayne. Originally produced for film magazines, how did those projects come about?

DM: I love teaching. When an author or an actor or a singer fascinates me, I try to learn as much as I can about them—and then I enjoy telling other people what I learned. Because I have a background in music and theater, I have the advantage of being able to talk about technical details. Most of my profiles (John Wayne, Marilyn Monroe, Nelson Riddle, and so forth) were written for the *Perfect Vision* and the *Absolute Sound*—high-end video and audio magazines to which I contributed in the 1990s.

JBK: Had you the pleasure of ever meeting Sinatra?

DM: I never met him, but I saw him perform twice. The first time was in the 1970s after he came out of retirement. He was splendid. His eyes were like lasers, spellbinding his audience. The next time was a decade later, and by then, sadly, his health was fading as were his skills. My e-book, *Frank Sinatra: The Artist and His Music*, demonstrates how he learned to sing—his breath control and his phrasing and so on. Many people don't know that when Sinatra was getting started, he took voice lessons from a Metropolitan Opera singer. My goal was to demonstrate that Sinatra was truly the finest interpretive singer of the recording era.

JBK: In your essay, you mention how impressed you had been that Sinatra embraced—celebrated—getting older, mentioning his album *September of My Years* as a pivotal point in his career. You've been at your own craft beyond that celebration point of Frank's. Is David Morrell as thankfully older, smarter, more seasoned and satisfied? Was any particular book the same pivotal point in your career?

DM: I'm entering my fifth decade as an author and am learning all the time. My goal is to grow and evolve. All my books have action and suspense, but after that, I try to expand the idea of what a thriller can be. Every book is a new beginning. For example, in 1984, *The Brotherhood of the Rose* was one of the first novels to merge the authentic espionage of the British spy novel with the action of the American spy novel. Before that time, British spy novels had almost no action while American spy novels had preposterous espionage tactics. Other titles have been equally experimental: *Double Image* with two plots on top of each other and *Creepers*, which fused elements of thrillers and horror until they were indistinguishable. *Murder as a Fine Art* is an imitation Victorian novel that uses a highly unusual viewpoint, the third-person omniscient. You seldom find that viewpoint any longer, and yet it was common in Dickens's work.

JBK: We have read that you enjoy writing many different sorts of things, screenplays being one of those you mention. None are listed in the vast pool of information about you easily found online. Are you still waiting for that first screenwriter credit, or are we just overlooking them?

DM: I've been hired to write screenplays and teleplays since 1979. As I mentioned, there are all sorts of reasons why a project never gets to the screen. I did a lot of work for Laurel Entertainment in the 1980s, particularly an adaptation of Michael Palmer's excellent medical thriller, *The Sisterhood*. We were ready to go into production, but then Laurel discovered that their rights to the property had lapsed. I wrote three drafts of the miniseries of my novel, *The Brotherhood of the Rose*. Then NBC hired another writer, and another writer after that—a common pattern. The third writer received the credit, even though I asked for arbitration from the Writers Guild, which hilariously ruled against me because the third writer had changed plot points of my novel and hence was considered to be more creative. I wrote a script for the third Rambo film, which was initially about revolutionaries in Central America—but then the producers decided to use the Soviet war in Afghanistan. Some projects didn't get made because the head of the studio was replaced or because a director's previous film was a flop. I worked on a lot of projects over the years—but my only credit is for "Habitat," a half-hour episode of Laurel Entertainment's *Monsters* series. This is a common experience with screenwriters, getting hired and paid but not seeing anything on screen.

JBK: In looking about the internet for tidbits of your career, I ran across a YouTube book trailer for *Creepers*, apparently created for an English project by a student. That video represents a powerful shift in public interaction that did not exist even a handful of Morrell books ago. You just completed another book tour for your latest novel, and a few years back that was the only way you and your readers could connect personally. What do you think of the modern age, in respect to how readily your readers can contact you now?

DM: I resisted joining Facebook until I realized that it could be used as a way to discuss books, movies, music, and other aspects of popular culture. I think of my Facebook page as a version of the seminars I taught at the University of Iowa. One week, I even discussed the reading lists that I used for my various literature courses. Facebook allows me to have plenty of contact with my readers, as does my website www.davidmorrell.net, which has a ton of information as well as a way for people send emails to me. I answer all of them.

JBK: For generations, magazines and newspapers were the only producers of book reviews. Word of mouth excluded— the public had no voice to praise or deride a book. The huge retailer Amazon.com has been changing that paradigm in recent years by allowing their website to be a platform of public opinion about anything in print and readers went nuts with their thoughts. Yet, in just the last year, Amazon has been removing reviews from retail pages in some very odd, lopsided form of marketing control. Have you heard of the controversy, and do you have an opinion what is happening? Do you follow your own reader reviews?

DM: I never look at my Amazon reviews, and I never try to persuade people to post positive comments. But I know many authors who give readers free books in an effort to induce them to post positive comments. Also, there are companies who are paid to post positive comments. The process is so suspect that I stay away from it. Years ago, on Amazon, some idiot said that I had died and that my family concealed my death and hired someone to write my later books but that they hired someone who didn't know anything about my work. That's when I stopped looking at Amazon reviews. A friend told me that recently on Amazon someone objected to *Murder as a Fine Art* because there are a lot of murders in it. This is lunacy.

JBK: *First Blood* took you three years to write. All the while an eager agent was satisfied with updates of your progress. Even your novel *The Totem* was extensively edited from its first manuscript before initial publication. You are certainly prolific, but obviously very patient. How do you recognize that a book is complete? Who does the larger share of revising…you or your editor?

DM: I never submit a novel until I try every possible way to make it professional. My wife, an expert reader, contributes comments. After that, I send it to my agents, Jane Dystel and Miriam Goderich, who offer comments. Then the book goes to my editor. The editing is usually fairly light. *The Totem* in 1979 was a special case because my then-editor didn't "get" what I was trying to do. The novel was about mysterious events in a mountain valley. I tried to give the book an epical feeling by characterizing the entire valley. But my editor wanted to restrict the book only to a town in the valley. I rewrote the book, compressing the narrative, but in 1993, I was able to publish the big version that I prefer.

JBK: Which came first in your career…success with novels or short-stories? Which is more gratifying for you to complete?

DM: I finished *First Blood* in the summer of 1971. Then I wrote a short story, "The Dripping," that I sent to *Ellery Queen's Mystery Magazine*. The magazine bought the story about a week before a publisher bought *First Blood*, so "The Dripping" was my first sale. I was proud to join the *Ellery Queen* "first" club and was featured in an anthology of their "first" authors, which include Jack Finney, Stanley Ellin, William Link and Richard Levinson, and Robert L. Fish. I've written about 70 short stories, two of which received Stoker awards from the Horror Writers Association, and two of which were finalists. Another of my stories was nominated for a World Fantasy Award. Because of their compression, they require more time per page than a novel does. Mostly I use short stories to explore subjects and techniques that wouldn't be appropriate for a novel. For example, one of them, "The Beautiful Uncut Hair of Graves," was written in the "you" viewpoint. Another, "Elvis 45," consisted entirely of dialogue without "he said, she asked" speech tags. "The Dripping" turned out to be my most reprinted story, in nearly 20 anthologies, most recently in 2012's *The Best American Noir of the Century*.

JBK: You have been called "the mild-mannered professor with the bloody-minded visions", and knowing you were already teaching while creating *First Blood* we cannot imagine you traipsing through the woods wearing camo for that research. It seems first-hand knowledge of John Rambo's skill came much later after the book was published. What was it like for you, finally experiencing a walk in his shoes…with warriors embracing you as a comrade-in-arms?

DM: Actually I did spend a lot of time in the woods while researching *First Blood*. I wrote much of the book while I was a graduate student at Penn State, and one of my professors, a hunter, often took me into the Pennsylvania mountains so I could get a feel for the locale (the novel is set nearby in the mountains of Kentucky). I enrolled in a firearms class, and I spoke to a lot of Vietnam veterans who were suffering from what we now call post-traumatic stress disorder. It's an odd feeling to have created a character who turned out to be one of the top five thriller characters, based on the criteria of characters in novels who became recognized worldwide because of movies about them: Sherlock Holmes, Tarzan, James Bond, Rambo, and Harry Potter. At a recent bookstore event, a man told me that he was part of the first-responder team when the World Trade Center was hit in 2001. He said he briefly panicked, but then he asked himself what Rambo would do. In 2010, I was part of the first USO authors' tour to a war zone: Iraq. I met a lot of military personnel who said that they enlisted because of Rambo. That's a lot of responsibility for an author and character to bear. It's the movies, of course. The novel itself has an anti-war theme, and I can't imagine anyone joining the military after reading it.

JBK: We've read that you love the processes of research, to discover something new to put into your project. Is writing 'work' for you, at all? Or, does the work come after the writing?

DM: I compare myself to a Method actor. I can't begin a project unless I know how the characters talk and dress and behave in the context of their work. Before each novel, I always immerse myself in the subject. In fact, I often choose a subject because I want to learn about it. Protective agents, undercover operatives, knife experts—a lot of people have been generous in teaching me. The first draft is an uncertain process because the book is still taking shape. I often think of it as a person and ask, "What can I do to help you?" The third draft, when I'm fine-tuning, is always fun because I can see the book's shape. At that stage, small changes can produce massive results.

JBK: Some years back you wrote a story series for Marvel Comics *Captain America: The Chosen*. Not long after that, you penned a two-part series called *Spider-Man: Frost*. Are you getting hints that delayed project is about to go into production? What was the original delay?

DM: The artist assigned to *Spider-Man: Frost* is legendary illustrator Klaus Janson. He produced some excellent early artwork for my project but then was transferred to various other Marvel projects as deadline emergencies occurred. This went on for a long time. But recently I heard from my Marvel editor that Klaus is again working on my *Spider-Man: Frost* project. I'm excited to see it move forward again. I don't have a publication date, though.

JBK: How did your invitation to work for Marvel come about?

DM: A Marvel editor contacted me with the idea of pairing the creator of Rambo with another military icon, Captain America. I'm a fan of the creative possibilities in comics, but I needed to educate myself about writing for the form. Marvel sent me several sample scripts, which reminded me of the format for film scripts, so I felt at home. When *Captain America: The Chosen* was released as a book, I included my script for the first issue so that people could see the detail that's involved. The writer chooses the number of panels per page and can even make suggestions to the colorist. For example, I wanted the first 16 pages to feature windblown desert colors so that when Captain America made his first appearance, all the red-and blue primary colors of his costume (seen for the first time) would be more dramatic. Also I chose to use a full-page panel for his first appearance in the series.

JBK: How many books have you completed which have never seen print? Do you have any narratives that just never seemed to work, either in your opinion or your publishers?

DM: Only one complete book was never published. It was an early attempt at an espionage novel, and it didn't work because at that time I didn't know enough about that world. For me, 100 pages is the point at which I know whether a book can sustain my interest to the end. A couple of times, I stopped working on a novel at that point because I saw where it was going and I knew that there'd be narrative problems. But this is rare. Now that I think of it, my biggest disappointment was a novel about spouse abuse at a time when no one talked about it. I wrote several hundred pages about a woman who was pursued by her husband all the way across the United States, an epical hunter-hunted story. One of the scenes involved the husband attacking a battered-women's shelter. I wrote this in the early 1980s. It was one of the few times when I submitted a partial draft. Editor after editor rejected it because the topic was too controversial. One even said that

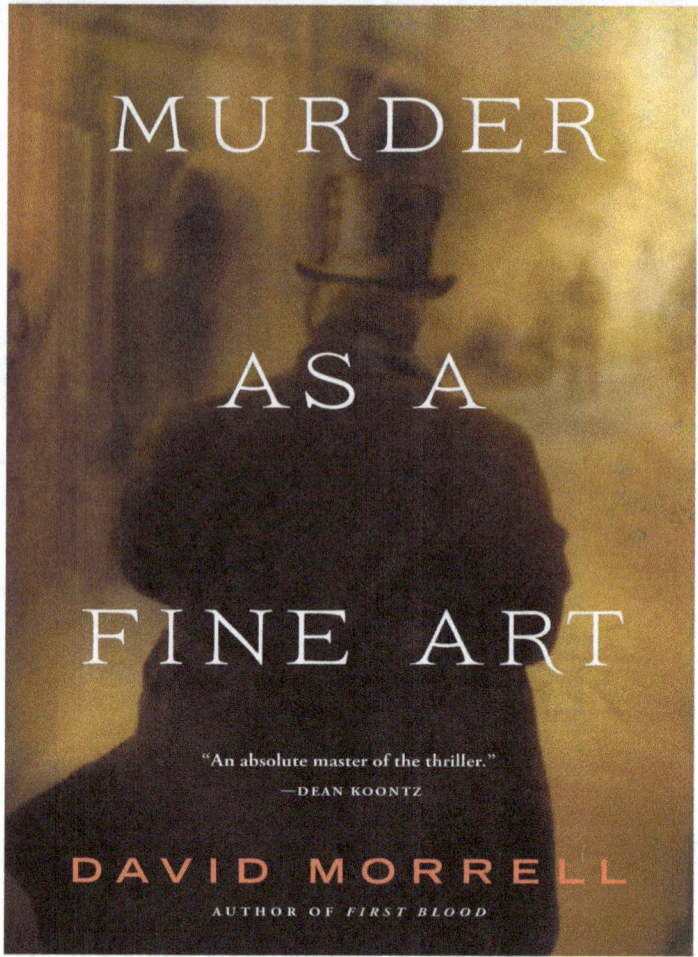

MURDER AS A FINE ART

"An absolute master of the thriller."
—DEAN KOONTZ

DAVID MORRELL
AUTHOR OF *FIRST BLOOD*

my heroine deserved to be beaten. A year later, Julia Roberts appeared in the hit film, *Sleeping with the Enemy*. Suddenly the topic was acceptable, and all kinds of books and films used that subject. My novel, which had been ahead of its time, was now old fashioned. I never completed it. That's my biggest disappointment.

JBK: Will you rest now that *Murder as a Fine Art* promotion has completed, with its last appearance in Denver this week? Are you juggling other projects? How many books can you have in the work at any one time?

DM: I'm working on a follow-up to *Murder as a Fine Art*. I rarely do sequels, but in this case, I have a lot more to say about Thomas De Quincey and 1850s London. As for working on multiple projects simultaneously, it's not my way. I lose focus if I switch back and forth, although occasionally I'll interrupt a novel to work on something short if I feel I need some distance from the main project.

JBK: Thank you, sir, for your kind participation.

❦ ❦ ❦

THEY

By David Morrell

Papa was clever. In the spring, when the sod roof thawed and the snakes fell through, he hooked blankets to the ceiling and caught them. Usually, they were bull snakes, but sometimes, they were rattlers. They sounded like somebody shaking a package of seeds. Papa said they were still sleepy from hibernating, which was why he wasn't worried about going near them. He made a sack out of each blanket and carried their squirming weight to the far edge of the pasture, where he dumped them into our creek. The snowmelt from the mountains made the water high and swift and took them away. Just to be safe, papa warned us never to go downstream past where he dumped them. Mama wanted to kill them, but papa said they were too sleepy to mean us harm and we shouldn't kill what we didn't need to.

The snakes dropped from the ceiling because papa dug the back of the cabin into a slope. He piled the dirt over the sod on the roof beams. It kept us cool in the summer and warm in the winter, and shielded us from the wind that shrieked through the valley during bad weather. In time, grass grew up there, but while the dirt was soft, snakes burrowed into it. We always heard them moving before they fell, so we had warning, and it wasn't many, and it was only for a few weeks in the spring.

Papa was so clever, he made the best soap in the valley. Everybody knew how to make the soft kind. Pour water over wood ashes to dissolve the potash in them. Strain the water through a layer of straw to get rid of dirt. Add the potash water to boiling animal fat. Let the two of them cool and use the scummy stuff at the top. That was the soap. But we had an outcrop of salt on our property, and papa experimented by adding salt to the boiling water and fat. When the mixture cooled, it got hard. Papa also put sand in his soap, and everybody thought that was his secret, but they could never get their soap hard because his real secret was the salt, and he made us promise not to tell.

We had ten chickens, a horse, a cow, a sheep, a dog, and a cat. The dog was a collie. It and the cat showed up a day apart. We never knew where they came from. We planted lettuce, peas, carrots, beans, potatoes, tomatoes, corn, and squash. We had to build a solid fence around the garden to keep rabbits away. But birds kept trying to eat the seed, so papa traded his hard soap for sheets and tented them over the ground. The birds got discouraged. The rabbits that kept trying, papa shot them. He said they needed to be killed to save the garden and besides they made a good stew.

We were never hungry. Papa dug a root cellar under the cabin. It kept the carrots, potatoes, and squash through the winter. Mama made preserves of the peas and beans, using wax to seal the lids the way papa showed her. We even had an old apple tree that was there when we came, and mama made the best pies, and we stored the apples, too. All of us worked. Papa showed us what to do.

Hot summer nights, while he and mama taught us how to read from the Bible, we sometimes heard them howling in the hills. Yip, yip, yip, yip. Baying at the moon. God's dogs, papa said. That's what the Indians call them. Why? Judith asked. Because they're practically invisible, papa said.

Only God can see them.

What do they look like? Daniel asked. Silly, I said. If only God can see them, how can anybody know what they look like? Well, a couple of times people have seen them, papa said. They're brown. They've got pointy ears and black tips on their tails.

How big are they? Judith asked, snuggling in his arms. A little bigger than Chester, papa said. Chester was our dog. They weigh about thirty pounds, papa said. They look a little like a dog, but you can tell them from a dog because they run with their tails down while a dog runs with its tail up.

Sure sounds like somebody got a good look at one, I said. Papa nodded. I saw one a long time ago, he said. Before I met your mother. I was alone at a campfire. It came out of the darkness and stared from the edge of the light. It must have smelled the rabbit I was cooking. After a while, it turned away. Just before it disappeared into the darkness, it looked over its shoulder, as if it blamed me for something.

Were you scared? Daniel asked. Time for you to go to sleep, mama said. She gave papa a look. No, papa said, I wasn't scared.

The harvest moon was full. They howled in the hills for several hours.

The next year, the rains held off. The other farmers lost their wells and had to move on. But the drainage from the snow in the mountains kept water in our creek, enough for the garden. The aspens on the slopes had it hard, though. They got so dry, lightning sparked fires. At night, parts of the hills shimmered. Smoke drifted into the valley. Judith had trouble breathing.

At last, we had a storm. God's mercy, mama said, watching the rain chase the smoke and put out the flames in the hills. The morning after the first hard freeze, Daniel ran into the cabin. His face was white. Papa, come quick, he said.

Our sheep lay in the middle of the pasture. Its neck was torn. Its stomach was chewed. Blood and chunks of wool lay everywhere. The other animals shivered, keeping a distance.

I saw the veins in papa's neck pulse as he stared toward the hills. At night, we'll fence the cow and the horse next to the cabin, he said. There's meat on the carcass. Ruth, he told me, get the ax and the knife. Daniel and I need to butcher the sheep. Get the shears, he told mama. We'll take the wool that's left.

The morning after that, papa made us stay inside while he went outside to check the rest of the animals. He was gone quite a while. Mama kept walking to the only window we had. I heard papa digging. When he came back, his face looked tight. The chickens, he said. They're all killed. He turned toward mama. Heads and feathers. Nothing else left. Not enough meat for you even to make soup from. I buried it all. What about eggs? mama asked. No, he said.

That night, papa loaded his rifle, put on his coat, and went out to the shed beside where the horse and cow were fenced. Yip, yip, yip, yip. I stared at the ceiling and listened to them howl. But they were far away, their echo shifting from one part of the valley to another. When papa came inside the next morning, the breeze was cold. Snow dusted the ground. His eyes looked strained, but he sounded relieved. Seems they moved on, he said, putting his rifle on a shelf. We'll trade soap for more chickens, mama told him, and gave him a cup of coffee.

By noon, it was colder. Clouds capped the mountains. Looks like an early winter, papa said. Thank God, mama said. As dry as it's been, the mountains need moisture. The creek needs smowmelt, she said. At supper, we heard wood snapping outside, the horse whinnying. Papa dropped his fork and grabbed his rifle, which he hadn't unloaded. Mama handed him a lantern. From the window, we watched his light jerk this way and that as papa rushed toward the corral next to the shed.

He kept running. He passed the fence. The light from the lantern got smaller until I couldn't see it in the darkness. I listened to the wind. I flinched when I heard a shot. Then all I heard was the wind again. Snow was in the air. Mama whispered something as she stared through the window toward the night. I think she said, Please God. We waited. Ruth, get Daniel his coat and a lantern, mama told me. He needs to go out and see if papa wants help.

But Daniel didn't need to. Look, Judith said, standing on tiptoes, pointing. Through the window, we saw a speck of light. It got bigger, moving with the wind and papa's arm. Cold filled the room as he came in. Judith coughed. Papa locked the door and set down the lantern. Something scared the horse so bad it broke through the fence and tried to

run off, he said. Tried? Daniel asked. Papa looked toward the window. Whatever scared the horse took it down. Didn't get much to eat, though. When I shot, they ran into the dark.

They? I asked. No need to alarm the children, mama told him. But everybody has to know so you can all be careful, papa said. We're already careful, mama said. Need to be even more, papa said. They, papa? I asked. I think I saw five, he said. Judith coughed. Five of what? Daniel asked. God's dogs? Did they run with their tails down? Papa nodded again. But now they're the devil's dogs, he said. I think I hit one. I found a trail of blood, but maybe it was the horse's blood dripping from their mouths.

Nobody moved. Judith, get the ax and the knife, papa told me. Daniel and I need to butcher the horse before they come back. Butcher? Judith said. We're going to eat horse meat? Daniel asked. It's meat, papa said. When winter comes this early, we need all the food we can find.

With the dark around us, mama and I shivered and held lanterns that swung in the wind while papa and Daniel cut up the horse. Papa told us to keep staring toward the night, to watch in case they came back. He kept his rifle protected in a blanket beside him. Only Judith didn't work. She shivered too much to hold a lantern in the blowing snow.

Look at the paw prints in the snow, Daniel said. I know, papa said. Not natural. I took my gaze away from the darkness and frowned at the prints. I'd never seen anything like them. They were like huge blobs of melted wax, none of them the same size, all big and grotesque and misshapen. Ruth, keep watching the night, papa warned me.

We put big chunks of horse meat in burlap bags and carried them to the storage pit papa had dug next to the cabin. That's where the meat from the sheep was. Papa set planks over the hole and put rocks on them. The cold will freeze the meat all winter, he said. At least, we won't starve. But what about the cow? mama asked. We'll put her in the shed at night, papa said.

In the cabin, we found Judith coughing in a chair by the fire. Even though the logs roared, she couldn't get warm. Her face was red. Has anybody seen Chester? she asked. I thought a moment. I hadn't seen the dog since the morning. And where's the cat? Judith asked. I looked at the others, who frowned. Did they smell what was out there and run off? mama asked. They'd need to be awfully scared to do that, Daniel said. Maybe they didn't run off, I thought.

Yip, yip, yip, yip. We turned toward snow blowing at the window and listened to the howls. They were close. I'll make coffee and warm us up, mama said. Yip, yip, yip. The howls sounded closer. Papa stopped unbuttoning his coat. I'd better stay with the cow in the shed.

Dawn was only a few hours away. The morning light was gray from the clouds and the blowing snow. As Judith coughed, I peered through the frosted window and saw papa step from the shed, which was large enough to hold him, the cow, and bales of alfalfa stacked at one end. He looked pale. Stiff. His shoulders were hunched. It was the first time I thought of him as old. He peered around, ready with his rifle. Then he motioned for me to come out and start my chores and milk the cow.

The day was busy as we raced against the night. Daniel went with papa to the woods at the edge of the valley, rigged ropes to logs, and dragged them back for more firewood. They had the rifle. I washed clothes and helped make mutton stew while mama used snow water for a sponge bath to try to lower Judith's fever.

The only smoke in the valley is from our chimney, papa said when he and Daniel got back. Through the window, I saw it snowing again, flakes hitting the pane. Mama turned from wiping Judith's brow. I guess more people moved on than we thought, she said. Maybe that's why those things are coming here. After the drought and the fires, there's no game in the mountains. And all the other farms are deserted, papa said. There's no other livestock in the valley.

After supper, Daniel put on his coat. He took the rifle off the shelf. You spent the last two nights in the shed, papa. Tonight, it's my turn.

Yip, yip, yip, yip. In the dark, I listened to them. Judith kept coughing. Mama came in with tea from bark that papa said would lower her fever. Maybe we should have moved on, I heard mama say to herself.

Just before dawn, I jerked awake when I heard a shot.

I'm okay! Daniel yelled from the shed. The moon came out! I saw them coming! Five like you said! One was limping! Probably the one you shot, papa! I put a bullet into it! The others ran off!

In the morning, we all dressed warm, except for Judith, and went out to see what Daniel shot. The sky was cold blue. The sun glinted off the snow, making me squint. A breeze numbed my cheeks. We let the cow into the pen next to the shed and fed her. Then we walked a hundred yards, following more blobby, misshaped paw prints. We came to something in the snow. Fine shot, papa said. At night, with no sleep, at this distance. Daniel looked pleased. I had the moon to help me, but thank you, papa, he said.

The snow was red. The thing was brown with pointy ears and a black tip on its tail, just like papa described. Its sharp teeth were bared, as if it died snarling. The cold wind blew snow across the ground. Hard to tell, Daniel said, but that looks like a bullet wound in its right front leg. Probably my shot, papa said. And that's your shot through its chest. That's what brought it down.

The reason it was hard to tell is that the animal had been chewed on. Its stomach was gnawed open. Its left flank was raw. Damned things ate one of their own, papa said. That's how hungry they are, mama said. I didn't know they got this big, papa said. It was five feet from the tip of its nose to the end of its tail. Must have bred with something else.

But the mutilation isn't just from being eaten, Daniel said. What happened to its paws, its ears, and the snout? From the fires in the mountains, papa said. I couldn't make myself look at it any longer. Its paws had awful scars as if a fire had melted the pads. Its fur was singed. Its ears had ragged edges. Its snout was deformed from having been burned. This one got trapped up there in the flames, papa said.

Yip, yip, yip.

We turned toward the nearby hills. In daylight? papa asked. They're howling in daylight? I never heard of that. Yip, yip, yip. They're watching us, Daniel said. Yes, papa said. Ruth, get the knife so we can skin what's left of it, he told me. Even if it's scarred, we can use the pelt. There's no point in wasting anything, including this. Plus, I want them to see what we do to them. I want to put the fear of God into them. Mama said, You talk as if they're smart and can think. Oh, they're smart, all right, papa said. When I was a kid, a trapper told me these things hunt in packs better than wolves.

That night, as Judith coughed, I used the knife to scrape the last of the meat from the pelt. Then I stretched it on a frame, the way papa taught me, and put it just close enough to the fire so it would dry without shrinking. Mama gave Judith more of the bark tea. Daniel sharpened the knife and the ax. As their metal scraped on the stone, I went to the window and looked toward the lamplight in the shed, where papa guarded the cow.

Judith died in the night. She kept coughing, and her chest heaved, and she couldn't catch her breath. Her cheeks were scarlet, but she kept fighting to breathe. Then her lips got blue, and her face, and after two hours, she died. Mama held her, sobbing. Daniel kept looking at the floor. I stood at the window and stared at the dark of the shed.

A shadow ran between the cabin and the shed. Another shadow, dark against the snow on the ground. The howls were very close. I heard a shot, but mama didn't react. She just kept sobbing. I'm all right! Papa yelled. They're running away! But just in case, don't open the door!

Then the night was silent, except for a rising wind and mama's sobbing. We need to tell papa, I said. When it's light, Daniel said. It won't help Judith if we bring him in now. Mama started murmuring, In the valley of the shadow. I went over and took her hand. I'm sorry, mama, I said. Her eyes were red. Fear no evil, she murmured, holding Judith.

When papa came in at dawn, he stopped in the doorway and knew immediately what had happened. His face looked heavy. He closed the door and crossed the room. He knelt in front of mama, who was still holding Judith. Lord, give us strength, he said. Through the window, I saw more tracks in the snow. Papa sobbed. I wanted him to know I was brave. I'll do my chores, papa, I said. I'll take care of the cow.

My coat barely kept me warm as I milked the cow, then fed her in the pen. I took a pitchfork to the manure in the shed, throwing it in a pile at the side of the pen. Four brown specks watched from the rim of a hill.

Mama dressed Judith in her best clothes, her "church clothes," mama called them, although we hadn't see a church in two years. Papa set Judith on the kitchen table. We took turns reading from the Bible. About Job and Lazarus and Jesus on Easter morning. Except mama. She sobbed and couldn't bring herself to read. Then papa and Daniel put on their coats and went to the shed, where they got the shovel and the pickax. They spent the rest of the day digging. I was reminded of when they buried my other brother and sister when we lived in another valley. This grave was in a nice spot near the apple tree. Judith would like that. Judith loved apples. The ground was frozen hard, and Daniel and papa were soaked with sweat when they came back to the cabin.

Daniel spent the night in the shed with the cow. Papa and I stayed up with mama as she held Judith's hand. We prayed more. Eternal life, papa said. I expected to hear them howling, but there wasn't any sound, not even a wind. Daniel came in at dawn. I've never seen him look so exhausted. I went out and took care of the cow.

Then we said our last prayers. Judith's face was gray now. She seemed a little swollen. Papa carried her outside into the cold. The rest of us followed. Mama sobbed as Daniel and I guided her. When papa set Judith into the ground, mama murmured, Not even a coffin. Don't have the wood, papa said. She'll be so cold, mama said.

Papa and Daniel took turns shoveling dirt. Mama couldn't bear to look. I took her back to the cabin. Papa carried stones from a fence he was making and put them on the grave. Daniel went to the shed. I heard hammering, and Daniel came out with two branches nailed to form a cross. Papa pounded it into the ground.

Papa stayed in the shed that night. At dawn, we heard him wailing. Daniel and I ran to the window. No! papa screamed. He charged toward the apple tree. No! he kept screaming. Daniel and I raced out to see what was wrong. Dirt was scattered over the snow. Rocks were shoved aside. The grave was empty. Papa's voice broke. Fell asleep! No! Didn't mean to fall asleep!

Eternal life, mama said. I didn't hear her come up behind us. She wasn't wearing boots or a coat. Judith has risen, she said. A swath in the snow went across a field and into the woods. Monstrous paw prints were on each side. The sons of bitches dragged her that way, papa said. I never heard him speak that way before. Daniel hurried to the cabin to put on his coat. He and papa followed the tracks. Risen, mama said. I helped her back to the cabin. From the window, I saw papa and Daniel disappear into the woods.

It snowed again. I stood at the window, straining to see. I leaned against the wall and must have dozed. The gust woke me. The door was open. Snow blew in. Papa! I cried. Daniel!

Thank God, you're back! You had me so worried! But no one came in. The wind blew more snow. Mama? I swung toward the chair by the fire. The chair was empty. Mama! I rushed to the open door and saw footprints going away. I grabbed my coat and hurried outside. The snow filled the footprints. I tugged the door shut. The quickly vanishing footprints led me toward the apple tree. They went past the apple tree. Then I couldn't see them any longer in the gusting snow. Mama! I screamed. But the wind shoved the word back into my mouth.

The snow swirled thicker. The air got darker. I stumbled forward but didn't know which direction to take. Then I realized that I didn't know how to go back even if I found her. I couldn't see the cabin. My tracks were almost full. I followed them as best I could. The wind seemed to push me to the ground. I thought I saw a low moving shadow. I struggled to my feet and ran, only to bang into the corral near the shed. But I knew where I was now and stumbled forward, whispering Thank God when I bumped into the cabin. Inside, I sank to the ground before the fire.

I woke in the dark and heard them. I heard the cow panicking. Then the only sound was the wind. In the morning, there was two feet of snow. It took me a long time to stamp through it to get to the shed. Somehow they got the latch open. The cow was all over the inside. Mostly blood, hide, and bones. Hooves. The head. Its eyes were wide with shock. I saw where the tracks went off in the snow in single file. The first one made it easier for the second, and the second made it easier for the third and fourth. Oh, they're smart, all right, papa had said.

They'll eat mama next, I thought. They're probably already eaten papa and Daniel. When there's nothing else left in the valley, they'll come for me? For a moment, I couldn't move. What am I going to do? I thought. What would papa do? Think like papa. I don't need to go out, I realized. I could stack wood in the cabin. I could bring meat from the storage pit. I had carrots, squash, potatoes, and apples in the root cellar. I could stay inside all winter. I'd need water, but if I was careful and I opened the door real quick and scooped a pail of snow, I could close the door before they got me.

I dug my way down through the snow to the boards across the storage pit. Unlike the rocks on Judith's grave, the ones on the boards were still there, maybe because they were heavier. I pried two parcels of horse meat from the frozen pile. The rest was stuck together so solid, I couldn't get at the lamb meat under it. I stacked the parcels in a corner of the cabin. I planned to stuff myself on it before it rotted. I carried tools from the shed–the shovel, the pickax, the hammer, and the pitchfork. I spent the day bringing in wood. I kept looking over my shoulder as I split logs. My arms ached. Too soon, it was dark. I went in, cut away a slice of thawing meat, and cooked it over the fire. It was tough and bitter, but I didn't care. I ate it in a frenzy and fell asleep.

In the night, I needed to relieve myself. I used a pail in a corner. In the morning, the smell was so bad that I wanted to carry the pail outside and dump it. But it stormed in the night, and now there was three feet of snow. I was only a foot taller. Besides, I knew it wasn't safe to go out. There were animal tracks in the snow. Across from the cabin, eyes glared from the shed's open door. I was forced to relieve myself in the pail again, and the stench got worse. I knew I wouldn't be able to bear it for a whole winter.

What would papa do? I thought. I got the pickax, went to a corner, and chopped the dirt floor. I got the shovel and scooped out the dirt. I kept chopping and scooping. My arms ached worse. But eventually I had a hole deep enough. I dumped the pail of waste into it, covered the waste with dirt, and still had plenty of space to dump more.

I heard scratching on the other side of the wall. They must have heard me digging and burrowed down through the snow to the bottom of the wall. I put my ear against the logs. I heard them out there trying to dig under. But clever papa had built the wall with two logs below ground to guard against flooding. I listened to them working to claw through the frozen ground. But it was too deep. They clawed and clawed, and at last I no longer heard them.

Again it snowed. In the morning, the drifts were close to the window sill. Deformed paws scraped glass. One of the things stared through the window, its dark eyes, scarred ears, and teeth-bared, misshaped snout making me think of the devil. In a rush, I closed the inside shutter. I was frightened and sickened, yes, but I also closed the shutter because the thing was so smart I didn't want it to see what I was doing. I went to the shelf where papa kept the box of poison he used on prairie dogs. We need to kill them so our animals don't break a leg in one of their holes, he said. I cut off a slab of horse meat, sliced it open, filled the cavity with poison, and squeezed the meat together. As I went toward the door, I heard wood creaking above me. I saw that the beams were bent from the weight of the snow and dirt.

Need to be quick, I thought. While the thing scratched at the window, I went over to the door. I lifted the latch as quiet as could be. Then I said a prayer, jerked the door open, hurled the meat over the top of the snow, and slammed the door shut. Or tried to. Some of the snow fell, blocking the door. Panicking, I scooped frantically at the snow. I heard one of them straining to run through the drifts toward the open door. My heart beat so fast, I thought I'd be sick as I scooped the rest of the snow away and slammed the door. Something banged against the top and growled.

I trembled. Then I opened the shutter. Sunlight off snow almost blinded me as I saw three of them fighting over the meat. They had burn scars all over them. One didn't have a tail. Another didn't have lips on the left side of its jaw. The fourth, the biggest, was the most deformed of them all. Its scars made it seem it had huge warts all over iis snout. It glared from the door to the shed. When it snarled, the others stopped fighting and turned to it. With another snarl, it moved forward, its mashed paws finding purchase in the snow. It sniffed the meat and growled for the others to leave the meat alone. Two stepped back. But the one without a tail took its chance, bit into the slab, and ran off. At a distance, it gobbled the meat and sat contentedly. In a while, it squirmed. In a while longer, it writhed, vomited blood, and died. This took a long time.

Gathering clouds brought darkness swiftly. As snowy wind shrieked past the cabin, I cooked horse meat, but not before I used papa's soap to wash my hands. Make yourself clean, he often said. It's the difference between us and animals. I pushed the blanket from the wall at the back of the cabin and went down the sloped floor to the root cellar, from where I brought back potatoes and carrots. I set them on a clean spot next to the fire. I listened to the shriek of the wind and the creak of the roof beams.

After a while, I had an idea. I filled a lantern with coal oil and lit it. Certain that the storm was too fierce for the things to be prowling out there, I went to the door. I had a moment's doubt. Then I knew that papa would be proud of me for being so clever. Breathing quickly, I put on my coat, opened the door, closed it behind me, and crawled up through the snow to the top of the drift. The wind was so cold, it made my face feel burned. Shielding the lantern, I squirmed through the gusts. When I saw the dark outline of the shed, I hurled the lantern through the front door and raced toward the cabin. Glass broke. Behind me, flames whooshed as I slid down the trough I had made. I fumbled at the latch, shoved the door open, kicked fallen snow away, and slammed the door.

Outside, one of them wailed. So numb I didn't feel the cabin's warmth, I ran to the shutter, opened it, and saw the fiery shed. A thing raced from the door, its fur ablaze. Yelping in agony, it fled into the darkness. The flames on it got smaller in the distance as it raced away. The alfalfa in the shed ignited. The fire grew larger, the shed's walls and roof collapsing, sparks erupting. Soon, the wind and the snow killed the blaze. I closed the shutter and went to the fireplace, where I discovered the potatoes and carrots were getting soft. The horse meat tasted better as I got used to it. I dozed on a blanket near the hearth. Sometimes, the creak of the roof beams wakened me.

Then silence wakened me. I raised my head and saw cracks of sunlight through the boards of the shutter. It was the first quiet morning in several days. I went to the pit in the corner, relieved myself, shoveled dirt down, and washed my hands with papa's soap. I nibbled on a piece of leftover potato, the skin crusty, the silence encouraging me that the fire had killed the remaining three. I went to the shutter, swung it open, and one of them charged through the window. The crash of glass, the rage in its eyes made me scream and stumble away, knocking against the table. The force of its attack carried it two-thirds through the window. Spit flying, it dangled, thrusting with its paws to get all the way through, and suddenly yelped, blood spurting, a shard of glass in its stomach holding it in place.

It squirmed, determined to reach me, the hate on its face giving it strength. Its snout had fresh blisters and burns. I grabbed the pitchfork. As the thing broke free from the window, landing on the floor, I charged with the pitchfork. A tine caught its throat. But the thing was as big as I was. Wrenching free, it snarled and lunged. I stabbed with the pitchfork, piercing one of its eyes. Twisting away, leaving a trail of blood, it braced itself, leapt, and caught the pitchfork straight in its chest. The force against the pitchfork's handle knocked me down. The handle twisted this way and that as the thing snarled and writhed and bled.

A noise brought me to my feet. I staggered and barely reached the shutter in time to slam it shut before something crashed against it, almost breaking the shutter's hinges. The thing out there growled like the devil's creature it was. Hearing a scrape behind me, I turned and saw the thing on the floor struggling to stand despite the pitchfork in it. I stepped back as it tried to crawl. Its eyes were red with fury, dimming, going blank. I vomited.

For a time, I didn't move. Then I went to the water pail, where I rinsed my mouth, spat into the fireplace, and drank. The water soothed my throat which was raw from screaming. Four dead, I thought. But I knew the last one was the smartest, and I decided it didn't want me only for food now. I'd killed its companions. I'd destroyed its den. It hated me.

Without shelter, it'll freeze out there, I thought. I seemed to hear papa say, No. It'll dig a cave in the snow.

But if I don't go out again, it'll need to move somewhere else to find food, I thought. Again, I heard papa say, The stench of the decaying carcass will poison you. You'll need to open the shutter to breathe. It'll charge in.

No, I told papa. I can stand anything. The shutter stays closed.

I cooked more horse meat. It tasted delicious. As shadows gathered beyond the cracks in the shutter, I decided that the thing on the floor was truly dead. I lit the lantern on the table, edged toward the carcass, and tugged the pitchfork from its chest.

The roof creaked. Be clever, I heard papa say. I pushed away the rug on the wall and hurried to take the ax and the knife down the ramp to the root cellar. I carried down a pale of water. I rushed back to get the lamp and the rest of the tools, but I never got that far. With a massive crack, the roof collapsed. The crush of dirt and snow sent me rolling down the ramp. My head struck something hard.

For a moment, colors swirled inside my mind. Then my vision cleared, and I saw that the top of the ramp was almost entirely blocked by wood, dirt, and snow. Dust made me cough, but as it settled, I saw a gap behind which flames rose. The collapsed roof had knocked the lamp over. The table was on fire.

The flames will suck the air from the cellar, I thought. I climbed to the top. Because the shovel was still in the cabin, I had to use my hands to push dirt into the gap. As the space got small, I saw the flames grow brighter. Smoke filled the opening. Frantic, I pushed dirt until the space was closed. Surrounded by darkness, I retreated to the bottom, sat, and tried to calm myself. My breathing echoed. I shivered.

Hunger woke me. I had no way of telling how long I'd slept. I was slumped against potatoes. My back ached. The cellar, which was about five feet wide and high had wood across the top to keep earth from falling. It smelled damp and like rotted leaves. Darkness continued to surround me. My hunger insisted. Papa used to say that raw carrots were bad for digestion. But it was either them or raw potatoes or squash, so after waiting as long as I could, I felt for a carrot and bit into it, its hardness making my teeth hurt. I didn't choose the apples because they felt soft and wormy. I was afraid they would give me the runs. Continuing to shiver, I chewed until the piece of carrot was mush in my mouth. Only then did I swallow. I did that for a long time, hoping I wouldn't get sick.

I tried to count the passing seconds, but my mind drifted in the stale air. For all I knew, it was now day outside. I needed to relieve myself but forced myself to wait. Finally, I crawled up the ramp. About to dig through the blockade of dirt and snow, I heard noises beyond it. Where the gap had been, dirt began to shift. Stomach tightening, I backed away.

At once, I saw a speck of daylight. A snout poked through, clustered with whorls and outcrops of scars and blisters. The thing growled. As the light widened and the head thrust into view, its ears merely nubs, I grabbed a potato, hurling it as hard as I could. It thudded off the creature's snout. I threw a second potato and heard a snarl. The creature clawed to widen the hole, shoving its neck through as I grabbed the pail of water and threw its contents. Water splashed over the raging head but made no difference. Its eyes burned. I banged the empty pail against the head, but the creature was halfway through. The handle on the pail broke. The creature's hind legs were almost free. I raised the ax but didn't have room to swing, so I jabbed, but the thing kept coming, and abruptly it wailed.

It snapped its head to the side, staring wildly behind it. Its wail became a savage yelp as it whirled and bit at something. The fierce motion widened the hole, allowing it to turn and bite harder. Daylight blazed in. I heard a noise like someone shaking a package of seeds. As the creature spun, the snake came into view, flopping like a whip, rattling, its fangs buried in the creature's haunch. The snake must have fallen when the roof collapsed. The heat of the fire wakened it. It kept its fangs sunk in as the creature whirled and yelped. The poison made the creature falter. Breathing heavily, it steadied itself, as if it knew it was dying and had to concentrate on unfinished business. It took a step toward me. It opened its mouth to bite. I shoved the ax handle between its jaws and leaned forward, thrusting the handle down its throat.

Choking, the creature thrashed. I struggled with the ax, pressing harder, feeling vibrations through the handle. Gagging, the thing frothed, wavered, slumped, trembled, and after a while lay still. Only then did the snake stop rattling. It released its fangs and dropped to the ground. Papa said, Its poison sacks are empty. For a while, it can't hurt you. But I didn't believe papa. As the snake slithered down the ramp, I pressed against the wall, trying to keep a distance. The snake crawled over the pile of squash and disappeared behind it.

I edged around the carcass, fearing that any moment it would spring to life. The cold air smelled sweet. Wary of other snakes, I stood among the dirt and snow and surveyed the wreckage. Clouds hovered. Knowing I needed shelter before the next storm, I saw that beams had fallen on an angle in front of the fireplace, forming a kind of lean-to. I found the pelt that papa had cut from the creature he and Daniel shot. I secured the pelt over a hole between beams. I tugged down the scorched blanket from the entrance to the root cellar and hooked it over another hole between beams. I found other blankets and did more of the same.

But there were still holes, and the blankets wouldn't keep moisture out, so I clenched my teeth, went into the root cellar, found the knife, and skinned the creature. Damn you, I said all the time I cut away its pelt. I stuck it over other holes between beams. Then I skinned the carcass of the thing that had come through the window, and I crammed that pelt between beams. In time, I would look for the creature I had poisoned and use its pelt, but snow was falling, and I had to complete my shelter. A few embers glowed under charred wood in the fireplace. I layered kindling and logs and blew on the embers. I was almost out of breath before the kindling sparked and the logs began to burn.

As the snow thickened, I went down to the root cellar and carried as many potatoes and carrots as I could, all the time keeping a wary eye on the pile of squash. While a potato cooked next to the fire, I bit a chunk from a carrot. Papa was wrong that uncooked carrots would make me sick. Maybe papa was wrong about a lot of things. Darkness settled, but despite the falling snow, my shelter felt secure. Tomorrow, I planned to make it stronger. I chewed another carrot and watched the potato sizzle. I thought about papa, about the many valleys in which we lived and how he was never satisfied and we always had to move past every town. I thought of the brother and sister who were buried in one of those valleys. I thought about the bark tea papa gave Judith for her fever. Papa always told us how clever he was, but maybe he didn't know as much as he thought about bark, and it made her sicker. Maybe papa wasn't so clever when he and Daniel chased after the things that took Judith. Maybe he should have kept control and stayed home and mama wouldn't be dead and he and Daniel wouldn't be dead.

I think about that a lot. I sit in this tiny room and listen to motor cars rattling by outside. Eighty-eight years is a long time to remember back. You ask me what it was like living in the valley when I was twelve. The old days as you call them. For me, the young days, although I was never really young. Streets and houses and schools and churches are now where our farm was, where everyone died, where I spent the winter eating carrots, potatoes, and horse meat. But never the squash. I never went near the squash. Damned stupid papa.

THE END

Thrill-Seeking with Eric Red

By Aaron J. French

Photo Courtesy of Eric Red

Aaron J. French: Hi, Eric. Thanks for taking the time to answer a few questions for Dark Discoveries. When did your love of horror stories and thrillers first begin?

Eric Red: As a kid. My mother and grandmother took me to see a re-release of *Psycho* when I was nine, which traumatized me and set me on a track for life. No film ever scared me as much. I loved it. Today, when my mother sees one of my films and says, "Where does that come from?"I say, "Remember when you took me to *Psycho*?" She'll never live it down.

AJF: Could you tell us about your experience working on the *Near Dark* and *Hitcher* scripts? Did horror fiction writing play any part in building the scripts?

ER: With *The Hitcher* I set out to write a propulsive narrative that began at the beginning, ended at the end, and had no subplot or back-story—nothing to distract from the main action. As a young writer, I figured you only have two hours to tell the story and if you cut out all the crap there could be an increased intensity for the audience. While I didn't have a term for it at the time, *The Hitcher* was one of the first horror action pieces. *Near Dark*, on the other hand, was about mixing the western and vampire genres. In thinking what vampires would be like if they really existed, the American outlaw thing came organically.Fiction didn't play a part in any of my scripts because I didn't start writing fiction until 2008—not even short stories. Everything was screenplays, teleplays or film and TV treatments, with the exception of one comic series.

AJF: You wrote *and* directed *Cohen and Tate*, *Bad Moon*, and *100 feet*, while *Body Parts* is based on the French novel "Choice Cuts." What pressures or concerns did directing these films add to the writing process?

ER: None at all. A script's a script. It's the same job writing it whether you're directing that particular screenplay or not.

AJF: With *Don't Stand So Close*, you've released your first full-length fiction novel. How long did you work on getting the book completed and published? Did you have some short stories published in the meantime?

ER: It took me a few years to write the book—I worked on it on and off between films—then it took about another year to get it published. During that time I wrote and had six short stories published in magazines such as *Weird Tales* and anthologies like *Dark Delicacies III: Haunted*.

AJF: In your films, there is a large psychological focus aimed on your characters. *Don't Stand So Close* follows a similar trend. What about psychological horror and thrillers resonates with you as an artist?

ER: For the reader or the audience to maintain a suspension of disbelief, they have to believe, at least somewhat,what they are reading on the page or seeing up on the screen. The characters have to be realistic and the psychology truthful. It's all about generating audience involvement. It interests me to explore the mythological underpinnings of various monsters and genres and why they resonate—and that all circles back to the psychological thing.

AJF: Why don't you tell us about the two main characters in your book, Matt Poe and Linda Hayden? Stories similar to theirs have appeared in the national news. Was this your inspiration for the characters? If so, what is it about the psychology of these incidents that inspired you?

ER: Matt Poe is a seventeen-year-old east coast high school senior transplanted to a Midwestern town. He is a total outsider and at that age when impressionable young guys are very preoccupied with sex. And he's lonely, which makes him easy prey for his beautiful English teacher, Linda Hayden, a serial sexual predator. She is evil but has things in her past that make her actions understandable. Their relationship is the spine of the book and it goes to some pretty terrifying places.

Photo Courtesy of Eric Red

who just can't comprehend the things happening around him involving his daughter. He kind of wrote himself. Just having him hovering in the background of the story adds a tension to the secret affair between the teacher and the student.

The other of Matt's friends, Rusty, was the hardest character to write. He has identity issues with his sexuality and morality and an ambiguity as a character that was tricky. A lot of people tell me they find him the most interesting character because he's hard for the reader to get a fix on and we don't know what he's going to do next.

AJF: Now for the million-dollar question: Do you plan on turning this book into a film?

ER: I'd like to, if anybody would give me enough rope to hang myself. It'll require a financier with guts because it's not a "safe" movie. But it's exactly that edgy aspect I think audiences would connect with.

AJF: Before we close, could you take a minute to talk about future projects, whether film or fiction?

ER: My second novel, a horror western called *The Guns of Santa Sangre* is coming out this November with Samhain Publishing. It's about three outlaw gunfighters in turn-of-the-century Mexico who take a mission where they get to keep all the silver in a church that's left after they use the rest of the silver to kill werewolves who have taken over a small peasant village. It's a pulp western with cowboys, wolf-men, fangs, claws, silver bullets and plenty of blood and action.

Also, I have a five-issue comic series called *WildWork* being published this year by Antarctic Press. In it, Professor Van Helsing pursues Count Dracula into the American West of the 1880s. The doc has to recruit a group of tough cowboys who don't believe in vampires to be vampire slayers. It's an epic, spectacular, action-packed saga, and lots of fun.

Guess this is my western period!

I didn't model the characters on any of the notorious teacher/student relationships in the news. I did base it somewhat on a few friends' experiences when I went to high school. The coming-of-age subject matter, and the good and bad sides of sex when you're a kid, resonated with me as a writer.

AJF: You've never shied away from portraying sexual encounters in your movies, and now with *Don't Stand So Close* the sexuality has been taken to an extreme. The most interesting thing, for me, is how the sexual material in this book can, in one sense, be thought of as any young boy's fantasy, and in another real sense it's very dangerous and illegal. Could you talk about that?

ER: In telling the book from the point of view of a normal male teenager with sex on his brain, it was important to describe what he thinks and feels honestly, or it would have been a cop out. A teenage student having sex with an adult teacher is not just illegal but only a screwed up adult would cross that line—the whole point of the book is lots of young guys have fantasies about teachers, but be careful what you wish for!

AJF: Another thing that struck me was the vivid use of language in describing the book's rural setting, Wayland, Iowa. Did any particular place from your life serve as the inspiration? What difficulties did you encounter having to paint each scene with words, rather than rely on the camera's lens?

ER: I made it all up, combining a number of small towns I've driven through or location scouted over the years, but it was a total Iowa of the mind. Fully rendering a setting is something one learns in horror, where atmospherics are an essential ingredient. The town was a character in the book—the heartland and sense of the earth was intrinsic to an elemental story about primal human urges and behavior. It would not have been the same book set in a city.

AJF: A number of secondary characters play an integral part. Any of them more pleasurable to write? Did any pose difficulties?

ER: I really enjoyed writing Matt's girlfriend Grace's father, Sheriff McCormack. He's this rural, hard-nosed, decent man

Photo Courtesy of Eric Red

DO NOT DISTURB

The Do Not Disturb sign had hung on the door of room 510 for three weeks straight. It had been up the entire time since Jane Williams had joined the housekeeping staff of the Route 9 Hotel in Provo, Utah. Berry, the Latino girl who had the maid job before her, told her the room was occupied and the Do Not Disturb sign had been there the whole time she had worked there, and that had been the full summer. The hotel manager Mr. Sweeny told Jane when she took the position to just leave the guy alone, that his credit card was good and he was all paid up. The only time they heard from him was when he called room service and asked for the big bucket of ice. He did it three times a day and housekeeping was to leave the bucket outside the door. A few hours later the empty bucket would be returned and housekeeping would refill it with ice and put it back.

From the beginning, cleaning the rooms on the 5th floor, that constant Do Not Disturb sign made Jane uncomfortable. Why would somebody never come out of their room? Those linens must not have been changed in a long while. If she were the owner of the hotel she would have at least requested that housekeeping changed the bedding. But she wasn't the owner, Sweeny was, and he was paying her and the one time she said something he told her to shut up about it. The guy paid his bills and business was intermittent off the Interstate during the fall months. Berry had told her over drinks at the local Ramada Inn bar that it bothered her too. But it wasn't Jane's business and she needed the job. Berry's leaving the open housekeeping position came at a fortuitous time for the twenty-year-old single girl, even though it paid little more than minimum wage.

Jane put the fresh bucket of ice outside the room.

Pushing the cart of housecleaning supplies into room 504, Jane changed the bedding, switched the towels, replaced the little soaps and shampoo, turned down the bed, disinfected, cleaned the trash buckets and set out new mints, flushing a used condom she found under the bed. She rolled the cart out into the stained gray-carpeted hall.

The ice bucket was gone. Room 510 had taken it and the Do Not Disturb sign was still there.

Jane couldn't resist. She snuck up to the door of 510 and put her ear against it, listening for what she could hear inside. At first nothing. Then she heard a hissing sound. The hiss was regular, coming at intervals, a hiss then silence, a hiss then silence. What was going on beyond the door? She both wanted to know and didn't want to know.

She crouched down, eavesdropping and listening, gazing along the hall at the drab lane of doors leading off the elevators, the stairs and the soda and ice machines. The hotel, mostly used by conventions and businessmen in the Provo area, was like a million others. Jane thought the place smelled of mildew and bleach constantly. She kept listening at the door, hoping she wouldn't get caught or that whoever was in Room 510 doing who the hell knew what wouldn't walk out and see her.

The sound of a door opening down the hall made her snap to attention. She leaped up and ran back to her cleaning supplies cart, just as an elderly husband and wife left their room arguing and heading to the elevators.

Pushing her cart again, Jane froze as she heard the door open behind her and the *thunk* of an empty metal bucket placed on the ground. Before she could whirl to see inside the room, the door had shut, the Do Not Disturb sign swinging lazily on the latch.

And the next week it was still up. Jane filled the ice buckets, cleaned the other rooms, and stewed. Her mind wandered as she busied herself with her chores, wondering what lay beyond the door to room 510. The occupant must go out at night, she decided. He had to eat and all he ever ordered from room service was ice. At the end of her shift as she walked through the parking lot to her car, she glanced up at the side of the 5th floor of the hotel, looking at the window of 510, but the shades were always drawn. Over drinks at the Ramada Inn, Jane asked Charlene, one of the night shift housecleaning crew, if she had ever seen Room 510 leave and she said nope, she hadn't. Sweeney said leave the guy alone and just deliver him the ice. It didn't make sense to either girl. What did the guy eat if he didn't have food stockpiled in there? He couldn't live on ice. Actually, Jane had read that guys in India could live on ice. Charlene wondered if 510 was a vampire. Jane reminded her that vampires didn't drink ice. Three drinks later, Jane was still wondering about that Do Not Disturb sign.

One day Room 509, directly across from 510, was vacant. Jane brought the filled ice bucket and set it according to routine outside the door. Quickly, she ducked into 509 and quietly closed the door. Pressing her eye against the peephole that stared across the hall to 510, she watched the door with the ice bucket in front of it. It was a long wait. Then the Do Not Disturb sign twitched as the latch slowly turned. The maid's heart jumped in her chest as she squinted through the peephole to see the door crack just a little, then a little more, the room dark beyond with no lights on inside. Soon, the long, marble pale fingers of a hand reached around through the crack, grabbed the ice bucket, and pulled it in, closing the door. It reminded Jane of a toy she'd had as a kid where you put a coin on a box and a mechanical glow-in-the-dark plastic hand would slowly crank out of the box, grab the coin, and snap back in.

Now the door was shut again. Moments later, Jane tip-toed out into the hall, noticing a fresh scent of Lysol in the air, and put her ear to 510. At first nothing. Then from inside she heard the squishing. A wet slushy sound.Then a snap. Her eyes widened, disturbed, and she pressed her ear harder to the door. She heard the hissing. She heard the slushing, squishing sound. A sharp pop.A crunching.Then a hissssssssssssssssss. Then silence. That was enough. Jane fled, truly creeped out.

For the next hour, she preoccupied herself with cleaning up the puke in the corner of a room on the 4th floor. Then she changed the towels in the bathroom and wiped the counters dry. Suddenly, there was a loud thud on the ceiling above her, like somebody falling down.

It was only then that she saw the open door of the room she was cleaning and the number 410, and realized she was directly below 510.

Hours later the empty ice bucket had not been put outside the door as usual.

Towards the end of her shift, Jane found herself standing outside 510 with the perpetual Do Not Disturb sign, knowing full well that she should rightly go down to the front desk and tell Sweeny she thought the occupant had fallen or had an accident. But she knew that if she did, there was a chance the manager would tell her not to do what she was about to do now, which was to knock and then if there was no answer, use her key and let herself in. Then she would never know.

So she knocked. No answer. Knocked again.Silence. Jane listened at the door. Nothing. She reached past the Do Not Disturb sign, pushing it aside, grasping the door handle and slowly opening it.

The smell of Lysol air freshener, incredibly thick and floral, assaulted her through the opening door, where it sat in the air. Jane gagged. She said hello. Nobody answered. It was black as pitch beyond the door as she stepped inside to a completely darkened room with the drawn curtains. Entering cautiously, throwing the wall switch, she turned on the standing lamp. Many boxes of Lysol aerosol cans were stacked floor to ceiling by the wall, and more boxes of discarded ones. The room was surprisingly neat. The bed was made. The light cast a dim illumination over the bed, which was empty. The bathroom door was closed. The maid approached step by step. Hello, she said apprehensively. Jane noticed how wet the carpet was as the cold water soaked through her sneakers as she opened the bathroom door. It was empty, but the shower curtain was drawn. Jane pulled it back.

Berry lay dead in the tub, naked in a state of gray semi-decay, eyeballs black with hematoma. Her legs had been eaten, the flesh and bone chewed off below the knee on the left and a huge meaty shag around her exposed femur. The ice cubes dumped over the body, to preserve it for feeding and keep it from rotting, had largely melted. The tub was brimming red with blood and foul cold water. The sink was lined with knives, forks and cleavers, cleanly washed and gleaming sharp. Jane took all this in and started to scream in a split second, but that was all it took for the Cannibal to rush out of the closet and grab her from behind. The pale, naked figure covered her mouth and broke her neck with a quick, violent twist. Jane Williams died instantly. Her body dropped into his arms and he eased her onto the closed toilet seat, where she slumped into her own lap like a discarded rag doll.

The Cannibal lit a cigarette and fretted over the situation. At least he had food for a month. It wasn't his fault. The last two maids would still be breathing if they had just paid attention to the sign on the door.

Three simple words, familiar at every hotel.

Couldn't people read?

❦❦❦

Adventures in Screenwriting: Jeffrey Reddick

Interview by Cyrus Wraith Walker

Michael Welch and Jeffrey Reddick hanging out on the *Day of the Dead* set. Image courtesy of Jeffrey Reddick

If you are not immediately familiar with the name, you should be. He is a screenwriter, actor, and producer, all rolled into one. Jeffrey Reddick is one of America's most respected screenwriters for film and TV currently. Working primarily in the horror genre, Reddick is best known for creating the Final Destination film series. His bio includes Final Destination, Return to Cabin by the Lake, Final Destination 2, Tamara, A Life's Work, Dante's Cove and Day of the Dead (remake). Seldom do we see such brilliance during a time when horror seems to have lost its spontaneity.

As a child, Reddick wanted to be an actor, as a teenager he was already writing films and presenting them to the head of New Line Cinema. A decade and a half later, he created the major blockbuster, Final Destination. Writers and student screenwriters and filmmakers alike are as excited about Jeffery Reddick's inspirational career as are his movie fans. I first met Jeffrey Reddick at ZomBcon in Seattle in October 2010, and I must admit I embarrassed myself a little. Despite his appearance on a panel with William F. Nolan (*Logan's Run*) and Jason V Brock (Dark Discoveries' former managing editor and art director), I remember approaching Jeffrey at his booth adjacent to ours and introducing myself, then promptly asking, "What do you do?" I had seen his Final Destination films multiple times as well as Tamara and here he was with some promotional material for *Day of the Dead* (2008) and I did not know who he was. In my defense, I was but an intern with Dark Discoveries at the time and rather new to all this. Later in my hotel room, it dawned on me and I could have hid under a gravestone. But Jeffrey was cool, probably one of the most humble and good natured individuals I met all weekend (other guests during that event included George Romero, Bruce Campbell and Malcolm McDowell). Though it was a pleasure to see and even meet those people, I think my encounter with Jeffrey Reddick was the most delightful. He really is a great person: down to earth, engaging, personable, and in my case, patient.

CW: Jeffrey, thanks for taking the time to speak with Dark Discoveries; as before, and even now, it is as much a pleasure for me as I'm sure it will be for our readers.

JR: Thank you, Cyrus. It's my pleasure.

CW: There is quite a bit of information out there about your incredible rise in the industry, starting from your childhood on up to the huge success of the first *Final Destination* film. Nonetheless, for our readers' sake, could you tell us a bit about your passions as a child and young adult?

JR: When I was growing up...back in the old days...we only had three TV stations. I loved to watch TV, but my mom was strict about the hours I watched it. We also had a local drive-in, where I would go to watch films. So, I would see everything I could at the theatre. Then, when we got a VHS player, I was ecstatic. I mostly watched horror films with a small group of friends. I also dreamed of being an actor. I loved...and still love...comic books. I've always been kind of a geek in that regard. When I was younger, I loved to read. Horror and Greek/Roman mythology were what I read most. But, as far as dreams go, I always knew I was going to be involved in the movie business. I just thought it would be as an actor.

CW: I've heard tales that you snuck peeks at Stephen King's Salem lot on TV though forbidden to watch such shows by your mother, and that it left a lasting impression that may have stirred a brilliant career. Is that true?

JR: Oh yeah, total true story. The movie scared me so bad that I snuck in my mom's room and slept by her bed for a week. I never told her about that. But my sister knew and ribbed me endlessly.

CW: Are there any older, forgotten television shows or movies that also inspired you?

JR: The biggest TV show that inspired me was "V" and "V-The Final Battle." They were two groundbreaking mini-series and they blew me away. As for movies, the original "Nightmare on Elm Street" is my favorite of all time. It was so imaginative and fresh. Even with the cheesy 80's style...I think it really holds up well.

CW: When I saw your version of *Day of the Dead* I was terrified, because the zombies are much more agile than they are in any other movie I'd seen. Tell us what stirred your desire to make that movie, if you would.

Jeffrey Reddick as a zombie in *Day of the Dead*. Courtesy of Jeffrey Reddick

JR: Actually, the producers contacted my agent about the project. They had Steve Miner attached to produce. He'd directed "Friday the 13th Part 2" with my final girl of the series...Amy Steel - "House," "Warlock," "Lake Placid" and "Halloween H20." The producers had a start date, so I knew the movie was going to happen. I knew some fans would be upset because I was remaking a classic. But the original pitch I did, which got me the job, was very faithful to the original. So, I was excited to make a move that updated the film and pleased fans of the original. Things changed during the development process and the film got further away from the original. But it was still a fun movie.

CW: It is an incredible film, and equally an incredible script. I've read your script, courtesy of you, and I must say it was as enjoyable to read as any novel I've read. For the screenwriters out there can you tell us a little about your process in writing such a dynamic screenplay?

JR: I'm glad you liked the script. Honestly, that script is one I read and can't believe I wrote it. One, because I never wrote action before. Two, because the writing style is different than my normal stuff. I had a lot going on when I wrote that script; my mom was really ill, so I was back in Kentucky dealing with that and trying to get the script in on time...with the producers breathing down my neck. That whole time was crazy.

As for my process, I read a lot of action/horror films before I started writing. I really focused on "Aliens" and saw how James Cameron wrote these great action scenes, with compelling characters. It made me raise the bar with my writing. But I just tried to keep the action sequences brief and brisk. If you get too bogged down in describing every bit of action, it can get boring for a reader after a while. I was always told to choose the shortest amount of words that have the greatest impact when writing a horror or action script.

CW: What's the hardest part of that? What's the most difficult aspect of writing a screenplay of this caliber?

JR: Well, for "Day of The Dead," the pressure was strong. Of course my mom's health was my main concern. But when writing this, I knew the fans were gonna be brutal if it didn't live up to the original. So it was hard when the producers started making me cut things, or add things, that weren't connected to the original film.

CW: You seem to outdo yourself with every film, so I personally have been greatly anticipating your next move. Can you tell us anything about what's brewing on the fire? What's next for Jeffrey Reddick?

JR: I'm adapting a young adult horror novel called, "The Undertakers." It's like an edgier "Spy Kids" meets "The Walking Dead." I'm really excited about getting that script finished. I've also got a few other movies that may be going soon. I'm also getting financing together to direct my first feature, which is really exciting. They're all horror. One of these days I'll write a comedy. But for now, I love horror.

CW: On behalf of Dark Discoveries and dark fiction fans everywhere, I'd like to thank you for taking this time with our magazine and hopefully we'll see you around the con circuit again real soon.

JR: Again, thank you. And thanks to all the fans out there. I wouldn't have a career without your encouragement and support.

☙ ☙ ☙

Jeffrey Reddick, Chad Donella, and Devon Sawa on set of *Final Destination*. Image courtesy of Jeffrey Reddick

RAY HARRYHAUSEN'S
GOLDEN VOYAGE

By Aaron J. French

WHILE GREAT ADVANCEMENTS have been made in the field of cyber-based technologies, which have done a good deal to enhance our modern culture—the rise of the internet and independent media, the availability of hard-to-find esoteric texts, computer gaming, social networking and the overall linking of humankind together in one unified, cybernetic bond—an area that seems to me to still be lacking is the rampant use of computer-generated imagery in motion pictures.

Of course I do admit to being overcome with joy when I first saw *Terminator 2: Judgment Day*, and I do appreciate a *Lord of theRings* trilogy or two. But when it comes to *Snakes on a Plane, Deep Blue Sea, Van Helsing,* and others, the sense of utter fraudulence becomes marked, and in a very real sense movies appear to be getting *worse* as technology develops, rather than better.

But can this be true? Well obviously it isn't *totally* true, and there are exceptions. Yet no one can deny that the employment of both egregiously bad and exceptionally good CGI is on the rise, appearing in almost every film that involves action sequences or special effects. CGI is the key term here, because what is not so much on the rise includes on-set location shooting (green-screen compositing has become the norm), real-life models and costumes, and even human actors (think Jar Jar Binks and the Na'vi of *Avatar*).

It is strange to think that the man who started this evolution, Ray Harryhausen, has now passed on, leaving behind a fierce legacy of ingenious films and special effects work, while back here on Earth the CGI craze continues to propel filmmaking down a road of phoniness and PKD unreality. Harryhausen's films—though saplings for what would become CGI special effects—in no way feel inorganic to me. Oddly enough, even though his creatures—such as the seven-headed hydra, the kraken, medusa, one-eyed giant centaur cyclops,or the skeletons from *Jason and the Argonauts*—appear less "real-looking" than most CGI transformers or superheroes, to me they actually thrum with more vitality and life. They have personality and character, rendering them, in my mind, more memorable and interesting.

But maybe I should backtrack. For those who may not have heard of Harryhausen, he is the visual effects artist and producer behind the classic films *The 7th Voyage of Sinbad, Clash of the Titans, One Million Years B.C.*, and many others. He was born June 29, 1920, and sadly died this past May 7, 2013. During the 1950s he pioneered his own brand of stop-motion model animation using armatures—articulated metal, wire, or wooden figures that can be made to hold various poses. He also invented a technique known as "Dynamation."

In the recent online blog post "Why Ray Harryhausen's stop-motion effects were more real than CGI," author Ethan Gilsdorf describes Dynamation as"… [combining] foreground and background footage by photographing miniatures in front of a rear-projection screen [which allows] the creature or creatures … to exist in the midst of 'real' human-scaled action, or even appear to move in front of and behind 'live' elements."

Thus we have the amazing Talos scene in *Jason and the Argonauts*, and Perseus riding the Pegasus in *Clash of the Titans*, and my personal favorite, Sinbad's battle with the six-armed Kali idol in *The Golden Voyage of Sinbad*.

But Ray Harryhausen really began his visual effects career with a love for dinosaurs, making short films of the prehistoric creatures in his garage. This love would eventually find fruition in *One Million Years B.C* staring Raquel Welch. And it would also spawn a lifelong friendship with the great Ray Bradbury, who made a promise with Harryhausen to always remain kids and to love dinosaurs forever.

Following his hobbyist work in the garage, Harryhausen created some truly original short fairy tale shows for George Pal's *Puppetoons*, but was eventually pulled onto more professional film projects, including *Mighty Joe Young* and Bradbury's own *The Beast from 20,000 Fathoms*.

However Ray truly hit his peak period when he "went Greek," as it were, and entered into the classical period of world history with *Jason and the Argonauts*, two more Sinbad films, and his opus, *Clash of the Titans*(1981).

This latter was the last feature film to showcase his effects work, and it is truly a work-of-art piece of filmmaking. After that, more sophisticated technology was developed during the '80s and '90s, which began to eclipse Harryhausen's production technique and the man finally retired.

The aforementioned CGI craze currently dominating Hollywood and the recent passing of Mr. Harryhausen seem to suggest the close of an era—perhaps even a Golden Era—of special effects in film. From here on out the digitization of what we watch up on the screen will increase, until we might not be able to mark the difference between what's real and what is not—or what's proxy and what is genuine. Is this a bad thing? Hard to say. I do know that lately I watch fewer movies than I used to, and as a kid I could've watched *Clash of the Titans* a zillion times without tiring of it.

But is this a product of childhood itself, or the way that Harryhausen created his effects? Probably both, but in his interviews Ray admits to consciously implementing the childlike form of imagination in his work. And there was that whole eternal-kids pact between him and Bradbury.

So maybe that's what's needed, then. Not more, or less, realistic special effects and CGI, but more child-driven imaginative qualities in films. Only time will tell if this is true. For now all I can say is rest in peace, Mr. Harryhausen. May your films continue to inspire wonder in those who watch them.

Ray Bradbury, Ray Harryhausen, Forry Ackerman - Jan 1963, Photo Courtesy of the Ray & Diana Harryhausen Foundation

Photo Courtesy of Gene O'Neill

Gene O'Neill:
Living Within His Characters

By Joel B. Kirkpatrick

Common men writing uncommon words; it's been the hallmark of bookmaking for thousands of years. Uncommon words can eventually elevate the common man to a richer standing among his peers. It takes an uncommon man to accept that new position unchanged. A changed man might write common words. That would unravel the illusion of greatness entirely.

Gene O'Neill might call that the *fog* of greatness. He sounds wary of praise, and of status, and of illusion—when common words can be given up instead. And he is wary of fog; it can hide some horrible things within.

O'Neill prefers to show things in a clearer light—to bring them out of the shadows. He looks for overlooked people, hidden figures, and hardened faces, extreme conditions that twist and bend the human spirit. He looks for something in-common, from every uncommon character. He has seen a lot, and done a lot, and written a lot. Not a bit of it…common.

Congratulations on the Stoker Gene, from Dark Discoveries.

JBK: Your son once said of you, *"My father likes faces with character…He likes soulful, damaged people—at least on paper. In real life he doesn't like anyone…"* That bit of wry teasing speaks volumes about your writing. You've been revealing an otherwise overlooked group of people in your stories, haven't you?

GO: Yes, and that is reflective of my personal beliefs. You won't find classic heroes or villains in my work. Like real life, my characters all struggle doing the best they can.

JBK: Readers have found a lot to praise in your body of work. You've earned eight Stoker nominations, and with one of those the prize. Do you have fans who have become just good friends over the years?

GO: Sure. In addition to often including family members' names in my stories, I include their friends' names, and sometimes fans' names. It's always fun to meet fans at conventions, readings, or singings. Many are like family.

JBK: With more than a hundred-twenty stories and close to five novels in print, you still avoid writing deliberately to a genre. That means your devoted readers may adore some of your stories and really dislike others. You aren't shy about that at all, are you? Is that a deliberate method of yours to reach the largest audience, or is it purely the result of writing what you like best?

GO: Well, from the beginning I haven't written pure genre stories. In fact I probably am best known as a mixed-genre writer. Not the best career plan for a young writer by the way. Really all I care about is being known as a *good* writer.

JBK: When we first visited for this interview, you hinted that you might begin serious work on expanding your recently published *Operation Rhinoceros Hornbill* into a novel titled *White Plague*. Did that opportunity arise?

GO: Yes, I'm currently two thirds through completing *The White Plague*.

JBK: What projects are you currently shaping, besides *Plague*?

GO: I'm putting the finishing touches on a novelette, *Ridin The Dawg*, an invite to a five year anniversary anthology for a good small press. Story is a good one, I think.

For the last few years I've not had any inventory of short stuff, able to take advantage of a cool anthology that gets announced. But I've just finished a pair of short stories, "Coyote Gambit," and "Tight Partners." Both are spoken for already (*Ed*. The former one appears in this issue of *Dark Discoveries*). I'm going to work on some more short stories after *The White Plague* is complete (end of year, I hope).

JBK: Many writers hold dreams of writing professionally. It seems you took that bold step—putting other work aside to write full-time—years ago. In those early years, did you doubt it was a good decision?

GO: No. Even though I startedwriting fairly later in life than most, I think it was a good decision. I've had many life experiences to write about. And when I went full time, I'd earned enough financial resources to support my family, regardless of writing financial success. No regrets.

JBK: You once told Chris Morey of Dark Regions Press that, "…*everything a person writes is autobiographical.*" Do you feel that modern writers understand that well enough nowadays to avoid writing to formulas and trends?

GO: No, I'm not sure I initially believed it—the wonderful writer Kate Wilhelm told me that early in my career. Now, I know it's true. Lends the emotional weight to my work.

JBK: When you began writing thirty years ago, there were fewer avenues to get your stories into reader's hands. Today the reality is staggering—technology creates several million new authors each year. Do you believe this is the spark beginning to change the publishing industry, or is it truly the growing public demand for more books creating the changes we see? Are you amazed at the changes you have witnessed?

GO: When I began writing there were many more *print* opportunities for a young writer. I published initially in mass market magazines. Had several NY agents want to represent my longer stuff back then—I was working two

jobs and couldn't afford to devote myself to longer work. Now, there may be a lot of digital opportunities, some of that self-published, with no benefit of good editing. I think when I started was a better time for a good young writer.

JBK: Ted Klein called you in 1980 for your first fiction sale to *The Twilight Zone* magazine (1981-89). They purchased *The Burden of Indigo*. Did that spur a burst of new writing from you as a result of the attention? How forcefully were you marketing your work at the time?

GO: Yes, I came out of the blocks after that. Selling to good markets like F & SF. But I'm a slow writer, and I was working two jobs, supporting a family, and wasn't able to really capitalize and knock out novels. From the start, I sent my stories to what I thought were the top markets.

JBK: Twenty-two years later, Brian Keene was calling *The Burden of Indigo* the best post-holocaust novel ever written. It is now considered a classic. Have you been surprised at that story's permanence?

GO: It's immodest to say, no. But, *no*.

JBK: Please describe the path that *Burden of Indigo* took, from its beginnings as a magazine piece of fiction, to a full novel project twenty years later.

GO: I was working and writing short stories late at night. Maybe tried a pair of novelettes along the way. But I only decided to begin a long novel after I saw my daughter about to graduate from college. I began *The Burden Of Indigo*. Ha! After working in a medical clinic and before I could begin writing full time, she told me she wanted to go to medical school. Delayed my writing novels a bit. But she has probably made a bigger contribution to society as a Cardio-vascular surgical PA. And world-class mom!

JBK: You are published now by several small press publishers. Is that a bit of business management on your part as the author, or the luck-of-the-draw with stories and their life beyond your own efforts? Do your books seem to travel into the right hands by themselves?

GO: Honestly, probably an accident. In the early years I only knew about the major mass market magazines and NYC publishers. I never attended a convention until my daughter had graduated from medical school. So I came late to the dark fiction small press—where I have a good home now. In fact the small press has probably saved the novella—my favorite length.

JBK: Have you reached a point in your career where projects are shopped to you, or do you still create mostly from your own desire and imagination? Has a project ever made you feel that you were just doing a job at the time?

GO: No, I've been lucky in that my primary source of income wasn't dependant on my writing. So I've pretty much pursued what I felt like writing. Of course at this stage, I get all kinds of solicitations of short stories or even longer stuff. Either the project has to really appeal or rarely a convincing appeal from a friend. I listen to everything, but am very selective. (Sounds snooty—I'm not really.)

JBK: Can you remember any single project that seemed to not want to be written? Have you ever confronted a narrative that had to be forced?

GO: Sure, I think it is a common experience for writers to lose faith in what they're doing half way through a project. You think: *Oh, man this is terrible, I'm wasting time*. But I've learned to struggle on. I always have serious apprehensions about everything at the moment I hit *send*. There are good days when you are really in John Gardner's *fictive dream*, and days when you just soldier on.

JBK: You recently released *Jade* and *Double Jack* (Bad Moon Books. 2010 & 2011), both of which are series books on two of your popular themes. Do you find inspiration more easily for characters you have known well and visited several times before? Do they still surprise you with fresh angles to explore?

GO: I think my feelings are common with other writers. When I finish a project I'm sad, because I have lived— sometimes for a year plus—with the characters. No one likes to say goodbye to friends, even if they've done terrible things. Backgrounds are important to me, especially stuff with a SF tint. I think of my stories in terms of background—like, that's a Tenderloin story, or a Cal Wild story, or whatever.

JBK: Many traditionally published authors can bemoan the fact that they initially sold well, but were too soon out of print with their mainstream book. Does that eventually happen to short story writers in magazines and web-based publications? Do you ever hear from readers that

they cannot find certain of your stories anymore?

GO: Just happened in a review of *The Hungry Skull*, which appeared in the first issue of a promising new digest, Nameless Magazine. The reviewer said, *Wow! Where has this guy come from?* Ha. But you are right, when you shift direction, readers of, say a magazine you appeared in numerous times, soon forget your byline or can't find it. Surprising with the ease of Googling a name nowadays.

JBK: You are certainly an author that avid readers hope to add to their collections. Have you ever had a strong enough response to any material to prompt a specialty-press project? Which of your collections was driven purely by reader demand?

GO: I think that the second project you do for a specialty press publisher has to be driven by demand. The first one sold well! Yes, I've had a number of specialty press folks ask to see my next long piece—novella or novel. Funny, I've mentioned expanding a recently published novella, *Operation Rhinoceros Hornbill*, into a novel that I'd probably call *The White Plague*.

JBK: *In Dark Corners* (Genius Publishing, 2012) is a retrospective collection, with some of your personal favorite short fiction. But it also includes some little-known science fiction stories of yours. Was that collection purely your own idea?

GO: No, as I recall I met with the Genius Publishing folks at a convention, and they asked for something (Norm Rubenstein, an editor at JournalStone was involved with this one). *In Dark Corners* is the eventual result. Some of those dark SF stories weren't in obscure publications.

JBK: Which do you believe is more difficult...writing from the darker side of reality, or creating a new, dystopian environment? Can people be more monstrous, in your opinion, than any winged or fanged creation?

GO: Difficult? I don't usually think about that when starting something. And of course there are only a few monsters in my supernatural stories. I think I lean more toward psychological stuff. People and their reactions interest me most, whether the story is SF or something else.

JBK: Truman Capote took a shocking event, and gave the public one of its first tastes of journalistic style true-life horror (*In Cold Blood*). Given your own psychology background, have you ever wondered at a real event horrible enough to interest you in writing non-fiction? Aren't you writing, with your deliberately deep psychological themes, stories that are only thinly-veiled fictions anyway?

GO: You are very perceptive; much of the idea generation of my dark psychological stuff comes from reality.

JBK: How often do you wish that you had launched your writing career as a younger man? Would we still have the same Gene O'Neill stories we know, or might you have been a different writer by now?

GO: Funny, I just exchanged an e-mail with a young writer discussing this. Of course the young writer has passion and energy powering her work, often writing fast. The older writer has experience underlying his work, often writing slower. I think by starting later, I probably gained from experience. I know I'm very slow now, often spending as much time thinking as typing.

JBK: The web knows you well; it is not difficult to follow dozens of internet links directly to information about you and your published works. Try as we might, we cannot locate a personal website of your own. What keeps you deliberately out of that arena?

GO: You will actually find few personal interviews, no reviews, or me interviewing other writers. And for the same reason I don't maintain a website. I was drug kicking and screaming to Facebook. I had limited time when I was beginning, writing instead of sleeping. I had to decide where that time was best spent. I decided to be a writer, period. And that's what I still am now.

JBK: No mention can be found of any graphic novel adaptations of your work... Have you ever been approached for such a project? Would a pairing of your story with some outstanding artwork interest you at all?

GO: Sure that would be fun. Recently Evil Jester Press bought a short story, "The Masque of the Red Horde" they are adapting into a comic.

JBK: You told Harry Shannon of *Really Scary* that you had sold all your material yourself, for years. But in the same interview you also warn that no short fiction writer can make a living without writing novels as well. Your first novel was released twenty-one years after your first sale as an author. Short stories earned you a good living, did they not? Are you still your own, best agent?

GO: Yes, I've marketed all my work. That doesn't work now in the mass market. I have a new agent, Bob Fleck, who likes my stuff and is going to present some to the NYC establishment. He likes the idea of *The White Plague*. Of course I'd like it if he got solid interest/offers.

JBK: You mentioned in 2009 that some interest had been shown in adapting your book *The Burden of Indigo* for the screen. What became of that attention? Has it been the only time you were approached by the film industry?

GO: There has been inquiry about several pieces, including "The Confessions Of St. Zach". But *Indigo* has stirred the most interest. I was offered an option on it from Zen Films of London. But I declined after taking my family to a premier of one of their projects in San Francisco. Again, risking sounding snooty, I'm not interested in a few option bucks; if I don't believe the company can do my work well, I'm not signing.

JBK: You are known to indulge in re-reading Hemmingway when you feel the need. Have any modern authors captured your taste in the same way as your older favorites?

GO: Sure I read a lot, usually fiction on recommendation. Right now someone I like a lot, a South African, Bryce Courtenay, recommended by Chris Marrs. But the bulk of my reading is mostly non-fiction. I love writer biographies. Recently finished Jubilee Hitchhiker—life and times of Richard Brautigan, and one on JD Salinger. Looking for something in common, I guess. Nope, the only famous person I share a common background with is Mickey Rourke—now there is a dark story. Also, I like astro-physics and cosmology, writers like Kaku, Greene, and Ferris. Of course I don't understand the math, and barely grasp the ideas. But we definitely live in interesting times.

JBK: You once read the story "Tombstones in His Eyes"which is a fictional account of your son, Gavin, aloud to your wife. Do you do that regularly, or often, in front of your fans? Has anyone ever treated you to a listening of your own works read aloud, and how did it sound to you, coming from another voice?

GO: I rarely read anything to Kay, and only occasionally at cons to fans. I have heard my stuff read on the radio and podcasts. The Stoker finalist"Graffiti Sonata" (published in Dark Discoveries) was read/acted on the Chicago podcast—forget the name—by an actor. Funny, he had a London accent.

☙❧☙

COYOTE GAMBIT

By Gene O'Neill

The man rises up cautiously from the cluster of thick manzanita bushes camouflaging his entryway. With his head barely exposed, he slowly turns and examines his immediate surroundings. He notices that the area has been lightly dusted with snow since early last night. Unusual weather for the Greater Bay Area, even frost rare during the winters before The Collapse. He pulls down the bandana protecting his face and releases a steamy breath from his mouth. Even in his bundled-up garb he isn't able to restrain a slight shiver. He's venturing out an hour later than usual tonight, dusk already rapidly descending.

He's been delayed with cleaning up broken glass and a mess before leaving his obsessively neat basement stronghold hidden away behind him under the overgrown concrete rubble. Now, he will have to rush over to the old park to check his trap line before predators strip any of his successful snares. Usually the silent thieves operate under the cover of early darkness. Rabbits have best resisted the radioactive pollution of all the animal survivors, and they are now his major source of fresh meat. He can't afford to lose even one to thieves.

Nevertheless, for a few moments more he remains in place, carefully inspecting the wintry landscape. First, he checks around his hidden entryway for any footprints. He finds the thin snow crust undisturbed. Then, he slowly scans the surrounding shadows for movement of any kind, and detects none. He sucks in a deep breath sampling the air. The sweet stench of death has at last completely dissipated from over the city, and the air tonight is nothing but chilled freshness. Finally, he cocks his head, pinches his nostrils, blows through his nose, popping his ear canals.

Then, he closes his eyes and listens ever so intently for a few moments. Hearing nothing suspicious, he blinks, ready to go. But before taking a step, he compulsively touches first his sawed-off shotgun and then his long knife, both holstered on the cartridge belt tightened around his hips outside his ankle-length tan duster.

As confidant as he can be that no danger lurks nearby, he pulls up his bandanna, tugs down the ski cap over his ears, and begins to head over to the city park, three long blocks away.

***

Like other cities in the Greater Bay Area, the downtown streets of Vallejo are impassably clogged with abandoned, rusting vehicles and stacks of litter. To the west across 250 yards of water, a few steel ribs of buildings are silhouetted skeletal reminders of where Mare Island Naval Shipyard once stood. Piles of rubble, twisted metal, and burned debris are scattered about everywhere over there, replacing the long two-story shops, deep dry docks, and dinosaur-like cranes.

In the heart of downtown, the man passes a pair of flattened Muni buses that were caught and buried under the avalanche of collapsing buildings. The city has been almost completely leveled and burned over like most other towns as far north as Dixon and south as Crockett, but especially the Vacaville/Fairfield/Suisun/Vallejo east-west corridor running along I-80 between Travis Air Force Base and Mare Island Naval Shipyard—the sites of three major strikes during The Collapse.

The man moves cautiously, all his senses remaining keenly on full alert.

Just last week here in downtown, after blundering around the burnt shell of an RV while carelessly deep in thought, he'd almost stumbled into the arms of an unexpected man. Fortunately, the startled stranger was not a *Desperado*. They usually traveled in pairs or small groups, and were very heavily armed with superior firepower—some even carrying military weapons like M16s and AR-15s. This apparently unarmed man was most likely a solitary gatherer/scrounger like himself. The frightened stranger had turned and shuffled off as fast as he could. He was obviously hobbled by injury or malnutrition, perhaps both. Once it might have been a comical sight, watching the wretched man making his stumbling, labored, slow motion, and slapstick getaway. But now it's just sad. An injured or lame person on their own has little or no good chance of survival. Yet the man's feelings are guarded and hardened after witnessing so much death and tragedy during the last three years.

The man continues south toward the waterfront bordering Mare Island Naval Shipyard, which even though shut down for almost three decades had still been designated a prime target for a major strike. Encountering nothing alarming or obviously hazardous, the man proceeds to his destination. Arriving at the edge of the old Marina Park, he stops and again checks about cautiously. The shedding eucalyptus trees, madrones, oleanders, and manzanitas that have survived the holocaust after The Collapse are now prospering and overgrown. Tall field grass has sprung up shoulder high across the entire park, providing good cover for both man and animal. A protected feeding area for rabbits.

He sees, hears, or smells nothing suspicious. No human tracks of any kind in the snow powder here on the eastern perimeter of the park. So the man moves into the tall growth around the old playground to check his first rabbit snare.

Nothing.

But at that moment he hears them coming. Distant *baying, howling, barking, growling*.

The dogpack—probably good size—is in deadly pursuit of something, and coming straight down Georgia Street in his general direction, approaching the park's northeastern boundary.

The rapidly encroaching sounds raise the hair on the back of his neck, cause the

breath to catch in his throat, and elevate his pulse. Despite the frosty night air, he's beginning to sweat, his underarms and crotch already gritty and itchy under his protective clothing. Compelled to act defensively, he quickly checks around for something to climb up on.

But the closest eucalyptus trees have no low branches and he's too far away from the basalt restrooms still in place. Fortunately, one of the few surviving oaks in the park is not too far away, and a low limb beckons. He hustles over and adroitly hoists himself up into the cover of the tree. Deftly, he scoots higher until he can easily survey his immediate surroundings for 360 degrees through the waxy black-green leaves.

Dogpacks are one of the constant deadly hazards threatening his daily survival. But here far up the black oak he is perfectly safe from ground attack. Sweating even more heavily now under his bundled-up garb, he again tugs down his bandana to more easily catch his breath. Then, he sucks in the cold air deeply, gathering himself for what may be a long wait.

As it nears the park, the man sees that the pack is in close pursuit of a deer, a small one—perhaps a yearling. There are six, big, well-fed dogs in the pack, led by a huge tan-colored mix of mastiff and probably pit bull. Under normal circumstances the deer would've easily evaded this pack of dangerous but relatively slow dogs. But it is sick or perhaps has something wrong with its right foreleg, as it seems to list clumsily to that side as it runs. The deer veers suddenly left, cutting directly across the park, and easily avoids the larger obstacles. But as the pack rapidly closes in, it begins frantically dashing headlong through the thick grass, brush, oleanders, and manzanita.

The man rotates slightly to the south and watches as the obviously fastest dog, a sleek Doberman Pinscher leaves the pack and closes in on the heels of the hapless creature. But something suddenly diverts the dog's attention.

Abruptly, it halts as if it has run into an invisible wall.

The Doberman's head is cocked now, and even from a distance the man can see its nostrils flare as it intensely samples the breeze blowing across the park from the nearby Carquinez Straits. The dog obviously has caught the scent of something that immediately commands more attention and greater interest than the struggling deer that has by then disappeared into the darkness on the far southern side of the park.

By now all five other dogs have also caught a whiff of the attractive scent. And pack discipline has been seriously disrupted, as they break apart and begin turning in circles, while constantly sniffing the air. A few snap at their neighbors' heels as they jerk about.

Then, the man sees *it*.

A single coyote stands on the crest of the first of a double set of hills right at the center of the park. Sleek, brown, with just a hint of grayish rust on its shoulders and ear tips. Peering down almost nonchalantly at the distracted pack.

It has to be a *her*.

The dogs—obviously all males—have now spotted her. And even though they are excited into a *snapping, yelping, whining* frenzy, the huge mastiff maintains a semblance of leadership control and pack discipline. He prevents a mass breakout of individuals chasing off after the lone coyote by direct *threat*. Lunging, baring his huge yellow fangs, and growling aggressively up in the faces of individual pack members.

The man knows the coyote standing enticingly on the hillcrest is indeed female, because he has seen coyotes play this gambit before. He allows a thin, rare smile, appreciating the cleverness of the small predators. He shifts his position, easing the kinks in his back and legs, while continuing to watch the drama playing out below.

The female coyote is undoubtedly in heat. Her alluring scent so pervasive that it holds prisoner the attention of all six male dogs.

Dogpacks are almost *all* exclusively male now. Female dogs, which are much smaller and weaker, had been mostly cut out of the successfully surviving packs. Often attacked by the males and driven off, if not killed and eaten. A matter of immediate necessity. This began only a few months after the initial devastation and successive fires of The Collapse. Stray dogs soon dying by starving to death or from having eaten radioactive carrion. Only the most ruthless dogpacks survived by quickly honing their pack hunting kills, stalking and eating only fresh meat—any *kind* of fresh meat, including female dogs and weaker strays.

And something similar had also been happening to women survivors hiding out of sight. The last woman he had seen was almost a year ago. Near the waterfront, when he'd been on a routine scrounging expedition. He'd spotted the fairly neat and young woman crawling out from under the fallen roof shell of a *CVS's Drugstore*. He'd felt a strong surge of elation. But fortunately for him, he'd resisted immediately approaching her after he spotted the wide dog collar on her neck and a leash trailing down her back. The three men appeared only moments later, all heavily armed with M16s and holstered handguns, chests crossed with belts of ammunition. The woman was the property of *Desperadoes*.

***

Growling and continuing to threaten an attack, the huge male lead dog forces the pack to back down in subservience to his dominance—several eventually rolling over and displaying their stomachs. Then, nervously glancing back over his shoulder several times, the mastiff begins to creep up the hill by himself, stalking the lone coyote female in heat.

But, before he reaches her, she turns and coquettishly trots over the hill and out of sight. The great mastiff breaks into a mad dash, headlong up and over the hillcrest.

Where the man sees the huge, fearsome dog skid to an abrupt stop.

Waiting to ambush him, hidden by the dip between the two hills, are six other members of the female's coyote pack. Roughly half the size of their prey, the seven coyotes, including the female, aggressively encircle the huge mastiff.

They begin darting in and out, depending on their superior flexibility and speed to evade the lunges and crunching jaws of the stronger but slower and clumsier dog.

Over a short period of time, they wear down the mastiff's stamina. Its chest heaves, and its broad tongue lolls out of its drooling mouth…

At that point, the largest coyote, probably the pack leader, confronts the mastiff directly, commanding the tiring dog's undivided attention. While he's so occupied, two coyotes simultaneously sneak in close and attack him from the rear… and efficiently hamstring the mastiff with twin slashing, tearing bites high on its inner rear legs.

Dragging his bleeding hindquarters uselessly now, the mastiff struggles fiercely to protect himself. But he is soon being successfully savaged from all sides, bleeding heavily and weakened from a dozen ragged deep bites. After another harrowing minute or two, the coyote leader finally lunges in and locks onto the badly wounded mastiff's throat, and begins a slow, strangling maneuver.

The fight is over.

Now, for the spoils.

In a few brief minutes, like skilled slaughterhouse butchers, each member of the pack expertly tears off a huge chunk of the dog. Then, the individual coyotes scatter to the east, taking along their shares of fresh meat.

The coyotes quickly disappear off into the night, moments before the remainder of the cowed dogpack finally collects its wits and courage enough to investigate the prolonged absence of their leader. Only to discover a partially butchered carcass and

meat-covered bones and innards from their once fierce leader strewn about the hidden dip between the hillcrests. They immediately begin feeding on the bloody remnants.

At that point, off in the distance, the clever coyotes *yip* and *howl* with what seems like a triumphant victory yell to the man still crouching up in the safety of the black oak.

***

After the partially fed, but leaderless and disheartened, dogpack finally wanders off into the night, the man shimmies safely down the tree trunk.

He begins to finally run his trap line, finding a plump rabbit strangled in his fifth snare. But as he nears his final and ninth trap, located near the wild blackberries growing in a marsh fed by a broken water pipe, he slows with a growing sense of apprehension. Just as he has first suspected from a distance, he finally confirms that the snare is indeed tripped. But it is empty, only several drops of blood and a few traces of rabbit fur left behind on the thin dusting of snow. He doesn't have to search far or very long before he discovers the thief's footprint—small and *human*.

The sight of the human footprint is as frightening as the earlier moment tonight when he first heard the baying of the dangerous dogpack. Because the man realizes that someone has discovered his trap line; and that person now *knows* the man exists.

***

Safely back in his basement stronghold, the man lights candles and skins and cooks the rabbit on his propane-fueled camp stove.

Even though there is plenty of diesel and gas available in abandoned vehicles and a number of underground storage tanks, that fact does him little good. The man has never located a small undamaged generator. He has found several massive industrial ones several miles away, but hasn't figured out how to easily load and then get them around the nearly impassable streets to his hideout. And if he were successful, he would have to somehow mask the noisy sound of a large generator—*silence* his reliable guardian. So he has no electricity or refrigeration. But he usually only snares one rabbit every two or three evenings, at the most. So, he has developed the habit of gorging on that one rabbit at a late evening meal, thereby eliminating any possibility of the meat spoiling. Salting or drying preservation experiments are secondary concerns at the moment. Maybe when he establishes another snare run a mile farther south in the overgrown sports park and ball fields, he will begin experiments to salt or dry any surplus meat.

After thoroughly enjoying the fresh rabbit tonight, which always reminds the man of chicken with a slightly gamy taste, he stretches out on his sleeping pallet.

By candlelight he likes to read from his small valued collection of books. His favorite two are badly worn paperback copies of *The Old Man and the Sea* and *One Day in the Life of Ivan Denisovich*. Both books are really about man persevering under trying circumstances. He usually completes reading each of the novella-length pieces in one evening. He's always moved by the Cuban fisherman's or Russian prisoner's inspiring survival efforts, despite the almost impossible odds against them. Tonight, he grows really weary before the old man has even hooked the giant fish. And he is forced to lay the Hemingway book down unfinished and blow out the candle.

Almost immediately after closing his eyes and drifting off, the man has the recurring dream about his young wife, pre-Collapse. It's very late at night, and they are spooning after sex on their apartment bed, him enjoying her distinctive *spicy-lemon* scent. He eventually grows aroused again and begins passionately kissing her neck and back. Then, he enters her from behind, and she moans loudly as they make love together ever so slowly. When they climax almost simultaneously, she gasps and cranes around to kiss him.

Shock.

She has no features!

He always awakens after this horrifying moment in a clammy sweat, panting out of breath. And, then, the overwhelming guilt returns.

***

A few days pre-Collapse, he'd gone on a hunting trip with his cousin up into the Ruby Mountains north of Elko, Nevada, picking Joel up in Roseville in his new *Ranger*. They were isolated at their camp when the first strikes hit Northern California, completely unaware of what had happened. But they'd decided to break camp early and return home—the buck hunting exceptionally poor for some reason. Of course they noticed the abandoned vehicles and almost complete lack of people as they traveled back down

I-80. But it was only after they finally reached Roseville on the outskirts of Sacramento and stopped that they actually realized the enormity of what had happened. Nearby northern Sacramento around old McClellen AFB and most of southern Roseville were a flattened, badly burned-over mess. Nevertheless, Joel stayed there at his home to check on relatives.

The man continued in his *Ranger* pickup, successfully bypassing Sacramento to the far west and able to drive south; but eventually he was forced to abandon his pickup and start walking with backpack and hunting rifle near Vacaville, as the highway and surrounding roads grew impassable. He soon noticed the heavily bundled-up dress of the occasional paranoid survivor he encountered. He imitated their garb finding a longcoat, roll-down skycap, and face scarf in the debris of a shopping center near Fairfield and the Travis AFB turn-off. Surviving on the leftover freeze-dried food and fresh water they'd taken along on the hunting trip, he avoided *all* hazards on the way, including a large group of *Desperadoes* apparently looting around Cordelia. But, he'd had to flee from camp late that night after hearing approaching voices, fearing it was the *Desperadoes* tracking him. He was forced to abandon his pack and hunting rifle.

Finally, after being gone almost a month, he arrived back home to Vallejo, realizing he was indeed lucky to still be in one piece and not radiation sick. But a day later he found his wife's badly burned and almost unrecognizable remains buried in the ashes of their burned-out apartment building. Nothing important remained to be salvaged—not even any photographs of her.

Nothing.

***

But now, three years later, almost crazy with the palpable reminders of his isolated loneliness, he cannot really remember exactly what his wife looked like. Auburn hair, yes, and a petite build, and he thinks she smiled constantly… That is the extent of all he can conjure up with his eyes closed. His guilt and the lonely despair on a number of occasions have driven him to the brink of ending it all with the sawed-off shotgun. But, after twice getting to the point of tightly fingering the trigger with the barrel locked under his jaw, he manages somehow to back off, avoiding oblivion. He shoulders the nagging guilt, convinced that forgetting her face is a major betrayal on his part. But he suspects—actually *hopes*—that if he can ever totally recall her features, his guilt will instantly dissipate like air *popping* from a punctured balloon. But the passage of time continues to erode her memory, and suicide is now the constant dark companion of his nagging guilt.

Tonight he is again extremely agitated and depressed by the recurring dream. It lingers in his mind, the featureless image an open sore. Despite it being several hours before dawn, the man gets up and paces about his immaculate but confining basement sanctuary. Finally, he takes a piece of a brown paper bag from a neat pile and decides to completely inventory his six-foot long, floor-to-ceiling storage shelves of canned and packaged dry food and other supplies. He isn't really too low on anything. But he's been planning a visit to the old *Safeway* ruins today anyhow. Just to check around. So, he goes over his supplies and compiles a list to distract himself from the depressing thoughts.

***

Just after dawn, the man dresses, shoulders his empty backpack, straps on his cartridge belt, and checks his shotgun.

He'd used the weapon in the early days to hunt game. *Mistake*. It made too much noise and used up too many shells. Now he has only three shotgun shells left. Ammunition almost impossible to find anymore, the *Desperadoes* confiscating weapons and ammunition from their victims. And he always left one shell at home, for when he can no longer cope with the guilt.

Ready, he pushes back the heavy grill cover hiding the crawlspace leading out from his basement shelter. Noiselessly, he creeps along the narrow path shifting through the maze of rubble, which emerges in the stand of shoulder-high, thick manzanita bushes.

***

A half an hour later, the man pauses at where the *Marina Safeway Super-Market* had once stood, pre-Collapse.

***

Within a few weeks after the strike on the far southwestern end of the Shipyard, the almost flattened *Safeway* had been completely stripped of all the unspoiled packaged meat, wine, liquor, and medicine that surviving scavengers could dig out from under the rubble. But, fortunately for the man, a portion of the rear warehouse section containing mostly durable canned and packaged goods sealed in cardboard boxes had been sheltered away. A six-foot high pocket-like bunker had been created when four curved steel beams fell and crisscrossed together, mostly protecting the cache from roof remnants that collapsed down onto the beams. And more importantly the hidden hoard had been initially overlooked and bypassed by foragers. The man had found it later only by accident, stumbling through a weak spot in the leveled roof, falling six or so feet, and finding himself sprawled out in *Eden*.

As insurance, the night after the initial discovery of the stocked cache, the man had worked steadily for almost twenty-four hours to further protect and secret his trove of undamaged rations. That first night of work, he had completely sealed off the loading dock warehouse entryway to the ruined supermarket with heavy chunks of concrete rubble and a seemingly half ton of shoveled debris. A day or so later, he'd followed four National Guardsmen using a Geiger counter to place freshly painted **red skull & cross bone** signs—most of them along the closest three miles of waterfront stretching parallel with the nearby Shipyard. The Guardsmen mysteriously disappeared in a truck shortly after completing the placements of the radioactive warning signs.

The man had conspicuously relocated the stolen signs all around the burned debris pile surrounding the destroyed supermarket, especially near the now covered rear entry.

***

Around in back of the store, the man cautiously approaches the wooden hatch he's made that camouflages and conceals the small entrance into the tunnel he's reinforced with basalt blocks through the concrete rubble and debris.

Inside the tight, dark passageway, he takes out his flashlight and follows the beam into the rear warehouse pocket of the *Safeway*. It's quiet, cold, and dark inside the bunker. He makes his way past the smashed liquor and wine section, mostly only broken empty bottles remaining. He glances at his list, stopping at the now often visited soup section, breaking open new cases of beef-barley, tomato rice, and another of chicken noodle. He puts five cans of each soup in his backpack. Then, he makes his way over to the packaged powdered drinks, to a half-full case of lemon-lime *Kool-Aid* he'd left opened during his last visit. He selects a dozen packages of the drink—his favorite. He finishes his food *shopping* at the section of packaged pasta, rice, and cereals, picking up a selection of ten sealed packages from recently opened cartons. Before he leaves the warehouse, he also gathers up four packages of double D batteries, two boxes of matches, and a carton of the large fat candles he likes to read by.

Finished now, he shrugs the stuffed and heavy backpack high on his shoulders, making sure his arms are left free enough to reach either of his weapons. Then, he crawls back out the tunnel and emerges minutes later through the hatch hole. Carefully, he replaces the camouflaged wooden plank back in place.

But before he takes even one step away, he sees the small footprint in the remaining frozen crust of snow. The sight causes him to gasp and flinch back, as if the print were a coiled rattlesnake. He sucks in a deep, settling breath, certain that the print is identical to the one he'd spotted yesterday at the end of his rabbit run. No question in the man's mind now: *He is definitely being followed and watched.*

For three years he's remained under the radar, coming and going with complete impunity. Undetected and safe, but also completely alone. This way he's managed to survive, escaping the attention of all others, including the occasional *Desperado* gang and the more frequent wandering dogpacks.

Fighting off a disabling sense of panic, he closes his eyes, takes several more deep breaths, lets the air trickle out past his dry lips, and tries to pull himself together.

Still unnerved, he carefully checks around…

…and sighs, thinking that whomever made the footprint is now out of sight.

Stiffly, the man begins to make his way home, on super alert. Stopping and furtively checking behind himself each time his paranoia flares.

Who's stalking him? What does the person want?

He feels perplexed, not sure what to think.

***

Later that afternoon before dusk, the man has to *force* himself to venture out and return to his rabbit run in the park near the waterfront.

***

Carefully, he advances along the trap line, inspecting each un-tripped snare, but also keeping on the lookout for more small footprints. But the crust of frozen snow has almost completely melted now. So he finds nothing, either game or footprints.

***

At the end of the run near the blackberries, along the perimeter of the park, off in the shadows, something moves ever so slightly, catching the man's eye. After squinting, he realizes it's a human figure.

His first inclination is to flee.

But he stands his ground, held in place by a strong smell…a *she-scent*—musky, sweaty, salty, and so sexually exciting. The overwhelming smell makes his eyes water, his nostrils flare and itch.

She-scent. He'd almost forgotten.

So it's definitely a female figure standing there, partially masked in the shadows, but boldly staring back at him.

Petite, bundled-up clothes, but exposed brownish hair with rusty streaks, and a broadly smiling face. Of course the man is instantly smitten. He has been alone so long, too long. His chest is tight with anticipation. He is eager to move close, greet, talk, and maybe even touch her.

But the tiny woman suddenly turns to leave.

"Wait, wait," the man attempts to shout, but manages only an inaudible hoarse whisper—his voice unused for nearly three years. "I won't harm you," he tries to add loudly, the unfamiliar vocal effort rasping his throat raw. He swallows dryly and whispers: " Please stop…"

But she ignores him and flees off to the south. Of course he breaks into a run and follows her. "Wait, wait," he says faintly at her back, massaging his aching throat with a hand.

The tiny woman is agile and fast, distancing herself initially from him, leading him away from his familiar turf.

But he spurs himself on, faster and faster, paying little attention to the increasingly unfamiliar surroundings, having thrown all caution to the wind. *He has to catch this woman*, he thinks, ignoring any hazards on the path where his striding feet are landing—

"Ugh!"

The air is driven sharply from his lungs as he is jerked off his feet into the air, folded in half, his uplifted arms trapped overhead, preventing him from being able to reach either of his weapons. Stunned, the man feels himself sinking down, down into unconsciousness… But gasping for breath, he fights off the encroaching blackness, managing to partially collect himself, and avoid the shutdown of senses, which still tunnels his vision. He gasps loudly for more air. Blinks repeatedly, finally clearing his vision. Hanging upside down, the man realizes he has been caught in some kind of a huge net.

It dawns on him what exactly has happened here.

He has been trapped, like one of his rabbit prey, lured into a stupid, reckless dash by the powerful *she-scent* and sight of the tiny woman. Clumsily tripping the net. And now he is paying for his abandonment of good sense, hanging upside-down about eight feet off the ground, swinging slightly to and fro. Despite his best efforts, he's still unable to reach either his sawed-off shotgun or long knife.

Glancing down to his right, he sees the smiling, petite woman is moving a bit closer. Right below him now. He realizes something isn't quite right with her face. Her smile is odd, slack-jawed, and meaningless…and her wide-eyed gaze is actually childish, almost vacant, and lacking intelligence.

Then, the other two appear, stepping out from the shadows.

Both are women!

Older, taller, well-fed. Neither anywhere as comely as the smaller one, but obviously brighter. The first time he's seen so many women gathered in one place in three years.

All three females are directly below him now.

One, the largest, oldest, and plainest woman is taking something from her big backpack…unfolding what appears to be a broad plastic sheet. She spreads it directly under where he hangs helplessly.

The man sucks in a breath. The other, taller woman is carrying a rifle. What appears to be an old rusty .22, which she's now lifting and aiming up at his head.

Badly frightened, he squeezes his eyes tightly shut, sucks in another deep breath…and catches a familiar scent from the tiny woman, not quite completely masked by her powerful she-scent.

Yes! It's faint, but it's definitely the smell of *spicy-lemon*.

And it all rushes back now, overwhelming him.

For a moment, he vividly sees his wife's beautiful face in his mind's eye. All her features completely intact now: her lustrous auburn hair, the ice-blue wide eyes, the high rosy cheekbones, the sensuous lips, and the full, engaging smile.

His spirit briefly soars free before he hears the balloon *pop*—

Photo Courtesy of Kathryn Leigh Scott

An Interview with Kathryn Leigh Scott

By James R. Beach

Kathryn Leigh Scott is an actress most known for her portrayal of the character Maggie Evans from 1966-1970 on the original *Dark Shadows* daytime drama series, as well as appearing in the feature films *House of Dark Shadows*, *The Great Gatsby* and the TV film *The Turn of The Screw*. She's also appeared as a guest on many other television shows and written a number of books including *My Scrapbook Memories of Dark Shadows, The Bunny Years* and *Down and Out in Beverly Heels*. She recently took the time to chat with me about the impact *Dark Shadows* had on her, fond memories of acting and what she's up to now.

Dark Discoveries: What made you decide to get into acting, Kathryn?

Kathryn Leigh Scott: I have wanted to act and write since I was a child. Like most children I got together with neighbor kids to put on "shows" . . . but I always took the production a bit more seriously! I combined my twin interests in grade school when I wrote a play about George Washington and wrote the best part for Martha, the role I played. All through school I did both. Acting provided me with my first success (and paycheck!) so that's what took precedence in my early career.

DD: Was *Dark Shadows* your first role or did you have parts in other movies or shows?

KLS: *Dark Shadows* was my first professional job on camera. Prior to that I'd done theatre, but getting the role of Maggie Evans as a regular on *Dark Shadows*, and appearing in the very first episode of the show, was a huge breakthrough in my career.

DD: You're probably most known for your portrayal of Maggie Evans and Josette du Pres, but you actually played four characters on the series overall (Evans, du Pres, Lady Kitty Hampshire and Rachel Drummond). Did you find that to be challenging?

KLS: It was exciting to play several characters on *Dark Shadows* in different time periods. For an actor newly out of drama school, it was a treat to put so much of what you'd learned into practice. I'd studied Shakespeare, Restoration Comedy and appeared in plays by Ibsen and Chekhov, which certainly helped me with the period roles of Josette, Lady Kitty Hampshire and Rachel Drummond.

DD: You also starred in one of the two theatrical *Dark Shadows* features Dan Curtis did, *House of Dark Shadows*, as well as an excellent adaptation of Henry James' *The Turn of the Screw* for TV. How was it working for Curtis? Any interesting stories or memories?

KLS: Dan Curtis has been the catalyst for so many fine things in my life. Thanks to him, I got the plum role of Maggie on *Dark Shadows*, worked in England, Hollywood . . . and was inspired to start my publishing company, Pomegranate Press, with the publication of *My Scrapbook Memories of Dark Shadows*. He was always there for me

KATHRYN LEIGH SCOTT
DOWN AND OUT IN *Beverly Heels*

and I miss him. He was a larger than life figure, cantankerous, sensitive, instinctive and volatile . . . really quite a character.

DD: You continued to work in television and movies quite a bit over the years. What were some of your favorite shows you appeared on and movies you acted in? Favorite co-stars?

KLS: I loved working with Dirk Bogarde in *Providence*, and adored Jimmy Stewart. We worked together for seven months in London in the play Harvey. I truly loved playing Sally Decker in *Police Squad*, which was a whacky comedy with Leslie Nielsen. I also loved doing *Philip Marlowe, Private Eye* with Powers Boothe, *Murrow* with Dan Travanti, *The Last Days of Patton* with George C. Scott and *Big Shamus, Little Shamus* with Brian Dennehy.

DD: You're also a writer and have done a few books including: *The Dark Shadows Companion*, a 25th anniversary book on the show and even a book on your Playboy Bunny experiences, haven't you?

KLS: I've always been a writer. I'm very glad I wrote *The Bunny Years* because it allowed me to tell the 25 year history of the Playboy Clubs through the recollections of the women who worked as Playboy Bunnies . . . and I was one of them. I also had a chance to produce a 2 hour documentary based on the book for A&E. I've written and published many books on *Dark Shadows*, and the latest was co-written with Jim Pierson. *Dark Shadows: Return to Collinwood* covers five decades of the series, including the 2012 film, which Tim Burton directed, starring Johnny Depp. It was the last appearance by Jonathan Frid, and he wrote the Foreword to the book. I am very excited about *Dark Passages*, my novel about *Dark Shadows*. I am now offering the book in a special package for $9.99 that includes a signed photo, book mark and book cover. The ebook is available on Amazon for only $2.99! My newest book is *Down and Out in Beverly Heels*, a mystery romance that is very funny. I am currently writing the sequel. Please order it on Amazon and write a review!!!

DD: I read you also started your own publishing imprint a while back. Can you tell me a bit about it and what sort of books you publish?

KLS: I started Pomegranate Press in 1986 with *My Scrapbook Memories of Dark Shadows*. I've since published about 70 books by various authors, all of them nonfiction related to entertainment, including biography, coffee table books and companions to classic television shows. Please check my website: kathrynleighscott.com for the catalog of books I publish, as well as special offers.

DD: You had a cameo in the new *Dark Shadows* movie Tim Burton did with Johnny Depp. What did you think of the movie and the experience?

KLS: It was fun to do and also a poignant time for the four of us working together again. It was the last time we were to work with Jonathan Frid.

DD: So what else is happening for you lately? Any new books or acting roles?

KLS: I am working on several films with Ansel Faraj, a young director with great talent. Lara Parker, Jerry Lacy and Chris Pennock from *Dark Shadows* are all appearing in his various films and we're having a great time working together. I'm also at work on a sequel to *Down and Out in Beverly Heels*. When I finish that, I'll do a sequel to *Dark Passages*. I still love acting and writing!

DD: Thank you so much for your time!

KATHRYN LEIGH SCOTT

DOWN AND OUT IN
Beverly Heels

Down and Out in Beverly Heels tells the story of Meg Barnes, a beloved actress who has it all and loses everything—and ends up living on the streets of Tinsel Town in her Ritz-Volvo—thanks to her newlywed con-man husband. The novel is a fun, light-hearted romance, taking us into the Hollywood social swirl, but also delves into the gritty truth of what it is to be "homeless and hiding it" in one of the most glittering, fashionable cities in the world. It's also a story of redemption as Meg tracks down her fugitive husband and struggles to regain her reputation, career and friendships.

© Douglas Kirkland, 2012

Publishers Weekly:

*Scott (*Dark Passages*), best known for her star turn on the TV show* Dark Shadows, *delivers a unique novel about a Hollywood actress short on cash and down on her luck . . . Mystery and romance are craftily combined . . . Scott gives the readers a first-hand view of the fickle nature of Hollywood in a fast-paced story complete with eccentric characters and a plethora of mysterious twists and turns.*

Booklist:

Some women really do have it all: money, fame, beauty. But, just like that, it can all be taken away. That's the story of Meg Barnes in actress Scott's debut romance, a tale of a rich and famous woman reduced to desperately trying to prove her innocence to the police . . . Scott, who played Josette DuPres, the vampire bride in the television series Dark Shadows, *combines a classic story of love and loss spiced with mystery that will surely keep readers entertained until the very end.*

KIRKUS Reviews

This is the first novel by Scott, who starred in the original Dark Shadows *series, and the author's knowledge of the world of Hollywood is evident in the background details throughout the book, offering a fun, sly behind-the-scenes tour of a world most of us know little about . . . the book is an enticing, witty romp; a sparkling Hollywood-set tale that will entertain and satisfy.*

Dark Shadows: Dark Decades

By Stephen Mark Rainey

Dark Shadows. Cast 1968, Photo Courtesy courtesy of Dan Curtis Productions and Jim Pierson

If you grew up in the mid-to-late 1960s and didn't know anything about *Dark Shadows*, you probably didn't really grow up in the mid-to-late 1960s.

Virtually everyone who has even heard of the original ABC-TV series, which aired from June 1966 to April 1971, also knows that every school-age kid in America from that period "ran home from school to watch *Dark Shadows*." At least, that's what you'd deduce from the ubiquitous recollections of late-term baby boomers. Yeah, I did that. I ran — at least, once we got cable TV in my house so we could pick up the station that carried *Dark Shadows* (our local ABC affiliate did not). That was in the spring of 1969, midway through the series' run. Prior to that, to satisfy my blossoming passion for all things spooky, I frequently contrived to have myself invited over to friends' places who already had cable (it was hardly common in those days).

The fact I could watch *Dark Shadows* only sporadically made the show that much more enticing; the bits and pieces of the continuing drama I managed to catch left gaping holes that my hyperactive imagination *had* to fill in. To me — and so many other kids of my time — the great estate of Collinwood and the town of Collinsport, Maine, was a real place, populated by people who were at once larger than life yet readily identifiable as real folks, just like those we knew in our own hometowns. Some of them had deep, dark secrets. Some of them weren't human. First and foremost was Barnabas Collins, vampire. There were also ghosts, werewolves, witches, warlocks, Frankenstein-monster-inspired creations, even Lovecraftian beasties (thankfully, in the case of the latter, always off-camera). It was a magical time, a magical place, this world of *Dark Shadows*.

The original series consisted of 1,225 television episodes and spawned two theatrical films (*House of Dark Shadows*, 1970 and *Night of Dark Shadows*, 1971, both released by MGM Studios), which featured many of the television cast members. The franchise was the brainchild of producer Dan Curtis, who claimed that the inspiration for the show came from a dream about a young woman on a train, heading for an unknown destination. Convinced he was onto something special — and potentially lucrative — Curtis hired writer Art Wallace to develop a story from this spark of an idea. Wallace fleshed out a complex plot, with well-defined characters, and called it *Shadows on the Wall*, which soon enough morphed into *Dark Shadows*. Conceived as a dark, gothic mystery, the show differed from any other dramatic production of its time, particularly the ubiquitous daytime soap operas — although, at the beginning, there were few, if any, insinuations of the supernatural in the story. Engaged by Wallace's treatment and Curtis's hard sell, ABC-TV executives approved the project, and Curtis began to gather the people he would need to make his dream a reality.

Courtesy of Jim Pierson and Dan Curtis Productions

Curtis reserved the title of executive producer for himself and, in short order, he hired Robert Costello as producer; directors Lela Swift and John Sedwick; set designer Sy Tomashoff; and composer Robert Cobert for the music score.

The story was set, naturally enough, in a huge, brooding, 40-room mansion called Collinwood, located in a small fishing village on the coast of Maine called Collinsport — both, as you might guess, named after the locale's wealthiest and most prominent family. The family consisted of Roger Collins (played by Louis Edmonds), a wealthy but haunted, acerbic man, his wife "gone away" for mysterious reasons; his sister, Elizabeth Collins Stoddard (played by the legendary Joan Bennett), who had not left Collinwood since the equally mysterious disappearance of her husband, Paul Stoddard, 18 years earlier; Roger's adolescent son, David (played by David Henesy), a troubled, temperamental lad who could occasionally behave quite wickedly; and Elizabeth's daughter, Carolyn (played by Nancy Barrett), a rebellious, angst-ridden girl in her late teens. Into this rather foreboding household came Victoria Winters (played by Alexandra Moltke) — the young woman of Curtis's dream — who had lived in an orphanage in New York her entire life until summoned to Collinwood to become governess to David Collins.

On June 27, 1966, Victoria Winters arrived in Collinsport — by train — to assume her duties, despite vague but insistent warnings from a man named Burke Devlin (first played by Mitch Ryan, later by Anthony George), whom she met on the journey, and Maggie Evans (played by Kathryn Leigh Scott), a waitress at the Collinsport Diner. By the end of her first night at Collinwood, Victoria was already being drawn into the mysteries that lurked in its gloomy, secretive halls.

The early episodes were recorded in black and white, which accentuated the grim atmosphere of the setting. The focus on the characters and their unusual but distinctly real-life concerns lent the production a certain film noir quality, and the sharp portrayals of Roger Collins and Elizabeth Stoddard by Louis Edmonds and Joan Bennett, respectively, added unusual gravitas for a soap opera production. The interiors of Collinwood

— constructed on a very small sound stage at ABC Studio Two on West 67th Street in New York City — convincingly conveyed opulence, warmth, grimness, and isolation, all reflecting the complex moods of the characters, time, and place.

Seaview Terrace, a sprawling mansion built in the 1920s in Newport, Rhode Island, served as Collinwood's exterior. Patterned after a French chateau, perched atop a hill overlooking a rocky coastline, the house made Collinwood *real* to the show's viewers. While the exteriors and interiors never quite matched up, particularly in scale, one could never doubt that, if you walked through those doors you saw from outside, you would end up inside the familiar confines of the "real" Collinwood.

Perfectly complementing the visuals, Robert Cobert's eerie theme music is surely one of the most distinctive and recognized television themes ever composed. The show's opening, with huge waves crashing over craggy rocks (filmed in Newport, Rhode Island, just up the beach from Seaview Terrace) and fading to an image of the house with the *Dark Shadows* title materializing before it remains indelibly, impressively imprinted in my old brain. The title sequence heralded something special; an experience to anticipate and to remember. Cobert's somber soundtrack music perfectly set the mood for a "dark" show, with lots of bass, warbling woodwinds, whining strings, and staccato jabs to accentuate the drama.

That early period of *Dark Shadows* was both novel and frustrating, both for viewers and the producers. The plot moved slowly, as soap opera plots are wont to do, and despite oftentimes well-conceived moments of intrigue and top-notch acting, interest in the series waned to the point that ABC-TV executives were on the verge of pulling the plug. Curtis and the writers, with little to lose in the bargain, decided to pull out the stops, and those subtle hints of supernatural forces in the storyline quickly became more than just hints.

* * *

From the show's beginning, there was never an explanation for Roger's wife's absence and David's antisocial behavior. That soon changed by way of David's mother Laura Collins (played by Diana Millay) making an appearance and turning out to be a supernatural creature — a "phoenix," who, every hundred years, burned herself and her offspring to death, only to be born again from the ashes. This dramatic experiment proved noble, if not altogether successful; however, it was sufficient to tantalize viewers and inspire Curtis to try something a little farther out. I'm betting you already know the next "far out" happening: Yes, Barnabas Collins – daytime television's first vampire.

In early 1967, the main storyline involved a pair of drifters, Jason McGuire (played by Dennis Patrick) and Willie Loomis (first played by James Hall and then John Karlen), who came to Collinwood with less than honorable intentions. Eighteen years earlier, McGuire had been a friend of Elizabeth's husband, Paul, who was himself anything but a saint. Elizabeth, fearing

for her daughter and her life, supposedly killed her husband —
and Jason helped her cover up the deed. Having fallen on hard
times, Jason decided to return to Collinwood and earn some easy
money by blackmailing Elizabeth for Paul's murder. Unknown
to Elizabeth, however, her attempt to kill Paul had failed, and he
simply left Collinsport free and clear. Jason cruelly used her guilt
— for an act she had not actually committed — for his own gain.
Willie, as greedy as Jason, but considerably less clever, set about
searching for the Collins family's legendary hidden fortune. His
search led him to a secret room in the Collins mausoleum. It
wasn't fortune he found. Not good fortune, anyway.

Canadian actor Jonathan Frid took the role of Barnabas
Collins as a temporary job to earn enough money to move to the
west coast and teach acting. The storyline called for Barnabas
to wreak havoc and drink blood for several weeks and then
be killed off. As most of us already know, things didn't quite
work out that way. Barnabas Collins became the equivalent of
a television rock star, sending shudders through *Dark Shadows*-
addicted young children (such as myself), housewives tired of
the mundane soaps, and casual viewers who tuned in just to
see what the bloody fuss was about. Barnabas proved a dark,
intriguing, and memorable character, exceeding the producers'
wildest dreams and boosting ratings so that talk of the series'
cancellation was quelled almost overnight.

The other cast members had known all along their show
was a bit out of the ordinary, but few of them were pleased
about the introduction of a vampire to their company; it was a
bit *too* far out. However, without question, said vampire gave
the entire cast and crew new leases on their professional lives.

* * *

Barnabas, free after being chained in his coffin almost
200 years earlier, made the family's acquaintance, claiming to
be a distant cousin from England, and settled in the original
Collinwood — a mansion known as "the Old House" (in reality,
the Spratt House, located on the banks of the Hudson River
in Tarrytown, New York; the building burned to the ground
while the show was still in production). One of Barnabas' first

acts was to eliminate Jason McGuire,
ridding Collinwood of one lingering
inconvenience. Soon, Barnabas
discovered that diner waitress
Maggie Evans bore a remarkable
resemblance to his long-dead love,
Josette DuPres, and devised a fairly
twisted scheme to abduct her, use
his supernatural influence to make
her believe she *was* Josette, and
ultimately become his bride. Maggie
eventually escaped, but with severe
psychological trauma, resulting
in memory loss and, for a time, a

Courtesy of Jim Pierson and
Dan Curtis Productions

Courtesy of Jim Pierson and Dan Curtis Productions/MPI Home Video

reversion to adolescence. Dr. Julia Hoffman (played by Grayson
Hall), a gifted psychiatrist and blood specialist, in her study of
Barnabas's victims, discovered a unique cell — the "vampire
cell," so to speak — and decided the "monster" might be curable.

It was during these events that the audience began to see
Barnabas more as a victim of a curse — the equivalent of a
horrible disease — than an actual monster. Julia Hoffman, once
devoted to destroying the creature responsible for the attacks on
Collinsport's population, became first sympathetic to Barnabas
and then quite infatuated with him. Her attempts to restore
Barnabas to ordinary human being didn't quite pan out; in fact,
the experiment going awry caused Barnabas to physically age,
temporarily, to his full 176 years. As a result, he saw fit to murder
Julia and came very close to doing so. However, gradually, he
began to trust her and, finally, accept her as a friend.

* * *

As a character, Barnabas was intriguing because he *wasn't*
simply an evil, bloodthirsty predator. Yet, even on his better
days, Barnabas showed himself to be duplicitous, calculating
and cold-hearted, at least to strangers. To his family and a select
few with whom he became close, Barnabas showed at least
marginal respect, if not outright warmth. He could convincingly
feign kindness, even loyalty, yet he would never hesitate to use
another person — even those he cared about — if it suited his
ultimate aim. When it came to human beings, Barnabas' single

true weakness was his young sister, Sarah, who had died in her childhood. From time to time, Sarah's ghost appeared, often to warn Barnabas's potential victims. It was his reaction to Sarah that first clued audiences into the villainous vampire's gentler side.

This evolving and clearly appealing character became the show's centerpiece, and it was only fitting that the producers should relate the story of how Barnabas became a vampire. This was done in clever fashion, by way of a séance in which several family members attempted to communicate with Sarah's ghost. During the séance, Victoria Winters was suddenly and inexplicably hurled back into the past — specifically to Collinwood in the year 1795 — where she met the ancestors of the contemporary Collins family, all played by familiar regular cast members. From this point onward, the *Dark Shadows* cast essentially became a repertory company, with the core actors playing a variety of roles. In 1795, the family lived in the Old House, as the "new house" was still under construction. Victoria saw herself surrounded by a sea of strangers with familiar faces. Joshua Collins, Barnabas' father, was played by Louis Edmonds; Naomi Collins, Barnabas' mother, was played by Joan Bennett; Jeremiah Collins, Joshua's brother, was played by Anthony George; Millicent Collins, Barnabas' young cousin, was played by Nancy Barrett. Unable to explain her presence, Victoria led the family to believe she had been in an accident that had affected her memory. As in the present day, she assumed the role of governess, this time to young Sarah Collins (Sharon Smyth) herself.

In 1795, Barnabas was engaged to Josette DuPres (Kathryn Leigh Scott); however, much to his chagrin, he had once succumbed to the charms of her maid, a beautiful young woman from Martinique named Angelique. The consequences of this indiscretion were complicated by the fact that Angelique was a witch. Hell having no fury and all that, Angelique placed the vampire curse on Barnabas and proceeded to weave a web of deception that implicated Victoria Winters as the witch. Pursued relentlessly by a zealous witch hunter, Reverend Trask (played to perfection by Jerry Lacy), Victoria was eventually arrested and sentenced to hang. As a human, Barnabas had befriended Victoria; as a vampire, he poured out his wrath on those who persecuted her, including Reverend Trask, whom he bricked up inside a wall in the cellar of the Old House, and then on Angelique herself. As Victoria was led away to her fate, Joshua Collins, having learned of his son's true nature, set out to drive a stake through Barnabas' heart. However, unable to destroy his own son, he chained Barnabas in a coffin for what he thought would be eternity.

There was no last-minute reprieve for Victoria Winters. She *was*, in fact, hanged — only, at the moment just prior to her death, to return to the present, unable to understand or explain anything that had happened to her.

Courtesy of Jim Pierson and Dan Curtis Productions

* * *

This weeks-long flashback proved highly successful and provided some of the show's most memorable and well-conceived moments. Jonathan Frid, playing to this point a mostly evil character, now portrayed Barnabas as a kind if sometimes misguided individual, to excellent effect, the contrast accentuating the tragedy of the curse that would befall him. Lara Parker, with her mesmerizing aqua eyes, golden hair, and lilting laugh, made for a striking, sensuous witch. Thayer David, who in the present day had played a sinister caretaker named Matthew Morgan, took on the 1795 role of Ben Stokes, Barnabas' devoted servant, showcasing his formidable acting talent. In fact, between the series and the two spin-off movies, David would play no less than ten *Dark Shadows* characters — concurrently, on occasion.

Once Victoria returned from the past, the pace and tone of *Dark Shadows* underwent a noticeable change; the series had by now established itself as unabashed fantasy, and the scripts began playing the most far-fetched scenarios to the hilt. Gone were the true-to-life dramas, the subtle hints of things not being quite what they seemed. Now, everything was right up in your face. Correspondingly, where there once had been a fair number of location shots, adding a sense of *place* in the real world — not to mention numerous extra actors taking up space in Collinsport — stock photos of Seaview Terrace and the Spratt House became the norm, with fewer scenes taking place outside the confines of the estate itself. This lent the show a rather claustrophobic atmosphere, arguably accentuating its break from the "real" world.

From its beginning, *Dark Shadows* was essentially live television. Each episode was recorded on tape but because of its hurried shooting schedule and limited budget, editing was all but impossible. Thus, whatever happened during the performance made its way on the air. Sets were lavish but not necessarily sturdy, resulting in wobbling gravestones, toppling stone pillars, and swords falling off the wall and smashing table lamps. Jonathan Frid was an admitted "slow study" and often had difficulty with the vast number of lines he was required to memorize in such short periods of time. Thus, he relied heavily — oftentimes obviously — on the teleprompter, resulting in lines like "That night must go nothing wrong!" and "I am defending the right of this girl to be judged innocent until she is proved innocent!" Of course, Frid was hardly the only cast member who flubbed lines. Louis Edmonds gained some notoriety by quipping, while in a graveyard, "Some of my incestors are buried here." He gamely caught the error and made sport of himself. John Karlen as Willie Loomis once cracked himself up while saying, "This place gives me the willies." Viewers often found the bloopers, missed cues, and collapsing sets endearing, and many fans of my generation remember *Dark Shadows* more for its amusing gaffes than anything else.

* * *

Having tackled the vampire legend so lucratively, the producers decided to delve further into classic themes for material. Next in the queue came a unique take on the Frankenstein monster story, this one involving a creation named Adam (played by Robert Rodan). A certain Dr. Eric Lang (Addison Powell) stumbled onto Barnabas' secret but, rather than destroy him, proposed to cure Barnabas of the vampire curse — in exchange for his assistance in an experiment designed to give life to an artificially constructed man. In a bizarre twist, Adam, brought to life using Barnabas' life force, drained Barnabas' vampire affliction so that he might live as a reasonably normal human being. During these episodes, a secondary story ran involving the return of Angelique, now going by the name Cassandra, who — in a surprise turn — arrived at Collinwood as Roger Collins's new wife. Of course, her actual aim was to further exact vengeance on Barnabas. We also saw the introduction of Nicholas Blair (played with evil glee by Humbert Allen Astredo), a powerful warlock who came to Collinwood pretending to be Cassandra's brother. Clearly her superior in some hellish hierarchy, Blair was never pleased with Angelique's vendetta against Barnabas and, to punish her for her failure to bring about its swift resolution, turned her into a vampire as well. Blair envisioned Adam as the first in a line of powerful, remorseless semi-human creatures over which he would assume ultimate control. Thus came Eve (played by Marie Wallace), who took to Adam about as well as Elsa Lanchester took to Boris Karloff. Angelique, forever vengeful when thwarted, eventually made an end-run around Blair to their master, Diabolos, who summarily dragged an indignant Blair back to the underworld.

The Adam/Eve storyline came off quite poorly, despite actor Robert Rodan playing the artificial man with sincerity

and remarkable range. Angelique's return, the introduction of Nicholas Blair, and Angelique's transformation to vampire, short-lived though it was, fared better dramatically. The concurrent storylines switched back and forth mercilessly, only occasionally intersecting. Barnabas, though charismatic as an "ordinary" human, tended to be indecisive, even inept. During this period, Thayer David made a welcome return as the eccentric Professor Timothy Elliot Stokes, a direct descendent of Ben Stokes and one of the show's most well-drawn, long-lasting, and memorable characters.

As *Dark Shadows* became more and more focused on supernatural themes, the character of Victoria Winters diminished in importance and, apparently, in mental sharpness. She became the perpetual victim, her most-expressed sentiment being "I don't understand." Alexandra Moltke, dissatisfied with the direction her character had taken, opted to leave the show when she became pregnant in real life. She was briefly replaced by actresses Betsy Durkin and Carolyn Groves, neither of which proved satisfactory, and, finally, Victoria was written out of the story — transported once again to the past, where she evidently died.

Early in the series, there were many hints that Victoria might have been Elizabeth Collins Stoddard's daughter, which certainly would have explained the reason she had been brought to Collinwood, but the question was never resolved. When the *Dark Shadows* novel, *Dreams of the Dark* was written for HarperCollins (by Elizabeth Massie and myself), Dan Curtis Productions directed us to reveal that Victoria *was*, in fact, Elizabeth's daughter. This is not necessarily canon, but clearly a fact the producers wished to impart.

Now that *Dark Shadows* had presented its own interpretations of *Dracula* and *Frankenstein*, it was time to move on to the Wolfman — not to mention more witches, ghosts, zombies, and horrors from the past.

* * *

In December 1968, David Selby, a West Virginia–born actor, joined the cast as Quentin Collins, who initially appeared at Collinwood as an evil ghost. To tell Quentin's story, the writers again opted to visit the past, and this time Barnabas himself journeyed back to the late nineteenth century — 1897, to be exact — intending to change events and prevent Quentin's ghost from terrorizing the Collins family. This time, with assistance from Professor Stokes and a set of I Ching wands, Barnabas sent his spirit back in time, only to awaken in his own vampire body, trapped in the chained, hidden coffin. Naturally, he managed to escape this inconvenient situation and return to Collinwood as another cousin from England.

The 1897 flashback was very long and involved, running for many months without returning to the present day of 1969. There were numerous subplots, one involving Barnabas's romance with a young governess named Rachel

Maggie & Barnabas Lyndhurst Video Sleeve Color Art

it back, and his search led him to Collinsport.

Count Petofi proved one of the series' most popular villains. He was educated, erudite, remorseless, occasionally sympathetic, and, mostly, Thayer David in top form. Not to mention he made Quentin look like a good guy. In fact, Quentin, for all his wickedness, could be quite charming, even likable, thanks in no small measure to David Selby's masterful portrayal. Petofi made it his business to commandeer Quentin's body, learn the secrets of time travel from Barnabas, and forever escape the gypsies who relentlessly pursued him. To insure Quentin's longevity, Petofi had one of his pupils, artist Charles Delaware Tate (Roger Davis), paint Quentin's portrait, which, in *Dorian Gray* fashion, not only aged while Quentin remained youthful, on nights of the full moon also took on the aspect of the werewolf, essentially freeing him from the curse.

Although Barnabas had ventured back into the past to alter events and prevent the devastation wrought by Quentin's ghost, he found himself sympathetic to Quentin's plight. Having suffered a hellish curse himself, Barnabas knew all about being driven to commit acts he found personally heinous. The dynamic between these characters proved irresistible to audiences of the day, and even now stand out as among the series' high points. In the end, Petofi was foiled, and Barnabas — after a brief but bizarre side trip to the year 1796 — returned to 1969 to find Collinwood free of malevolent ghosts.

* * *

A character as popular as Quentin could scarcely be relegated to the past. Made immortal by the Tate portrait, he was able to reappear in the present day. However, despite the portrait, the werewolf curse had not been extinguished. Collinsport resident Chris Jennings suffered the curse and, from time to time, was responsible for considerable bloodletting. Chris, it turned out, was directly descended from Quentin and mad wife Jenny.

In late 1969, a new threat arrived in Collinsport, in a storyline inspired by H. P. Lovecraft's unique brand of cosmic horrors. Just before Barnabas's return to the present, he encountered strange figures in the woods around Collinwood, who seized control of his mind, turning him into a sinister character, much as in his early vampire days. These malevolent beings were known as Leviathans, a powerful race that had once ruled the earth. In their true forms, they were nebulous, horrifying things, but they could both assume the guise of human beings as well as possess others. Barnabas' ill-fated attempt to resist them resulted in his once again becoming a vampire.

A new couple in Collinsport, Phillip and Megan Todd (Christopher Bernau and Marie Wallace), appeared to have in their charge a quick succession of young boys — named Joseph, Alexander, and Michael, respectively — all blond, precocious, and thoroughly wicked. Soon, each child was gone, but an adult named Jeb Hawkes (Christopher Pennock) arrived, his

Drummond (Kathryn Leigh Scott), a Josette DuPres look-alike of the nineteenth century. Another was the return of Laura "the Phoenix" Collins, apparently no longer confined to a hundred-year cycle. For the most part, the complex storyline managed to succeed dramatically and commercially, enhanced by the richness of the characters and some superb acting. Quentin, essentially evil but given remarkable depth and humanity by David Selby, proved virtually as popular as Barnabas had been during his early vampire days. Quentin was the first character from the show to have his own theme song, titled *Shadows of the Night*, which was recorded by numerous artists of the day — such as Andy Williams, the Charles Randolph Grean Sounde and others — and given significant radio play. In 1969, the song was nominated for a Grammy award.

Quentin Collins, not exactly your proper Victorian gentleman, had numerous affairs, an affinity for the occult, and a mad wife, whom he imprisoned in the tower room of Collinwood and eventually killed. As it turned out, mad wife Jenny (Marie Wallace) was the sister of gypsy Magda Rakosi (Grayson Hall), who, in revenge, placed the werewolf curse on Quentin and his male descendants. Enter Count Andreas Petofi (the ever-versatile Thayer David), a master of occult powers. Petofi had once been a werewolf but was cured by Magda's gypsy tribe, who coveted his magical hand and proceeded to cut it off to keep for themselves. Needless to say, Petofi desired personality eerily similar to each of the boys'. Simultaneously, Paul Stoddard (Dennis Patrick), Elizabeth's long-missing husband, returned to Collinsport, ostensibly to make amends for the misery he had wrought so many years previously. In those earlier days, he had made a bargain with a stranger — a Leviathan, of course — to gain great wealth, promising in return his most valuable possession.

Much to his dismay, he learned that his daughter, Carolyn, was the object of the Leviathans' demand.

After Barnabas's long stint as a more heroic character, for many, his reversion to evil was a jarring change, welcome to some, not so much to others. It was almost ironic that a repentant Paul Stoddard should be played by none other than Dennis Patrick, the same actor who, in the role of Jason McGuire, had been his own partner in crime. In the early days, Frid and Patrick had an engaging chemistry between them, and it showed once again here, especially when a very sinister Barnabas appeared to remind Paul that he owed his daughter to those who had made his years of wealth possible.

The Leviathans intended for Carolyn to marry Jeb Hawkes — one of the original entities in human form — to produce a new race of offspring who would inherit the earth. If this sounds a bit like Nicholas Blair's scheme for Adam and Eve, it may come as no surprise that Blair should here make his return as a motivating force behind the Leviathans. The Collinsport constable, the Todds, and Paul Stoddard himself became casualties of the Leviathans' evil influence. However, at the end of the day, Jeb Hawkes' human side prevailed, for he actually fell in love with Carolyn, and the Leviathans — not to mention Nicholas — were once again relegated to the nether regions.

To many fans, the Leviathans sequence failed to engage, despite some fine dramatic moments and an element of dark dread that had been missing from the show for some time. Thankfully, Jeb Hawkes in his actual Leviathan form never appeared on screen, but his presence was nicely insinuated by the sound of heavy breathing and a trail of dark slime that remained wherever he had passed – all very fine Lovecraftian stuff. Still, the storyline never developed fully, as it too often homed in on the rather dull relationship between Jeb and Carolyn, and the Leviathans themselves seemed too distant, their aims too vague, to be truly menacing.

Since the show's first venture back into the past, the producers found a certain freedom in leaving Collinwood of the present day to explore different stories and different characters. This time, they didn't go back in time but *across* time… at least at first.

* * *

Even before the Leviathans were entirely vanquished, strange things were happening in the rarely used east wing of Collinwood. In a certain room, familiar characters would appear, but in altogether different roles, unable to see or interact with anyone on the other side of the door. In this odd parallel time, Quentin Collins was the master of Collinwood, now married to Maggie Evans. Roger and Elizabeth appeared to be the poor relations. Having witnessed this alternate reality, Barnabas believed that if he entered that realm, he might finally be free of the vampire curse. This, however, was not to be, as he discovered when he managed to make the crossover. Willie Loomis, an aspiring author in this universe, discovered Barnabas' secret and chained him in a coffin, hoping to force Barnabas to tell his life story so that he might be privy to some best-seller material. Here, the story's focus turned to Quentin, Maggie, and their inevitable issues with the supernatural. This was so that Jonathan Frid and several of the other stars might have time off-set to star in *House of Dark Shadows*, the theatrical feature that would re-imagine the story of Barnabas Collins, vampire, coming to Collinwood – a parallel-time version of the story, as it were.

A passel of various classical influences made their way into the parallel universe, including a storyline based on the Daphne du Maurier novel, *Rebecca*, with the redoubtable Grayson Hall in a role reminiscent of Mrs. Danvers, staunchly loyal to the recently deceased Mrs. Quentin Collins — Angelique herself. Angelique's twin sister, an altogether decent young woman named Alexis Stokes, resided at Collinwood, not realizing Angelique's spirit remained potent and malignant, seeking to drain her life force and take her place in the household. Then came the show's tribute to Robert Louis Stevenson's *The Strange Case of Dr. Jekyll & Mr. Hyde*, featuring Christopher Pennock as the benevolent scientist Cyrus Longworth, who, under the influence of a potion intended to banish evil within the self, became the dastardly John Yaeger. Barnabas, though still a vampire, retained his more heroic characteristics and helped sort out each of the plot complications before returning to his own universe.

* * *

By now, *Dark Shadows* had revisited many of the classic horror stories, with varying degrees of success, but appeared to be struggling to find itself all over again. Jonathan Frid had

Courtesy of Jim Pierson and Dan Curtis Productions

Courtesy of Jim Pierson and Dan Curtis Productions

grown weary of playing Barnabas, fearing he would be forever typecast. Kathryn Leigh Scott found opportunities waiting for her across the pond with her new husband, Ben Martin, and left the show. David Selby remained as popular as ever, but Dan Curtis and company appeared to have little appetite for further exploring his character in the present day. Instead — much in the manner of Quentin's original ghostly appearance — they introduced a pair of spirits, one a malevolent character named Gerard Stiles (played with sneering menace by James Storm) and a benevolent ghost named Daphne Harridge (Kate Jackson in her first professional acting role), who sought to possess young David Collins and Professor Stokes's niece, Hallie (played by Kathleen Cody). Gerard became quite the murderous force, prompting Julia Hoffman to seek refuge in the parallel time room. However, to her surprise, she discovered a stairway that had never previously existed and, in desperation, ventured down it.

Next thing you knew, we were back in 1840, with an earlier edition of Quentin Collins — an ancestor of the familiar character but, for all practical purposes, the same fellow. Quentin, a practitioner of the occult (or perhaps, to some, a master physicist), had constructed a staircase that led to different time periods, and Julia had unwittingly discovered it. Taking a cue from Barnabas, she passed herself off as a distant cousin and, not knowing what else to do, decided to free Barnabas from his coffin, hoping he might have found a way to transport his spirit from 1970 back to the past. Alas, this was not the case, and the Barnabas she unleashed was the same murderous vampire Joshua Collins had imprisoned in the year 1795. Luckily, before the 1840 Barnabas could do away with her, the 1970 Barnabas again used the I Ching wands and sent his spirit back to 1840, just in time to spare Julia's life.

Quentin's cousin, Desmond (John Karlen), had recently discovered the severed head of a 17th Century warlock named Judah Zachary. Quentin's friend, Gerard Stiles, took an interest in the grotesque souvenir, and it apparently took an interest in him, for Judah Zachary's spirit immediately overcame him, turning Gerard from a spirited, somewhat conniving character

to a distinctly evil one. Gerard attempted to have Quentin and Desmond executed by manufacturing evidence they were guilty of witchcraft (a bit of a stretch for the year 1840), and then set out to stake Barnabas in his coffin. Who should intervene, however, but Angelique. Yes, she too remained a force at Collinwood and was initially quite peeved to learn of Barnabas' escape; however, when his ultimate destruction was imminent, she decided to save him. Furthermore, as Quentin and Desmond were to be executed, she appeared again and created a distraction, allowing Desmond to fatally wound Gerard.

At this point, seeing Angelique in a new light, Barnabas realized he actually did feel love for her. Unfortunately, as the events of 1840 had unfolded, she had also complicated the life and love of one Lamar Trask (Jerry Lacy), of the original Reverend Trask stock, and he chose this moment to exact revenge and shoot her, leaving her to die in Barnabas' arms.

The whole 1840 storyline wandered far from the original threat of Gerard Stiles. There was even a brief trip back to the 1690s to relate the story of the warlock Judah Zachary's origin. Rather surprisingly — or perhaps not — this flashback revealed that Angelique, in her original incarnation as a woman named Miranda DuVal — was one of Zachary's followers. Her death at the end of the 1840 episodes was one of many paradoxes presented by the various time travel scenarios. Was Angelique of 1840 the same Angelique from 1795? If so, she died reconciled with Barnabas, thus negating her evil influence in the future. Or was she the more "experienced" Angelique, returned to the past from 1970, just like Barnabas and Julia? The series' writers never addressed these questions, and perhaps wisely so.

* * *

The series' final major storyline began with no characters whatsoever from the 1970 time period. Instead, we went directly to parallel time in the year 1841, where at least some of the characters resembled their 1840 counterparts. The plot was lifted primarily from Shirley Jackson's story, *The Lottery*, with the unlucky loser doomed to spend a night in a haunted room, from which the only escape was insanity or death. The main story focused on a love story between Bramwell Collins, son of the original Barnabas (Jonathan Frid in his only portrayal of a character other than Barnabas), and Catherine Harridge (Lara Parker), who was married to his cousin, Morgan (Keith Prentice). The room in question was haunted by the ghost of Brutus Collins, a 17th-century ancestor who had murdered his cheating wife and her lover. Aware of Bramwell and Catherine's relationship, Morgan closed them in the room, but because their love was true, they survived the night, thus breaking the curse.

Riled by this fact, Morgan attempted to murder both of them but was foiled — and killed — by Bramwell's friend Kendrick Young (John Karlen). Things looked to have fallen ever-so-nicely into place, but at the end of the final episode, on April 2, 1971, young Melanie Collins (Nancy Barrett) was found with suspicious, very familiar-looking bite marks on her neck. However, as the characters gave each other "oh, no, not again!" looks, Thayer David's distinctive voice came on, saying, "There was no vampire loose on the great estate. For the first time at Collinwood, the marks on the neck were indeed those of an animal. Melanie soon recovered and went to live in Boston with her beloved Kendrick. There, they prospered and had three children. Bramwell and Catherine were soon married and stayed on at Collinwood, where Bramwell assumed control of the Collins business interests. Their love became a living legend. And, for as long as they lived, the dark shadows at Collinwood were but a memory of the distant past."

On *Dark Shadows'* last day, I was exactly one month shy of my 12th birthday. I had heard the show was going to end. But when the closing credits finished rolling, and the final notes of Robert Cobert's main theme trailed away for the last time, I cried. I bawled as if my best friend had died. (In later years, I discovered I was far from alone in this.) On the following Monday, like just about every kid of my generation, I turned on the television at the prescribed time, hoping against hope that it was all a big mistake, and that *Dark Shadows* would be there. *Surely* it would still be on.

Nope. *Password* had replaced it.

For so many viewers, young and old, it was the end of a magic time. *Dark Shadows* was done, at least for regular daytime broadcast, but it was hardly dead and buried.

* * *

The series was still being aired when the initial theatrical feature, *House of Dark Shadows*, appeared in theaters. It was the first ever full-length movie based on a daytime soap opera, but it proved quite a different animal from its progenitor. Produced and directed by Dan Curtis, the movie re-told the story of the Barnabas' arrival at Collinwood and his obsession with Maggie Evans, whom he desired as his new Josette. Many of the events from the Barnabas's early days were re-created, though several of the characters were changed or combined. Collinwood itself was no longer the familiar Seaview Terrace but the Lyndhurst mansion in Tarrytown, New York. It was a somewhat unsettling alteration of setting but extremely effective as Lyndhurst is a striking example of modern gothic architecture with expansive and atmospheric grounds.

Most notably, *House of Dark Shadows* was far gorier than it ever could have been on television at that time. No one was spared in the movie; even those core characters who you *knew* would never die in the series. The overall production quite resembled a Hammer Production, which actually proved one of its strongest assets. The story itself was disjoint and oftentimes rushed, partly due to the script but partly due to MGM's decree that the film couldn't run over 90 minutes, requiring more streamlining than the story could comfortably accommodate. Still, *House of Dark Shadows* was a commercial success and, by some accounts, helped saved MGM from bankruptcy in 1970.

Night of Dark Shadows was made after the show ended, and starred David Selby and Lara Parker as completely different versions of Quentin and Angelique. It too was filmed at the Lyndhurst, to very good effect. The movie presented a rather surreal ghost story, even more disjointed and severely edited than its predecessor, to far more detrimental effect. *Night* didn't fare nearly as well as *House of Dark Shadows*, for numerous reasons. It came out six months after the series had ended, and interest was no longer at its peak. Jonathan Frid refused to appear in the movie, having sworn off playing Barnabas Collins ever again. At the end of the day, the finished product was simply a mess because of the studio's insistence on that 90-minute running time, which forced Dan Curtis to personally spend the 24 hour-period just prior to its release cutting out nearly an hour of the film.

Although a restored version of *Night of Dark Shadows* has been proposed, there are no current plans for a release of Dan Curtis' director's cut, though efforts continue.

* * *

After the theatrical films, selected episodes of *Dark Shadows* went into syndication at various times, though it wasn't until 1992 that the entire series was re-broadcast, on the Sci-Fi Channel. In early 1991, an all-new *Dark Shadows* primetime series, subsequently known as the "Revival" series, ran for half a season on NBC-TV. It starred Ben Cross as Barnabas, Joanna Going as Victoria Winters, Jim Fyfe as Willie Loomis, Roy Thinnes as Roger Collins, Jean Simmons as Elizabeth Collins Stoddard, and Barbara Steele as Julia Hoffman. Despite superior production values and a capable cast, the show didn't perform well in the ratings, in part because live coverage of the nascent Gulf War frequently canceled or postponed its broadcast. The production was something of a hybrid between the original series and *House of Dark Shadows*, retaining many of the original plot elements, including Victoria Winters' journey into the past. Original series composer Robert Cobert provided a new score for the show, reprising many of his original compositions,

Courtesy of Jim Pierson and Dan Curtis Productions

including a fresh arrangement of the opening theme.

In 2004, Dan Curtis produced a one-hour pilot for a new version of *Dark Shadows*, starring Alec Newman as Barnabas, Marley Shelton as Victoria Winters, Martin Donovan as Roger Collins, and Blair Brown as Elizabeth Stoddard. The pilot was not well received and has never been broadcast or given an official video release. It is occasionally shown at *Dark Shadows* Festivals.

2012 saw the premiere of Tim Burton's theatrical version of *Dark Shadows*, starring Johnny Depp as Barnabas, Bella Heathcote as Victoria, Michelle Pfeifer as Elizabeth, Jonny Lee Miller as Roger, Eva Green as Angelique, Helena Bonham Carter as Julia, Chloe Moretz as Carolyn, Jackie Earle Haley as Willie, and Gully McGrath as David. The movie was an uneven blend of dark fantasy and comedy, treading the line between tribute and parody, more often leaning toward the latter. Its theatrical release was only moderately successful. Fan reaction was quite mixed, though the overall consensus seems to be that it was generally an okay movie. Original series actors David Selby, Jonathan Frid, Lara Parker, and Kathryn Leigh Scott made very brief cameo appearances in the film.

* * *

In the late 1960s and early 1970s — not to mention far beyond — *Dark Shadows* proved to be a merchandiser's dream come true. Between 1966 and 1972, Paperback Library released a series of 32 *Dark Shadows* novels, written by Marilyn Ross (actually Dan Ross, using his wife's name), although any resemblance between the television series and novels was largely coincidental. Ross also wrote the novelization of *House of Dark Shadows*, released by Paperback Library in 1970. Other *Dark Shadows* merchandise included bubblegum cards, a ViewMaster disc set, a Gold Key comic magazine series (which resembled the show and its characters even less than the novels), board games, and replicas of Barnabas Collins' onyx ring and Josette's music box. In the 1990s, MPI released the entire television series on VHS and in the 2000s, on DVD. In the late 1990s, HarperCollins and Dan Curtis Productions teamed to publish a new novel series based on the original show, which resulted in *Angelique's Descent*, written by Angelique herself, actress Lara Parker, who has since authored additional *Dark Shadows* novels for Tor: *The Salem Branch* (2006) and *Wolf Moon Rising* (2013). In the mid-2000s, Big Finish Productions, based in the UK, began producing a series of *Dark Shadows* audio dramas, now numbering over thirty releases, all featuring original cast members as well as members of both the 1991 NBC-TV *Dark Shadows* revival series and the 2004 pilot.

During and after *Dark Shadows*, Dan Curtis produced numerous made-for-television projects, oftentimes partnering with renowned writer Richard Matheson, including *The Strange Case of Dr. Jekyll & Mr. Hyde* (1968) and *Dracula* (1973), both starring Jack Palance; *Trilogy of Terror* starring Karen Black

(1975); and, most notably, *The Night Stalker* (1971) and its follow-up, *The Night Strangler* (1973), both of which starred Darren McGavin as reporter Carl Kolchak and launched the well-remembered *Kolchak: The Night Stalker* series. Curtis achieved his greatest fame for producing and directing the pair of World War II miniseries *The Winds of War* (1983) and *War and Remembrance* (1988), the latter of which earned him an Emmy, Golden Globe and Director's Guild awards .

For countless fans, including me, myself, and I, *Dark Shadows* was and is a unique phenomenon — a product of its time that can never be recaptured, regardless of remakes, rehashes, or reboots. For me personally, having the opportunity to write "official" *Dark Shadows* episodes, in novel and audio drama script forms, even though many years after the original series, has been one of the joys of my life. In all those 1,225 episodes, different viewers found different characters and scenarios to latch onto and make their own. To each fan, *Dark Shadows* was something personal, and for many of us, it remains so.

Way back when, I used to say that if I were a good, faithful, and deserving person, when I died, I would go to Collinwood. I don't know, but that still seems to me a pretty decent deal.

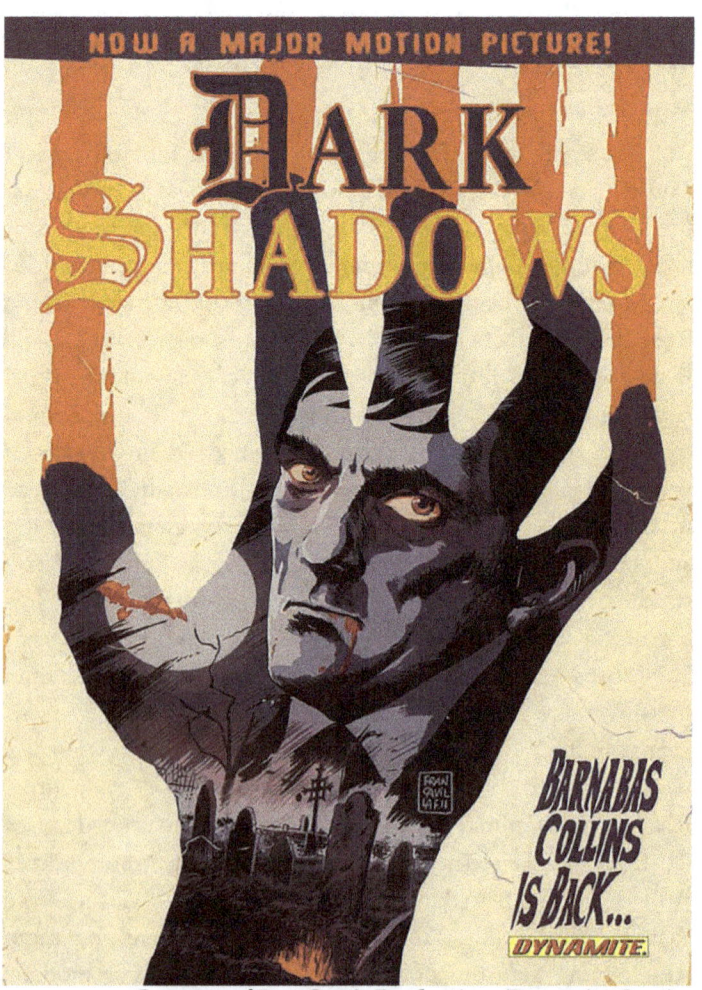

Courtesy of Dan Curtis Productions/Dynamite Comics

Darkroom

(TV Series: November 27, 1981 – January 15, 1982)

Trever Nordgren

"You're in a house, maybe your own, maybe one you've never seen before. Do you feel it? Something evil. You run, but there's no escape. Nowhere to turn. You feel something beckoning you, drawing you into the terror that awaits you in the darkroom!"

Darkroom was a short-lived anthology television series produced by Peter S. Fischer and hosted by actor James Coburn. It was based on the format of shows such as Alfred Hitchcock Presents, Night Gallery (both of which also included a host who introduced each tale), and The Twilight Zone. Darkroom, which ran for one season (seven episodes, sixteen stories),often included two or three stories within a single episode. Darkroom was intended to provide chilling, nightmarish scenarios already penned by famous authors, including some fresh tales of terror too. For whatever reason, though, it just didn't catch on with viewers.

Although some of us may have caught it in its initial TV run in late 1981 and early 1982, Darkroom has pretty much disappeared since then. It's rarely been seen since and was unavailable on VHS or DVD (until now, that is, with a 2-disc US and European DVD release). Overall, it had solid acting, moody cinematography, and a suitably creepy score. James Coburn was quite good as well and a bit menacing. Some of the actors that show up in episodes include: Ronny Cox, Brian Dennehy, Samantha Eggar, Rue McLanahan, Lloyd Bochner, Billy Crystal, and Helen Hunt. Also of note, several episodes were deemed "too intense" for television and later ended up in the rarely seen anthology movie Nightmares (1983).

Episode 1 (27/Nov/1981) "Closed Circuit" –Directed by Rick Rosenthal. Screenplay by Alan Brennert. Story by Carter Scholz. Starring John Randolph, Mary Frann, Richard Anderson, Robert Webber. A popular anchorman finds himself being slowly replaced by his own computer created image.

Episode 2 (27/Nov/1981) "Stay Tuned, We'll Be Right Back" – Directed by Paul Lynch. Written by Simon Muntner. Starring Bert Freed, Joanna Miles, Lawrence Pressman, Robert Grey. A man and his son put together an old crystal radio, but the father is shocked when he begins receiving broadcasts from the past.

Episode 3 (04/Dec/1981) "The Bogeyman Will Get You" – Directed by John McPhearson. Written by

Robert Bloch. Starring Helen Hunt, Arlen Dean Snyder, Gloria De Haven, R.G. Armstrong. A horror obsessed teenager begins to suspect that her handsome new neighbor is a vampire, but the truth may be far worse.

Episode 4 (04/Dec/1981) "Uncle George" – Directed by Rick Rosenthal. Written by Peter S. Fischer. Starring Claude Akins, June Lockhart, Dick Whittington, Dub Taylor. A financially strapped couple seeks someone to pose as their deceased Uncle George, in order to keep receiving his pension.

Episode 5 (11/Dec/1981) "Needlepoint" – Directed by Paul Lynch. Written by Violet Pullbrook. Starring Ester Rolle, Lawrence Hilton-Jacobs. A pimp's abusive ways lead to the death of a young woman, and earn deadly revenge from her voodoo practicing grandmother.

Episode 6 (11/Dec/1981) "Siege of 31 August" – Directed by Peter Crane. Screenplay by Peter S. Fischer. Story by Davis Grubb. Starring Ronny Cox, Gail Strickland, Pat Corley, Hank Brandt. A farmer finds himself tormented by the memories of his war experiences, after his son's toy soldier set comes to life.

Episode 7 (18/Dec/1981) "A Quiet Funeral"– Directed by Curtis Harrington. Written by Robert Bloch. Starring Eugene Roche, Misty Rowe, Robert F. Lyons. A double-crosser attends the funeral of his own victim, only to meet his comeuppance at the hands of the betrayed man's associates.

Episode 8 (18/Dec/1981) "Make-Up"–Directed by Curtis Harrington. Screenplay by Jeffrey Bloom. Story by Robert McCammon. Starring Billy Crystal, Brian Dennehy, Jack Kruschen. The powers of a magical makeup case transform a perpetual loser into an overnight big shot.

Episode 9 (25/Dec/1981) "The Partnership" – Directed by John McPherson. Screenplay by Christopher Crowe. Story by William F. Nolan. Starring David Carradine, Carole Cook, Jonathan Stark, Pat Buttram. A seemingly kind old man hides a terrible secret, one that allows him to live well in an otherwise desolate town.

Episode 10 (25/Dec/1981) "Daisies"– Directed by Paul Lynch. Screenplay by Peter S. Fischer. Starring Lloyd Bochner, Rue McClanahan, Elizabeth Halliday. A botanist develops a way to communicate with plants, all while committing adultery with his lab assistant.

Episode 11 (25/Dec/1981) "Catnip"– Directed by Jeffrey Bloom. Written by Robert Bloch. Starring Cyril O'Reilly, Jocelyn Brando, Michael V. Gazzo, Lynn Carlin. A ruthless young man accidentally kills an old witch, but her ominous black cat won't let him get away with it.

Episode 12 (08/Jan/1982) "Lost in Translation"– Directed by Rick Rosenthal. Written by Michael Scheff & Mary Ann Kasica. Starring Andrew Prine, Whit Bissell, Cindy Garvey. An archaeology professor blackmails a man into translating a powerful ancient formula for him, but isn't pleased with the results.

Episode 13 (08/Jan/1982) "Guillotine" – Directed by Rick Rosenthal. Written by Peter Allan Fields. Starring Patti D'Arbanville, Michael Constantine, Frank M. Benard. A married 19-century Frenchwoman desperately attempts to stop the execution of her lover.

Episode 14 (15/Jan/1982) "Exit Line" – Directed by Peter Crane. Written by Peter S. Fischer. Starring Samantha Eggar, Anne Lockhart, Stan Shaw, Jack Carter. A harsh theater critic finds that she has insulted one too many people, when a struggling actor takes her hostage.

Episode 15 (15/Jan/1982) "Who's There?" – Directed by Paul Lynch. Written by Brian Clemens. Starring Diane Kay, Michael Lembeck, Grant Goodeve. A suspicious husband sets a deadly trap for his unfaithful wife.

Episode 16 (15/Jan/1982) "The Rarest of Wines"– Directed by Peter Crane. Written by Jerry K. Siegel. Starring Judith Chapman, Henry Polic II. A jealous brother will go to any lengths to get his sister's share of the family fortune.

THE PARTNERSHIP

By William F. Nolan

INTRODUCTION TO "THE PARTNERSHIP"

By William F. Nolan

Of my 200-plus printed short stories, I'd rank "The Partnership" among the top ten. It worked out perfectly from mind to paper. Written in the summer of 1979, it was first printed in the anthology *Shadows 3* (edited by Charles L. Grant) and then televised on *Darkroom* on Christmas Day in 1981 (adapted by Christopher Crowe and starring David Carradine). It was also a featured selection in the U.K. for *The Television Late Night Horror Omnibus*, edited by Peter Haining, who dubbed it "creepy and frightening."

The story deals with a very bizarre partnership between Tad Miller and his buddy Ed that seems to work well for both parties. The main setting is a spooky amusement park funhouse – a direct recreation from my youth of the one in Fairyland Park back in my home town of Kansas City.

Happily (and this is rare in Hollywood) the *Darkroom* version is a totally faithful rendition of my story, right down to the dialogue and situation. I was very pleased with the result. Had *Darkroom* lasted there would have been more Nolan stories in the series. Alas, that was not to be. But at least we have "The Partnership."

***

THE PARTNERSHIP

Me and Ed, we're in business together. Which is what I want to tell you about eventually because I think you folks will find it interesting. But this is also about the stranger with the beard. And he comes first.

You like ghost stories? Bet you do! Everybody does. But this isn't one of those. Not a ghost in it. Still, it's a little spooky, I'd guess. I mean, to some it will be. Strange – that's a good word for it.

Strange.

Anyhow, Ed and me, we got ourselves a real nice partnership going. For one thing, we trust each other, and that's the basis you build on. No trust, no partnership. Learned that a long time ago. My Irish granddaddy, bless him, came over from County Cork. Bought into a saloon in Kansas City with a partner who "stole him blind." That's how he always put it: "That man stole me blind!"

Now, with Gramps long gone in Missouri earth, I'm as old as he was when I was a tad. That's how I got my first name. Ralph's the legal one, but I've always been Tad since Gramps called me that. Tad Miller. Simple name for a simple man.

I grew up in St. Louis and we moved to Chicago when I was still a boy – but you don't really want to know how I got here to this little town stuck down in god-knows-where country. It's in Illinois, a good piece out from Chicago, and we're on the lake. That's where it counts – not how I got here or what brought me.

I'm here. That's enough.

Name of the town's not important, so I won't give it out. If I did, some of you folks might come here one day, looking to say hello, and I wouldn't like that much since I'm not partial to meeting just anybody. No offense.

Ed's the same way. When he's ready to meet a stranger he'll go all out, but in between he's like me. Keeps to home.

Don't get me wrong. When a stranger comes to town, and I see he's lonely, I'll strike up a conversation as quick as the next fellow. I just don't *advertise,* if you know what I mean.

This town's on a spur highway into Chicago, and we get our share of hitchers. Road bums, sometimes. Others – like kids on the run from home, heading for life in the big city. Some on vacation. All kinds, drifting in for coffee and grub at Sally Anne's. They all end up at Sal's. Only eatery left in town, so she gets the business.

Real nice sort, too. You'd like her. Kind eyes. I always notice a person's eyes, first off. Windows on the soul sort of thing. And hers are soft and liquidy, like a deer.

Me and Sally we kid each other a lot, but we're both too old to have it mean anything. But she likes me. Most folks do. And that's nice. Person wants to know he's liked, even if he keeps mostly to home.

Well, before I tell you about the bearded stranger I met at Sal's last month you need to know some things about this town.

For instance, it's dying fast. Getting smaller every year. Most of the young ones gone now. Us diehards still hanging on. Me and Ed, we'll have to split up one of these days because this town's due to wink out like a star in the sky. Bound to happen. Be a sad day for me. Ed, too. We're not that close, understand, but there's a lot between us. Still, like my mama used to say, nothing lasts forever.

Anyhow, the town's slowed down a hellish lot since I first moved here from Chicago after Mama and Pop died. Super freeway gets most of the traffic. Put us in the backwash. The *big* change came when Moffitt Paper closed their factory. Town lost its main source of revenue, and things slowed way down.

That's when I had to leave Happyland. That's what they call the amusement park on the lake. All closed down now. Boarded up. Left to rust and rain.

I ran the funhouse out at Happyland. For twenty years. Slept there on summer nights. Knew every turn and twist of the place, every creaking board and secret passage and blind tunnel in it. Still do, for that matter. Which is where the stranger comes in, but I'll get to that.

First, a little more about me and this town if you don't mind. (I'm in no hurry, are you?)

I got married here. Surprise, eh? Guess, on paper, I don't come across as the romantic type – even though Sally still kids me that way. But married I was, and to a good woman who never liked kids so we didn't have any. When she died I was left alone. No family, not even cousins. (I didn't know Ed then.)

Her heart gave out. One day, fine, the next she's gone. Hit me hard. Made me kind of wacky for a while. But I got over it. We get over things, or things get over us, take your choice. Nowadays I'm used to being on my own, and I do fine. Enjoy my privacy. Enjoy the woods and some fishing in the fall. Like I said, a simple man. I miss her bad some nights, just like I do Happyland. But they're both gone – and everything has to die. Nature's way. Accept it. Flow with the tide.

She's buried out at Lakeside. Strangers think it odd, us having our cemetery right there on the lake, smack next to Happyland. Graveyard and amusement park snug-a-bug together on the lake. Odd, they say. Or *used* to, when Happyland was still open. "Spooky" is what they called it, having them together that way. But I never saw a ghost in twenty years out there. Oh, once in a while some big rats would wander in and give the ladies a real scare in the dark. (I'd always refund when it happened.) They'd come from the burrows under the cemetery, the rats, that is. Big suckers. And scared of nothing. That's the way of a rat; he scares you, you don't scare him.

Anyhow, my good wife's buried out there, or was. Guess the rats have her by now, though that isn't very nice to think about, is it? They got mighty sharp teeth, can gnaw right through the side of a coffin unless you can afford a steel one. Me, I've never had one extra dime to rub against another! Spend what I earn. To the penny. But I pay my way. No debts for Tad Miller.

Better get on to telling you about the big stranger who passed through here last month…

I was at Sally's, kidding with her – and we didn't see him walk in. She was joshing me about a new ring I had on. Big shiny thing, and Sal said it looked like I was wearing a street light. I was joshing her back about her new hairdo, saying it looked like a hive of bees could make honey in there. That kind of stuff. Just kidding around, passing the time of day.

Next thing, the stranger is banging the counter with a spoon, and yelling for some service. Sal broke off quick and moved over there to ask him what he'd have.

"Coffee and your special," he growled. "The coffee now. And a small tomato juice."

She told him no tomato juice, just orange. That made him madder than before.

He was big and mean looking. Maybe a lumber man. Had one of those shoulder-hike rigs, which he'd taken off and put on the counter next to him. Man of about forty, I'd guess. Muscled arms and a wide back. Thick dark beard. But honest eyes. I noticed his eyes right off.

He wore one of those space-age wristwatches with all kinds of dials and dates on it and little panels that light up. I'd never seen one like it before, and was plain curious, so I took the empty stool next to him. He gave me a scowl for doing that, because the rest of the counter was empty, and I guess he didn't want company.

"Hello, mister," I said. "My name's Tad Miller."

"So what's that to me?"

Hard-voiced. Not friendly at all.

"Want to apologize for all that jawing I was into when you came in. Customers come *first* in this place."

He grumbled "all right" while stirring his coffee, but he didn't look at me. Ignored me. Hoped I'd go away.

I leaned towards him. "Couldn't help but notice that timepiece you're wearing. Handsome thing. Never saw one quite like it."

He swung around slowly, holding up his left wrist. "Got it in Chi," he said. "You like it, eh?"

"Prettiest damn watch I ever did see!"

He was warming up fast. Like a woman will do when you tell her how cute her kid is. Works every time.

"What are all those dials and things?" I asked.

He worked back his sleeve so I could get a better look. "Tells you the time in ten parts of the world," he said. "Tells you the month of the year and the day of the week."

"Well, I'll be jinged!"

He twisted the doodad at the side of the watch. "Set this," he said proudly, "and it rings every hour on the hour."

By now Sally was spreading out his lunch special, and she couldn't resist getting into the conversation. "What's a thing like that cost?" she asked him.

Bad manners. I'd never have asked it that way, straight out. And he didn't like it. He scowled at her. "That's my business."

Watch could have been stolen, for all I knew. You just don't ask folks about how they get hold of a thing like that or how much they paid for it. But Sal was never one for laying back.

She huffed into the kitchen, all tight-faced.

He was eating in silence now. Sally's question had put him back in his sour mood. I felt bad about that.

"Look…" I said, "don't mind her. She don't see many new folks around here. Sticks her nose in too far, is all."

He grunted, kept eating. Really shoveling it in. It was beef stew. I knew Sally made good beef stew, so he was bound to be enjoying it. I tried him again.

"You just… passing through?"

"Yeah. Hitching. Can't hitch on the super so I'm on the spur. Not many cars, I'll tellya. Waited two hours for a ride this morning."

I nodded in sympathy. "Like you say, not many cars. But the fruit trucks go through this time of year. In the afternoons. One of those'll stop for you. Those truckers are good people. Just you give 'em a wave, they'll stop."

"Thanks for the tip," he said. "Usually, with trucks, I don't even try. Regulations about riders and all."

"Just give 'em a wave," I repeated.

There was some silence then. Him finishing Sally's stew, me sitting there sipping at my own lukewarm coffee. (I drink too much of the stuff, so I've learned to nurse a cup. Can't sleep nights if I don't.)

Then I said to him, "You ever go to amusement parks as a kid?"

He nodded. "Sure. Who hasn't? Every kid has."

"I ran the Funhouse in one," I told him. "Down by the lake just this side of town."

His face brightened. A smile creased it. His first of the day, I'd wager.

"Hell, I loved those frigging funhouses! Used to sneak into 'em when my allowance was all spent and I couldn't afford to buy a ticket. They had an air vent inside that blew the girls' skirts up. Used to hide in there and watch." He scrubbed at the side of his dark beard. "Haven't been in one since I was eleven – back in Omaha."

"Never made it to Nebraska, but I hear it's a nice state."

"Used to scare myself half to death in those places. Bumping around in the dark… Couldn't see a thing. Scary as hell!"

"Folks like to be scared," I said. "Guess it's part of human nature."

"Trick doors… blind tunnels leading nowhere… things that popped out at you!" He chuckled. "One had a big gorilla with red eyes… I musta jumped ten feet when that ape popped outa the floor at me! Had gorilla nightmares for a month after that. Wouldn't go to bed unless Ma left the light on."

I've noticed one thing in the years with Happyland: people love to talk about funhouses. It's a subject everybody just plain likes to talk about – how scared they got as kids, lost in the dark tunnels, with things jumping at them. Funhouses are just that – *fun*.

"I miss running the place," I told him honestly. "Used to get a real kick out of scaring the folks. I'd work all the trick effects… and how they'd yell and scream! Especially the girls. Young girls love to scream!"

He nodded in agreement.

Suddenly I turned to him, grinning. "I got me an idea."

"What's that?" he said, pushing away his empty plate. He put his hand on his stomach and belched.

"Why don't you and me go out there – to Happyland? I can take you through the funhouse!"

He blinked at me, a little confused. "You mean – right *now*?"

"Sure. The park's closed, has been for years, but I can get in. Be no problem for me to show you through my funhouse. Be proud to!"

The big man shook his head. "Well… I dunno. That stuff's for kids."

"Hell, we're kids, aren't we? Just wearing adult bodies. No man ever stops being a boy. Not inside. Not all the way." I grinned at him. "Want to have a go?... give it a try?"

"Sounds a little crazy."

"Funhouse is for fun!" I said. "It's not even noon yet. You can take the tour with me, come out of the park and still grab a hitch with one of the truckers."

He slapped the countertop. "Why not? Why the hell not?"

I grinned at him. "Be fun for me, too. Haven't been out to Happyland for a longish while. Be like going home."

I own a Ford pickup. Old, like I am. Got a missing taillight. Clutch is bad. Needs a ring job. Tires are mostly bald. And the paint's gone altogether. But it putters along. Gets me where I need to go.

Happyland's only ten minutes out from town. As I said, right on the lake, but it's quiet now. Just black water, and too cold to swim in most of the year. Deep and black and quiet.

I parked next to the gate and we slipped under the rusted chain fence. The park was sad to see, all deserted and boarded up and with old newspapers and empty beer cans and trash everywhere. Vines growing right into the boards. Holes in the ground. I told the stranger to watch where he walked.

"Break an ankle out here at night," I said.

"I'll bet."

We passed the old Penny Arcade. All the machines were gone. It was like a dirty barn inside. No color or movement or sound in there now. Just a rat or two, maybe. Or a spider trapping flies.

Sad.

We walked on in the noon heat – past the Loop and the Whip and the Merry-go-Round, with broken holes in the floor where all the painted horses had galloped.

"No gorillas today," I said as we approached the Funhouse. "Electricity's shut down, and they took all the trick stuff away to Chicago. But at least we can run the tunnels. They're still the same."

"This is crazy," said the bearded man. "I've gotta be nuts, doing a thing like this."

"Be proud of yourself!" I told him. "You're not afraid to let out the boy in you! Every man would like to, but most are chicken about it. You've got guts."

We stood outside, looking at the place. The big laughing fatman at the entrance was gone. I can still hear his booming Ha-Ha-Ha-Ha like it was yesterday. Twenty years of a laugh you don't forget. I knew I never would.

The ticket booth was shaped like the jaws of a shark – but now most of the teeth were missing and the skin was peeling in big curling blisters along the sides. The broken glass in the booth had two boards nailed over it, like a pair of crossed arms.

"How do we get in?" the stranger asked me.

"There's bound to be a loose board," I told him. "Let's take a look."

"Oke," he nodded with a grin. "Lead on."

I found the loose board, pulling some brush away to clear it. Illinois is a green state; we get a lot of rain here, and things grow fast. The Funhouse was being choked by vines and creepers and high grass. It looked a thousand years old.

Sad.

The sky was clouding over. Late summer storm coming. They just pop up on you. It would be raining soon.

More rain, more growth. At this rate, in another fifty years, Happyland would be covered over – like those jungle temples in Mexico. No one could ever find it.

"Watch that nail near the top," I warned, as the stranger stooped to squeeze through with me. "Tear your shirt easy on a nail like that."

"Thanks."

"Got to watch out for my customers," I said.

Now we were inside. It was absolutely tar-pit black in the Funhouse. A jump from daylight to the dark side of the moon. And hot. Muggy hot inside.

"Can't see an inch in front of me," the stranger said.

"Don't worry, I'll walk you through. I've got a flash. It could use a new battery. Kind of dim, but we should be all right with it."

For emergencies, I always keep a flash in the Ford's glove compartment, with a couple of spare batteries. Never know when a tire might let go on you at night. But I keep forgetting to put in the new batteries when the old ones wear out. I guess nobody's perfect!

"Lots of cobwebs in here," I said, as we moved along. "Hope you don't mind spiders."

"I'm not in love with 'em," said the big man. "Not poisonous, are they?"

"No, no. Not these. Mostly little fellers. I'll clear the way for you."

And I did that, using a rolled newspaper to sweep the tunnel as I moved through it.

"Where are we?" he asked. "I mean – what part of the Funhouse?"

"About midway through from where you start," I said. "But the fun part is ahead. You haven't missed anything."

"This is crazy," he repeated again, half to himself. Then: "Ouch!"

I stopped, flashed the dimming light back at him. He was down on one knee.

"Hurt yourself?"

"I'm okay. Just stumbled. A loose board."

"Lots of those in here," I admitted. "Not dangerous, though. Not the way I'm taking you."

As we moved down the narrow wooden tunnel there was a wet, sliding sound.

"What's that?" he asked.

"The lake," I told him. "This part of the tunnel is built over the shore. That's the sound the lake water makes, hitting the pilings. The wind's up. Storm's coming."

We kept walking – going down one tunnel, turning, entering another, twisting, turning, reversing in the wooden maze. Maze to him, not to me. It was my world.

The rain had started, pattering on the wooden roof, dripping down into the tunnels. And the end-of-summer heat had given way to a sudden chill.

"This is no fun," said the stranger. "It's not what I remembered. I don't like it."

"The fun's up ahead," I promised him.

"You keep saying that. Look, I think we'd better-"

Suddenly my flash went out.

"Hey!" he shouted. "What happened?"

"Battery finally died," I said. "Don't worry. I've got another in the pickup. Wait here and I'll get it."

"Not on your life," the stranger protested. "I'm staying alone here in the pitch dark in this damned place."

"You *afraid* of the dark?" I asked him.

"No, dammit!"

"Then wait for me. I can't lead you back without a flash. Not through all the twists and turns. But I know the way. I can move fast. Won't be ten minutes."

"Well… I-"

"One thing, though. I want to warn you carefully about one thing. *Don't* try to move. Just stay right where you are, so I'll know where to find you. Some of the side tunnels are dangerous. Rotting boards. You could break a leg. The tunnels are tricky. You have to know which ones to stay out of."

"Don't worry, I'll stick right here like a bug on a wall."

"Ten minutes," I said.

And I left him in the tunnel.

Of course I didn't go back to the pickup for any batteries. Instead, I went to the control room at the end of B tunnel.

The door was padlocked, but I had the key. Inside, feeling excited about the stranger, I let Ed know I was here. Which was easy. I'd rigged a low-voltage generator in the control room, and when I pulled down a wall switch a red light went on under the tunnels and Ed knew I was back with a stranger.

I'll bet that he was excited, too. Hard to tell with Ed. But *I* sure was. My heart was pounding.

Fun in the Funhouse!

I didn't waste any time here. I'd done this many times before, so it was routine now: unlock the door, go inside, throw the switch for Ed, then activate the trap.

Trapdoor.

Right under the bearded stranger's feet. Even if he moved up or down the tunnel for a few yards (som of the nervous ones did that) there was no problem because the whole section of flooring was geared to open and send whoever was inside the tunnel down onto the slide. And the slide ended on the sand at the lakefront.

Where Ed was.

He would come up out of the lake when he saw the light. It would shine on the black water and he would see it from where he lived down there in the deep end and he would come slithering up.

Ed wasn't much to look at. Kind of weird. Spooky looking. (Remember, I said *no* ghosts!) His father was one of those really big rats that live in the burrows under the cemetery – and his mother was something from deep, deep in the lake. Something big and ugly and leathery.

They'd made love – the rat and the lake thing – and Ed was the result. Their son. He doesn't really have a name, but I call him Ed the way Gramps called me Tad. It fits him somehow, makes him more appealing. More… human.

Ed and me, we get along fine as partners. I bring him things to eat, and he saves the "goodies for me. Like wallets, and cash and rings (that big one Sally was joshing me about came from one of Ed's meals) and whatever else the strangers have that I can use.

Ed is smart.

He seems to know that I need these things since I've lost my job and all. That's why the partnership works so well. We each get our share. After I take what I want (one time I got a fine pair of leather boots) he drags the body back into the lake.

Then he eats.

Lucky for me, one meal lasts Ed for almost a month. So I don't have to worry if no stranger shows up at Sally's for two, three, even four weeks. One always ambles along sooner or later. Like Mama always said, everything comes to those that wait. Mama was a very patient woman. But she could be mean. I can testify to that.

It gets bad in the winter – for strangers, I mean – when the roads are closed, but that's when Ed sleeps anyhow, so things even out.

By the time I got back to the stranger's tunnel that afternoon it was really coming down. Rain, I mean. Dripping and sliding down the cold wood, and getting under my collar. Most uncomfortable. Somehow, rain always depresses me. Guess I'm too moody.

The stranger was down there with Ed where I expected him to be. Sometimes there's a little yelling and screaming, but nobody ever hears it, so that's no problem either. One fellow tried to use his knife on Ed, but Ed's skin is very tough and rubbery and doesn't cut easy. The stranger was just wasting his time, trying to use a knife on Ed.

I took a ladder down to the sand where the body was.

Ed was off by the water's edge, kind of breathing hard, when I got there. His jaw was dripping and his slanted black eyes glittered. Ed never blinked. He was watching me the way he always does, with his tail kind of moving, snakelike. He looked kind of twitchy, so I hurried. I don't think Ed likes the rain. Ed makes me nervous when it rains. He's not like himself. I never hang around the Funhouse when he's like that.

The bearded stranger was already dead, of course. Most of his head was gone, but Ed had been careful not to mess up his clothes – so it was no problem getting his wallet, rings, cash, coins…

When I climbed the ladder again Ed was already sliding towards the body.

Guess he was hungry.

Three and a half weeks later the stranger at the counter in Sally's looking at my watch.

"I've never seen one like that," he said.

"Tells you the time in ten parts of the world," I said. "Tells you the month of the year and the day of the week. And it rings every hour on the hour."

The stranger was impressed.

After a while, I grinned, leaned toward him across the counter and said, "You ever go to amusement parks as a kid?"

THE "GROUP" AND TELEVISION

By James R. Beach

A number of you *Dark Discoveries* readers are probably familiar with the "California Writers Group" or "The Group" and their impact on movies. For those who aren't, buoyed by mentors Ray Bradbury and Robert Bloch, "The Group" consisted of: Richard Matheson, William F. Nolan, George Clayton Johnson, John Tomerlin, "hub" Charles Beaumont at the center and fringe members Jerry Sohl, Harlan Ellison, Charles Fritch, Frank M. Robinson and O.C. Ritch. Even actors like William Shatner were attracted to the Group and often hung around them. And their stamp on popular culture is immense with landmark films such as: *I Am Legend, Logan's Run, The Incredible Shrinking Man, Duel, Burnt Offerings, The Legend of Hell House, Trilogy of Terror, The Intruder, The Seven Faces of Dr. Lao, Ocean's 11*, the Roger Corman Poe movies (*The Fall of the House of Usher, The Pit and the Pendulum, The Haunted Palace, The Mask of the Red Death*, etc.) and many others.

But what about Television? Matheson, Beaumont, Bradbury, Johnson, Tomerlin, Sohl and Ritch all contributed to the iconic Twilight Zone television series (only core group member Nolan was left out of it by bad luck. He co-wrote an episode with Johnson called "Dreamflight" that was cut from the schedule when the new producer took over toward the end of the series). But did you know that many members of the "Group" also wrote for a number of other popular, and in some cases legendary, shows as well? Johnson, Matheson, Sohl (all a part of the "Green Hand" writer's group along with Theodore Sturgeon) and Ellison wrote for the original Star Trek series (*Ed:* See issue #17 of *Dark Discoveries*) and many of the episodes are still considered some of the best. Matheson, Tomerlin, Bloch and Beaumont also wrote for Boris Karloff's

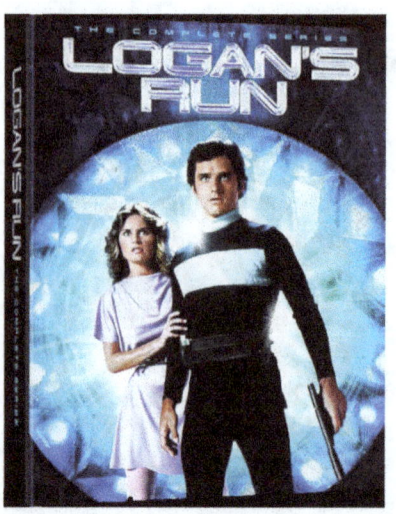

Thriller. Beaumont and Nolan wrote for One Step Beyond. Ellison and Bloch wrote for Outer Limits (and one of Beaumont's story ideaswas also adapted for the show). Johnson did episodes for Kung Fu and Honey West. Nolan and Ellison wrote for the Logan's Run series. Matheson, Tomerlin and Nolan wrote for the western series Wanted Dead or Alive. Matheson wrote for Night Gallery, Amazing Stories and Ghost Story/ Circle of Fear. Ellison and Matheson did episodes for the new Twilight Zone series in the eighties. Nolan and Bloch wrote for Darkroom (see article in this issue on the short-lived series). The list goes on and on…

Of course some of these shows are much more well-known than others, but you get my drift. There is hardly a fantasy or science fiction series in the last fifty years that one of these writers did not put their stamp on.Horror, science fiction, westerns, dramas – you name it, these guys did it. And did it well. The fact that many are still considered some of the best television series of all time is a testament to that fact.

Two of the main members of the Group, Richard Matheson and William Nolan, also struck up a very productive working relationship with legendary TV and movie producer Dan Curtis(best known for the original Dark Shadows series and a number of popular movies. *Ed:* see our Dark Shadows section in this issue of DD). Some of the all-time best made-for-TV movies and series came out of Dan's camp and many are still watched to this day. *Nightstalker* and *Nightstrangler*, both penned by Matheson, were the highest rated new TV movies at the time and both the movies and the subsequent series set the blueprints for shows to come later like *The X-Files* and *Supernatural*. Featuring a wise-cracking reporter played by Darren Gavin (A Christmas Story), Kolcheck investigated murders and crimes that turned out to be caused by vampires, werewolves, demons, etc. A popular TV series soon followed the two movies as well (a third movie script called *Nightkillers* was written by Matheson and Nolan, but was cancelled after the series was picked up instead. Eventually the script was published in 2003). Matheson also did Duel (Steven Spielberg's first full-length feature), Trilogy of Terror (with Nolanadapting two of Matheson's stories and a Philip K. Dick one that wasn't used, and Matheson adapting his own "Prey") featuring Karen Black playing all the female roles, Dracula (a great version with Jack Palance), Dying Room Only, Scream of the Wolf (with Peter Graves) and others.

For Curtis, William Nolan also did the aforementioned Trilogy of Terror with Matheson, Trilogy of Terror 2, Burnt Offerings (starring Bette Davis, Oliver Reed and Karen Black), The Turn of the Screw (starring Lynn Redgrave and Dark Shadows'Kathryn Leigh Scott), The Norliss Tapes (with Roy Thinnes and Angie Dickinson), Terror at London

Bridge,Melvin Purvis: G-Man, The Kansas City Massacre, and others. Even John Tomerlin scripted an excellent adaptation of The Picture of Dorian Gray for Dan Curtis that is often overlooked. I'd recommend checking this out if you can find a copy of it, as well as the majority of Matheson's and Nolan's work with/for Curtis.

Boris Karloff's Thriller only lasted two seasons (1961 – 1962) and sixty-seven episodes, but in its short run established itself as one of the scariest and best horror series of all-time. The first half of the initial season was pretty much an Alfred Hitchcock Presents clone of revenge murders, etc., but then the producers discovered the old issues of Weird Tales and it became much more than that. With memorable episodes adapted from Robert E. Howard, August Derleth and others, it's amazing what got past the censors in those days (the hatchet in the head scene in Howard's Pigeons From Hell is definitely one prime example). In his book Danse Macabre, Stephen King proclaims it the scariest show on TV ever. That definitely says something there. Charles Beaumont ("Girl With A Secret" and "Guillotine"), Richard Matheson ("The Return of Andrew Bentley"), John Tomerlin ("Dark Legacy") and Robert Bloch ("The Cheaters", "Waxworks", "Till Death Do Us Part", "The Weird Taylor", "The Grim Reaper", "The Hungry Glass", "Yours Truly Jack the Ripper") also wrote interesting episodes for the series and helped round things out. Many excellent actors appeared in the shows, such as William Shatner, Richard Chamberlain, Elizabeth Montgomery, Mary Tyler Moore, Rip Torn, Mary Astor Richard Kiel, Donna Douglas, Victor Buono, Alan Napier, Cloris Leachman, Beverly Garland, Leslie Nielsen, Reggie Nalder, Natalie Schafer, Susan Oliver, Ursula Andress, – and many from the Twilight Zone as well (and also directors like Douglas Hayes from TZ). Although it was out of syndication for many years, not long ago it finally came to DVD after occasionally getting played on Sci-fi Network.

One series virtually forgotten is Ghost Story/Circle of Fear from the early 1970s. Produced by legendary "gimic" movie producer William Castle (House on Haunted Hill, The Tingler, Strait-Jacket, etc.) and developed with Richard Matheson, this short-lived series features episodes written by Matheson ("The New House"), Robert Bloch ("House of Evil"), Harlan Ellison (an adaptation of his story "Shattered Like A Glass Goblin" with Star Trek writer D.C. Fontana), Henry Slesar, Stanley Ellin and even Jimmy Sangster of Hammer Studios fame. Memorable shows starred Janet Leigh, Angie Dickinson, Martin Sheen, Jason Robards, Tab Hunter, Jodie Foster, Gena Rowlands, Hal Linden, and others. I don't think this one is out on DVD in the US (I saw a Region 4 of it on eBay recently), but I'd encourage you to look for it in whatever format you can find. Many people especially remember being scared by "Death's Head" - where the faces of revenge victims are imprinted on the back of a moth after they die. The series only lasted twenty-two episodes (twenty-three total counting the pilot) and after thirteen shows they cut host Sebastian Cabot and changed the title to "Circle of Fear."

The torch was then passed on to the next generation. Richard Matheson's son, Richard Christian Matheson, has written for a number of popular television shows like The Incredible Hulk, The A-Team, Amazing Stories, Tales From the Crypt, Nightmares & Dreamscapes, Showtime's Masters of Horror and more. Charles Beaumont's son Chris Beaumont has also dabbled in TV writing for Fame and Highway To Heaven. Dennis Etchison, who tutored under Beaumont and Nolan at UCLA in the early sixties (and became a sort of junior member of "The Group"), collaborated on a treatment for the Logan's Run show with Nolan and now does Twilight Zone radio show adaptations of many of the original scripts (used and unused).

So, you can see the impact of "The Group" on the development of horror and science fiction television has been huge. There's hardly a show in that vein that they didn't work on, or influence. Or will continue to influence for years to come.

❦❦❦

THE ABC MOVIE OF THE WEEK

By Mark Sieber (list by James R. Beach)

There are many elements responsible for my lifelong obsession with all things horrific. The Universal Monster movies, to be sure. Dark Shadows. The Twilight Zone. Hammer Studios productions. The big-bug craze of the 50s. Edgar Allan Poe and Eight Tales of Terror. I don't know whether to be thankful for these things, or resentful.

These will be mostly unknown to all but the most ardent younger horror fan, those over the age of, say, 45, will surely remember those glorious Movies of the Week which came on the ABC network every Tuesday, from 1969 to 1976.

Nearly every type of movie was produced and aired. Bawdy comedies, timely stories of the hot topics of the day, action, suspense, romance. But the ones that seemed to be talked about the most were the horror movies.

Most of these aired for an hour-and-a-half, which made them only a little over an hour in length before commercial breaks were inserted. Nowadays in that time period they would probably only be forty-five minutes long. Many movies feel drawn out to feature length. An hour or so is about novella length.

ABC had been the third rated of the Big Three television networks for a long time, but The ABC Tuesday Movie of the Week played a big role in changing that. Most of the stories were, frankly, potboilers. But they were incredibly popular at the time. There was usually a lot of lunchroom talk about them on Wednesday at school. Especially the horror and action stories.

Not all of the Tuesday movies were low rent affairs. Spielberg had audiences riveted in their seats with his suspenseful adaptation of Richard Matheson's Duel. ABC was savvy enough to allow the writer to adapt his own story. There was one called Tribes, in which a hippie played by Jan-Michael Vincent was drafted into the Army.

And, of course, every horror fan worth his or her salt rightly reveres The Night Stalker. This classic was also penned by Matheson, but it was adapted from a then-unpublished manuscript by Jeff Rice. It was followed by a decent sequel, called The Night Strangler, and a silly but fondly remembered series that featured the Kolchack character fighting a different monster each week.

If you like Kolchack and have not read the Rice novel, you should make a point to do so as soon as possible. The character is quite a bit different, and the story is darker and more effective. Used copies are still pretty easy to find.

But I digress.

The producers were not only shrewd enough to hire the incomparable Richard Matheson, they also utilized the talents of Robert Bloch for some screenplays. They purchased and adapted stories by Theodore Sturgeon, John Farris, Zenna Henderson. Cult director Curtis Harrington did a couple of pictures with them.

Looking back, it was a golden time.

I've dreamed of having a chance to see some of them again. Of course it's easy to watch The Night Stalker, or Duel. Don't Be Afraid of the Dark was remade and isn't hard to find. But most were seemingly lost.

I have the fondest memories of shivering through ABC movies like Crowhaven Farm, Killdozer, The Cat Creature, How Awful About Alan, The House That Would Not Die, A Cold Night's Death, Moon of the Wolf, Satan's Triangle, Night Slaves, and so many more.

There are other famous ones that stand out in memory: Bad Ronald. Trilogy of Terror. When Michael Calls.

Some saint has uploaded a bunch of these on You Tube, and I have added hyperlinks to them. I haven't watched any yet, and I am wondering if I even should. Maybe some childhood memories should remain majestic. I'd hate to watch them and see that they are dated and corny. At the time they were so vivid and terrifying.

I may do so, but I'll wait for now. By all means, check a few out and let me know if I should take the plunge, or allow my sweetly dark memories to stay untarnished.

TV HORROR/SUSPENSE MOVIES OF THE WEEK (ABC & Other Networks)

Along Came A Spider (1970) – Directed by Lee Katzin. Produced by Aaron Spelling. Starring Suzanne Pleshette, Ed Nelson, Andrew Prine, Brooke Bundy, Richard Anderson, Barry Atwater. The widow of a scientist who was murdered by his colleagues goes undercover at the research lab where he worked to expose them.

Are You in the House Alone? (1978) – Directed by Walter Grauman. Starring Kathleen Beller, Blythe Danner, Dennis Quaid, Robin Mattson. Beller plays a shy high school girl plagued by a phantom secret admirer who eventually assaults her.

Bad Ronald (1974) – Directed by Buzz Kulik. Starring Scott Jacoby, Kim Hunter, Dabney Coleman, Pippa Scott. Jacoby plays a crazy teen hidden away in a secret room by mom Hunter after he accidentally kills a neighbor girl. After Hunter dies, the house is sold and another family moves in not realizing there's a psycho lurking behind the walls.

Black Noon (1971) – Directed by Bernard L. Kowalski. Produced by Aaron Spelling. Starring Roy Thinnes, Yvette Mimieux, Ray Milland, Gloria Grahame, Henry Silva, Lyn Loring. A traveling preacher & his wife are terrorized by a devil cult.

The Cat Creature (1973) – Directed by Curtis Harrington. Written by Robert Bloch. Starring Meredith Baxter, David Hedison, John Carradine, Gayle Sondergaard, Stuart Whitman. When a wealthy collector dies some items from his collection are stolen including an ancient Egyptian gold amulet from the mummy that was wearing it. The police consult scholars from the local University to help with the investigation.

A Cold Night's Death (1973) – Directed by Jerrold Freedman. Produced by Aaron Spelling & Leonard Goldberg. Starring Robert Culp, Eli Wallach, Michael C. Gwyne. Scientists suspect that there is someone other than their research primates inhabiting their polar station.

Crowhaven Farm (1970) – Directed by Walter Grauman. Produced by Aaron Spelling. Starring Hope Lange, John Carradine, Paul Burke, Lloyd Bochner, Patricia Barry. A young couple inherits a farm. Hoping that the rural location might help to patch up their strained marriage, they move into it, only to be confronted by the supernatural forces that inhabit it.

Curse of the Black Widow (1977) – Directed by Dan Curtis. Produced by Dan Curtis. Written by Earl Wallace. Starring Anthony Franciosa, Donna Mills, Patty Duke, Vic Morrow, and June Allyson. A detective is on the trail of a murderer whose male victims are found encased in silken cocoons. He eventually tracks the killer's path to Los Angeles, where he discovers her true identity - a woman who was bitten by black widow spiders as a child.

Daughter of the Mind (1969) – Directed and Produced by Walter Grauman. Starring Ray Milland, Gene Tierney, Don Murray, Ed Asner, John Carradine. A professor (Milland)comes to believe that his dead daughter is communicating with him from beyond the grave.

Dead of the Night (1977) – Directed and produced by Dan Curtis. Written by Richard Matheson & Jack Finney. Starring Ed Begley Jr., Patrick Macnee, Anjanette Comer, Joan Hackett, Elisha Cook Jr. Anthology that features three stories: a man buys a car that takes him back and forth through time; a tale of vampires; and a distraught mother asks for her drowned son to come back to life and gets more than she bargained for.

The Deadly Dream (1971) – Directed by Alf Kjellin. With Lloyd Bridges, Janet Leigh, Carl Betz, Leif Erickson, Don Stroud. A scientist keeps having dreams that he is marked for murder by a mysterious tribunal for something that he's not aware that he's done, and that his wife and his friends are part of the conspiracy. Soon he's not sure which is the dream and which is reality.

Death at Love House (1976) – Directed by E.W. Swackhammer. Starring Robert Wagner, Kate Jackson, Joan Blondell, Dorthy Lamour, Sylvia Sidney, John Carradine, Marianna Hill. Donna and Joel Gregory are staying at the estate of Lorna Love while researching a book about the long dead Hollywood goddess. Joel becomes obsessed with her and Donna starts to believe the house is haunted by her ghost.

Death Cruise (1974) – Directed by Ralph Senensky. Produced by Aaron Spelling. Starring Kate Jackson, Edward Albert, Polly Bergan, Tom Bosley, Michael Constantine. Several couples are notified that they have won an ocean cruise, but they actually have been lured onto a ship so that they can be murdered.

Death Scream (1975) – Directed by Richard T. Heffron. Written by Sterling Silliphant. Starring Raul Julia, Lucie Arnez, Ed Asner, Art Carney, Kate Jackson, Dihann Carroll, Tina Louise, Cloris Leachman, Sally Kirkland. A young woman is murdered in an alley. The crime is heard or seen by the residents of a nearby apartment building, but none of them did anything to help and they refuse to cooperate with the police during the investigation.

Death Takes A Holiday (1971) – Directed by Robert Butler. Starring Yvette Mimieux, Myrna Loy, Bert Convy, Melvin Douglas, Kerwin Matthews. Death takes a human form and visits Earth to try to find out why humans want so desperately to cling to life. He unexpectedly falls in love with a beautiful young woman.

The Devil's Daughter (1973) Directed by Jeannot Szwarc. Starring Shelly Winters, Jonathan Frid, Joseph Cotton, Robert Foxworth, Belinda J. Montgomery. A young girl whose mother had sold her soul to the devil in infancy is now called to the fold by Satan (Shelley Winters) who tries to marry her off to a fellow demon.

Dracula (1974) – Directed by Dan Curtis. Written by Richard Matheson. Produced by Dan Curtis. Starring Jack Palance, Nigel Davenport, Fiona Lewis, Sarah Douglas, Simon Ward. Matheson adapts Bram Stoker's novel Dracula with Curtis at the helm.

Duel (1971) – Directed by Steven Spielberg. Written by Richard Matheson. Starring Dennis Weaver, Jacqueline Scott, Eugene Dynarski. A business commuter is pursued and terrorized by a malevolent driver of a massive tractor-trailer.

Dying Room Only (1973) – Directed by Philip Leacock. Written by Richard Matheson. Produced by Dan Curtis. Starring Cloris Leachman, Ross Martin, Ned Beatty, Louise Latham. A couple are travelling by car and stop at a roadside diner to eat. When Leachman's husband mysteriously disappears, everyone assures her that she arrived alone.

Frankenstein (1973) – Directed by Glenn Jordan. Screenplay by

Dan Curtis and Sam Hall from Mary Shelley's novel. Starring Robert Foxworth, Bo Sevenson, Susan Strasberg, John Karlan, Willie Ames. Faithful adaptation of Shelley's novel about a doctor who harnesses electricity, via lightning, to reanimate a giant creature he has pieced together from dead body parts.

The Girl Most Likely To… (1973) – Directed by Lee Phillips. Written by Joan Rivers and Agnes Gallin. Starring Stockard Channing, Ed Asner, Jim Backus, Ruth McDevitt, Suzanne Zenor. An ugly girl undergoes plastic surgery and becomes beautiful. She then takes revenge on all the people who mistreated her when she was ugly.

Heatwave! (1974) – Directed by Jerry Jameson. Produced by Herbert F. Solow. Starring Bonnie Bedelia, Ben Murphy, Lew Ayres, John Anderson. The residents of an isolated mountain town must band together to survive during a devastating heat wave.

Hitchhike! (1974) – Directed by Gordon Hessler. Starring Cloris Leachman, Michael Brandon, Henry Darrow, Cameron Mitchell. A woman, on her way to visit her sister in San Francisco, picks up a hitchhiker who has just killed his stepmother.

Home for the Holidays (1972) – Directed by John Llewelen Moxey. Written by Joseph Stefano. Produced by Aaron Spelling. Starring Sally Field, Julie Harris, Jessica Walter, Jill Haworth, Walter Brennan, Eleanor Parker. An ailing man summons his three daughters home for Christmas and tells them he suspects his new wife of poisoning him. After his claims are mostly ignored, a psycho in a rain slicker and gloves begins killing them off one by one by pitchfork.

The House That Would Not Die (1970) – Directed by John Llewelyn Moxey. Produced by Aaron Spelling. Adapted from a novel by Barbara Michaels (Ammie, Come Home). Starring Barbara Stanwyck, Richard Egan, Michael Anderson Jr., Katherine Wynn, Doreen Lang. Ruth Bennett and her niece Sara Dunning move into the house of Ruth's recently deceased aunt and shortly thereafter they learn the house is possessed by two ghosts of the original owners who were from the time of the Revolutionary War.

How Awful About Allan (1970) – Directed by Curtis Harrington. Produced by . Starring Anthony Perkins, Julie Harris, Joan Hackett, Robert H. Harris. Perkins plays a man suffering from hysterical blindness after the accidental death of his father. Harris is the embittered, disfigured sister and Hackett the old girlfriend trying to rekindle the flame. Guess which one is trying to drive him crazy with stories of a shadowy boarder in the house and may or may not be trying to kill him?

The Invasion of Carol Enders (1974) – Directed by Burt Brinckerhoff. Produced by Dan Curtis. Starring Meredith Baxter, John Karlen, Charles Aidman, Christopher Connolly. Baxter plays a hospital patient possessed by the spirit of a fellow patient who was a murdered.

Isn't It Shocking? (1973) – Directed by John Badham. Starring Alan Alda, Louise Lasser, Edmund O'Brien, Ruth Gordon. A small-town sheriff is confronted with the deaths of local senior citizens and strange goings-on in his town.

Killdozer (1974) – Directed by Jerry London. Produced by Herbert F. Solow. Screenplay by Theodore Sturgeon and Ed MacKillop Starring Clint Walker, Neville Brand, Carl Betz, James Wainwright. While working on the island the work crew finds a large blue rock that they cannot move. Unknown to them is that it is a meteorite that fell to earth (Seen at the very opening of the movie). When one of the workers rams the rock (meteor) with a Cat D9 a large blue light is emitted which cause the D9 to stop running. Later when one of the workers goes to use the D9 it starts running on its own and starts killing the workers.

Live Again, Die Again (1974) – Directed by Richard A. Colla. Teleplay by Joseph Stefano. Starring Donna Milles, Cliff Potts, Walter Pidgeon, Mike Farrell, Geraldine Page, Vera Miles. After being cryogenically frozen for more than 30 years, a woman wakes to find her husband an old man and her children older than she is.

The Moon of the Wolf (1972) – Directed by Daniel Petrie. Based on the novel by Leslie H. Whitten. Starring David Janssen, Barbara Rush, Bradford Dillman, John Bernadino. After several locals are viciously murdered, a Louisiana sheriff starts to suspect he may be dealing with a werewolf.

Night of Terror (1972) – Directed by Jeannot Szwarc. Starring Donna Mills, Martin Balsam, Chuck Connors, Agnes Moorhead. A hired killer hunts down a schoolteacher to get something she has. She doesn't know what it is, but he's already killed twice to get it.

Night Slaves (1970) – Directed by Ted Post. (Adapted for a Jerry Sohl novel). Starring James Franciscus, Lee Grant, Andrew Prine, Leslie Neilson. Clay and Marjorie take a vacation together while Clay recuperates from a serious auto accident. They end up in a sleepy little town which seems to be normal, except at night when the townspeople (and Marjorie) turn into zombies, file into trucks and head out of town. They always return by morning, and no one has any memories of the night before.

The Night Stalker (1972) – Directed by John Llewelen Moxey. Written by Richard Matheson. Produced by Dan Curtis. Starring Darren McGavin, Carol Lynley, Simon Oakland, Barry Atwater. An investigative reporter, Carl Kolchak (McGavin), comes to suspect that a serial killer in the Las Vegas area is in fact a vampire.

The Night Strangler (1973) – Directed and Produced by Dan Curtis. Starring Darren McGavin, John Carradine, Joann Pflug, Wally Cox, Simon Oakland. Reporter Carl Kolchak is now in Seattle, Washington, trying to solve the mystery of several strangulations that recur every few years where the victims are drained of blood in this second made for TV pilot.

The Norliss Tapes (1973) – Directed by Dan Curtis. Written by William F. Nolan. Produced by Dan Curtis. Starring Angie Dickenson, Roy Thinnes, Don Porter, Claude Akins. Thinnes stars as Dan Norliss, an investigative reporter specializing in the supernatural. Norliss' tapes consist of his observations when tracking down a report about a "walking dead man." As it happens, the tapes seem to be all that is left of Norliss, who has completely disappeared.

The Picture of Dorian Gray (1973) – Directed by Glenn Jordan. Written by John Tomerlin. Produced by Dan Curtis. Starring Charles Aidman, Shane Briant, Nigel Davenport, John Karlan. A very attractive young man is given a portrait of himself by an admiring artist. Soon after this he treats a young woman cruelly and then notices that his portrait seems to look meaner than it used to. Eventually he cannot endure the portrait and hides it in the attic. As the years pass, he becomes ever more unscrupulous and dissolute. His friends remark how he is as handsome as ever and never seems to age. But up in the attic his picture becomes uglier and uglier.

The People (1971) – Directed by John Korty. Produced by Francis Ford Coppola. Starring William Shatner, Kim Darby, Diane Varsi, Dan O'Herlihy. A young woman is assigned to teach school in a secluded valley whose inhabitants appear stern, secretive and anti-pleasure. Following two children who disappear to play in the woods, she finds that this is actually a community of extraterrestrials with mild paranormal powers who are attempting to repress and deny their heritage for fear of arousing prejudice and hatred in their human neighbors. Based on a series of novels by the late Zenna Henderson.

Satan's School For Girls (1973) – Directed by David Lowell Rich. Produced by Aaron Spelling. Starring Kate Jackson, Cheryl Ladd, Pamela Franklin, Roy Thinnes, Lloyd Bochner, Jo Van Fleet. A young woman investigating her sister's suicide at a private girls' school finds herself battling a satanic cult.

Satan's Triangle (1975) – Directed by Sutton Roley. Starring Kim Novak, Doug McClure, Alejandro Rey, Ed Lauter, Jim Davis. The female survivor of a shipwreck and two Coast Guard helicopter pilots sent to rescue her find themselves trapped in a mysterious part of the ocean known as Satan's Triangle.

The Screaming Woman (1972) – Directed by Jack Smight. Adapted from a story by Ray Bradbury. Produced by William Frye (Thriller). Starring Olivia DeHavilland, Ed Nelson, Joseph Cotton, Larraine Stephens, Alexandra Hay. A wealthy former mental patient goes home to her estate to rest and recuperate. While walking the grounds one day she hears the screams of a woman coming from underneath the ground who has been buried alive. Her family, however, refuses to believe her story, and sees the incident as an opportunity to prove the woman's mind has snapped so they can take control of her money.

Scream of the Wolf (1974) – Directed by Dan Curtis. Screenplay by Richard Matheson from a David Case story. Starring Peter Graves, Clint Walker, Jo Ann Pflug, Philip Carey. A big-game hunter comes out of retirement to help track down a killer wolf, and begins to suspect that it isn't a wolf but an animal that can take human form.

Search for the Gods (1975) – Directed by Jud Taylor. Starring Kurt Russell, Stephen McHattie, Ralph Bellamy, Victoria Racimo. Two young people search for a valuable medallion, which they believe will prove

that aliens from outer space visited Earth in prehistoric times.

She Waits (1972) – Directed by Delbert Mann. Written by Art Wallace (Dark Shadows). Starring Patty Duke, David McCallum, Dorthy McGuire, Lew Ayres. Widower McCallum brings his new bride (Duke) to his bedridden mother's (McGuire) mansion where Patty is possessed by his first wife.

Snowbeast (1977) – Directed by Herb Wallerstein. Starring Bo Sevenson, Yvette Mimieux, Clint Walker, Sylvia Sidney, Annie McEnroe. A barely glimpsed Abominable Snowman terrorizes a Colorado ski resort.

The Strange Case of Dr. Jekyll and Mr. Hyde (1968) - Directed by Charles Jarrott. Produced by Dan Curtis. Starring Jack Palance, Denholm Elliot, Leo Glenn, Elizabeth Cole. Dr. Henry Jekyll experiments on himself with a concoction that he'd hoped would neutralize his baser instincts, but instead releases his long-repressed animal inclinations.

The Stranger Within (1974) – Directed by Lee Phillips. Written by Richard Matheson. Starring Barbara Eden, George Grizzard, Joyce Van Patten, David Doyle. A woman whose husband had a vasectomy becomes mysteriously pregnant and gives birth in record time while talking in strange languages and wanting very cold temperatures.

A Taste of Evil (1971) – Directed by John Llewellen Moxey. Written by Jimmy Sangster. Produced by Aaron Spelling. Starring Barbara Stanwyck, Roddy McDowell, Barbara Parkins, William Windom. On her way home from a stay at a mental institution after a rape, a woman realizes that someone is deliberately trying to drive her insane.

Trilogy of Terror (1975) – Directed by Dan Curtis. Written by William F. Nolan and Richard Matheson. Starring Karen Black, Robert Burton, John Karlen, George Gaynes. Three bizarre horror stories all of which star Karen Black in four different roles playing tormented women.

The Turn of the Screw (1974) – Directed by Dan Curtis. Screenplay by William F. Nolan from Henry James novel. Starring Lynn Redgrave, Kathryn Leigh Scott, John Barron, Eva Griffiths. An English governess is hired to take care of two adorable orphans, who turn out to be not exactly what they seem to be.

The Victim (1972) – Directed by Herschell Daugherty. Produced by William Frye (Thriller). Starring Elizabeth Montgomery, George Maharis, Sue Ann Langdon. A wealthy woman is trapped during a storm in a house with no electricity or phone and a killer is now after her.

Where Have All the People Gone? (1974) – Directed by John Lewellyn Moxey. Starring Peter Graves, Kathleen Quinlan, Verna Bloom. A strange series of solar flares proves fatal for inhabitants of the Earth, except for the fortunate few who are somehow immune from the effects. A handful of survivors attempt to rebuild their lives on the de-populated Earth.

Masks

By Brian M. Sammons

The little boy sucked in a breath and his eyes went wide when he saw Paul's face.

It was the fact that Paul didn't *have* a face that caused him such alarm. The boy's grip tightened on his mother's pudgy hand. She had been content to take sidelong peeks at Paul when she thought he wasn't looking. He didn't blame the mother or son for staring. Everyone likes to look at a freak. Rarely will someone admit it, but deep down everyone likes to see some misshapen, hideous, *thing*, if for no other reason than to silently thank God that it wasn't them drawing the stares.

As if to prove the point, Paul caught the fat British mother peeking at him again out of the corner of her eye. His head was turned slightly so the woman thought she could steal a glance without being seen. But Paul spotted her. That was the only good thing about Paul's mask; it hid his eyes in wells of shadow. No one could ever tell where he was looking.

Or what he had seen.

"Mummy, mummy." The little boy had finally found his breath and was now urgently tugging on his mother's hand. Paul knew what was coming as the child's wide eyes were still locked on his tin mask. He decided to play dumb and let the woman squirm.

He smiled at that. No, it was more of a grimace. A grimace is the best you can do when you don't have lips.

Paul took a moment to look around the packed post office. Two months after the end of the war and it was still a major event when mail made it to Britain from the continent. A boat from America with mail on it practically made the newspapers.

The mother in front of Paul was now trying in vain to hush her inquisitive child, but there was no way she could avoid the coming question.

"Mummy, why is that man wearing a mask?"

"Hush, Gilbert, Mummy's tired."

Nice try, mom, but that's not going to work, Paul thought and decided to up the discomfort level for the woman by staring back at her. Paul knew he was being a bastard, not that he cared. When you don't have a face you had to find your fun where you could.

"But Mummy, that man's got a mask on. Why does he have a mask on?"

"Shhh, don't bother him."

Paul could tell by the way the woman blushed that she felt his eyes on her. He knew it wasn't a good feeling. Even after months he still wasn't used to it.

"But Mummy, he's scary. Why does he have that ugly thing on?"

That got the mother's attention. Nothing gets the Brits more upset than the possibility of being impolite. The mother turned around, grabbed her son's chin so that his gaze was torn from Paul, and the two of them locked eyes.

"Now you be quiet, Gilbert, and leave that man alone. His face was hurt in the war. He's probably a hero and he does not need you staring at him. Is that understood?" The mother made sure she spoke the part about Paul being a hero extra loud, to be certain he heard it.

Then at last the mother acknowledged Paul's presence by looking at him. She offered a week smile and stared at Paul's chest. That was as high as she would raise her gaze in public. "I'm sorry. You know how children can be."

"Yesssh, ma'am, I know. Ssshildren can be curiousss. It'sssh alright." Paul made sure to slurp and drool his words at her as much as possible. He figured the mother deserved the whole effect.

"Th…thank you, sir," she whispered and quickly turned back around.

Paul stuffed his hands into his GI trench coat, shuffled his GI boots, and fumed beneath his GI mask. Everything he had on was new. The clothes Paul had worn in the trenches didn't make it out of France, much like his face. Upon coming to London to recover from his wounds he was given all new stuff. That included a new face made of dull tin held in place with leather straps. The mask was General Issue for anyone whose mug was so badly mangled that the sight of it caused delicate people to faint or become nauseous.

Nice of the military to be so thoughtful, Paul thought. *After all, we don't want innocent people getting too good a look at the real face of war, right? So for their sake, there's probably an entire company of men with uncomfortable, cold, tin masks instead of faces. Men who sacrificed their very identities for these ungrateful cows and their bugged-eyed, gaped-mouth, staring little brats…*

Paul caught himself getting worked up and tried to calm down. He had almost slipped his mask and that just wouldn't do.

Not here. Not now.

He counted the people between himself and the package pick up window. There were seven, not counting the children. At the rate the elderly postmaster behind the counter was moving, Paul guessed he had plenty of time to kill. So he turned to his daydreams. Anything was better than the soggy, gray tedium that now encompassed his life, even if it was memories best forgotten.

***

The captain blew the whistle, and up and over the soldiers went, like fools. Leaving the moderate safety of the filthy, disease ridden, rat infested trenches, frightened boys and crazy, would-be heroes ran through the darkness towards the flashing German guns. They were told that this attack was vital. No doubt some general wanted to claim a major victory by gaining a few more feet of blasted earth.

Across the aptly named No Man's Land they charged. Legs were caught and shredded by rusted barbed wire. Soldiers fell into craters filled with filth and stumbled over the rotting bodies of those who had gone before them. Some splashed into puddles with the remains of mustard gas floating on the surface. Those men came up screaming, eyes streaming, and coughing up blood. Then there was the opposing army shooting at them. At first the range was too great and the darkness provided cover, so most shots missed, but every step forward gave the Huns a bigger target to shoot at. When the flares went up the Americans were robbed of their lifesaving darkness. That's when the dying really began.

David, all red hair, freckles and laughs, was right beside Paul one moment, and the next he was simply gone. Paul never knew David's fate, but he saw what happened to Sam. The big man from Montana fell into a fresh, smoking crater clutching his guts. As he ran past, Paul saw the man desperately trying to push coils of pink intestines back inside his belly. Johnny, the trumpet player from Chicago, was found when Paul stepped on his chest, but by that time the former musician was beyond caring about such things.

A loud *TING* rattled Paul's skull as a bullet ricocheted off his helmet. This caused him to stop for a moment and look around in confusion, and that's when Mike ran into him from behind. Mike was screaming into Paul's face to *go, go, go* when all of a sudden Mike's head disappeared in a thick red mist. Something stung

Paul's cheek at that same instant and he dropped his riffle so he could touch it and see what it was. It was small and hard, and after Paul pulled it out of his face he saw in the orange glow of the drifting flare that it was a tooth. One of Mike's molars.

That's when Paul decided to run. He had to get away, anywhere but towards that meat grinder the officers were herding everyone toward. All thoughts of honor or duty or showing the Europeans how to really fight were quickly replaced with the image of one of Paul's own teeth sticking out of some other guy's cheek. So he ran, not ducking for cover or sneaking away, just all-out running in any direction that took him away from the flashing German guns.

Paul ran until his legs ached and his lungs burned. He ran over the bodies of his dead and dying comrades. He ran through the barbwire that clutched at his legs and tore his trousers and flesh. He ran through the smoke and the blood and the screams. He ran until the first red light of dawn crept over the horizon.

That was when he saw the church.

It stood alone in a vast expanse of desolation like something once hidden and best forgotten. The building was a white, one room affair, with a steeple at the rear. Although it had suffered some damage, it had largely escaped the ravages of war. Of the town that had no doubt once encompassed the church, there was no sign. There weren't even any notable piles of rubble. It was as if a giant hand had plucked the church up from some far off place and set it down here.

The surprise of finding a standing church in the middle of a blasted wasteland caused Paul to pause long enough to catch his breath and look around. He was still in No Man's Land and otherwise lost. From where he stood, Paul could not see trenches or fortifications in any direction and that was surprisingly unnerving. Odder still was the complete lack of the sounds of war sounds. He had long ago become accustomed to the gunshots, artillery fire, and the noise of soldiers as they prayed, cried, laughed, cursed or screamed in pain. Their absence now was keenly felt.

After untold moments trapped in the foreboding silence, Paul finally heard something other than his own rasping breath. It was music of a sort, with some odd singing accompanying it. Both were coming from the church.

Griped by a strangely compelling sense of curiosity, Paul carefully made his way in that direction. As he got closer the voices became clearer, but strangely the music did not. The haunting melody remained at a constant faint level as if someone was turning down the volume of a phonograph as Paul walked towards it. As for the voices, Paul was forty yards from the church when he recognized they were speaking French.

Paul was thirty yards away when he hit the muddy ground after he heard someone speaking German. A woman replied in French and although Paul didn't understand a word of either language, a shiver went down his spine nonetheless. Paul was thinking about crawling away and giving the church a wide berth when he heard a man speak up in English with a British accent.

"Carcosa? Pray, sweet Cassilda, tell what you know of lost Carcosa."

At that the German man spoke again for some time and it was while the kraut was talking that Paul noticed something strange happening to him. His vision had gone blurry, his eyes felt heavy, and a great tiredness was spreading over him like a warm blanket. In contrast, his breathing picked up and at the back of Paul's neck he felt an itching sensation like scurrying ants on his skin. He felt sweat gather on his brow and under his arms. When the German spoke again, Paul somehow knew what he was saying. Not the exact words, but the meaning behind them. The German was speaking about a terrible loss that could never be replaced.

Then the French lady, Cassilda being her name, spoke again and Paul could understand her too. She spoke about an empty city of shadows called Carcosa and a lake called Hali and of other places and people that were both unknown yet familiar. When she started to sing about the unending dark and the cruelty of time, her voice was filled with such anguish and hopelessness that Paul began weeping, after years of not shedding a single tear for anyone or anything.

When Cassilda's joyless aria ended the Englishman, who Paul now knew was Thale, yet he had heard no one address him as such, said, "And what of the Tattered King? Does he come for the Grand Masque tonight?"

Then Camilla, Cassilda's daughter in mourning, said that her brother Yoht would know. Next came…nothing. Only silence. None of the unseen people in the church spoke; the faint music had stopped, and even the outside world seemed to hold its breath. This went on until Yoht suddenly answered.

"Yes, dear sister, I know, and let what I share with the court bring some happiness to these gray halls."

It was only after Paul stood up and had taken his first steps toward the open doors of the church that he realized the last voice he had heard was his own.

As Paul crossed the remaining distance to the Great Hall of Cassilda's castle, he heard the royal court bid him to hurry and bring the joy that had become such a stranger to them. Before he could enter, Paul had to become more appropriate, so with the use of his trench knife and a yielding arm, he painted his face with the Crimson Sigil befitting of his station. Only so adorned did he enter.

There were six men and two women in the Great Hall. Some dressed in civilian clothes and others in military uniforms of gray, brown, and tan. All bore crusting Crimson Sigils upon their faces to identify themselves, but Paul did not need the smeared symbols to recognize the members of the High Court. There was Paul's mother, Queen Cassilda, and his older sister, Camilla, not to mention his best friend Aladar and the rest. All were instantly identifiable despite the strange masks they now wore in perpetration for the Grand Masque.

And likewise, they recognized him as Yoht, the eternally late messenger prince.

Shame filled Yoht as he looked upon the court, for he knew they had been waiting for him a long time. They were all too thin and obviously exhausted. Some wobbled on unsteady legs, others had stomachs that growled like angry dogs, and all smelled of spilt bowel and bladder. Yoht knew he was the reason for their pitiful state. They had been through the First Act time and again, always reaching this same point, always waiting for Yoht's entrance that never came. After waiting for untold hours they would have started all over from the beginning. They would have continued to do this until at last the prince made his entrance.

Now that the cast was fully assembled, Yoht pushed shame from his mind and strode into the Hall to deliver good tidings. After all, it wasn't really his fault that he was late; it was the part he was playing.

And what joy did Yoht share, with news that the Yellow King would indeed grace the Grand Masque with his presence. This news caused Camilla to sing for the first time since the deaths of her children and old Thale danced for the Court, even though his wife was gone and unable to join him. Even Aladar seemed to forget his father's suicide for a while and he smiled after frowning for far too many days.

Only Queen Cassilda did not join in the forced merriment. Instead she stared at the Yellow Sign painted on the nearby wall, a gift and a promise from the King of Yellow Tatters. As Yoht watched her, she sat stock still, expressionless, with only her eyes trying to follow the twisting, restless Sign as it flickered and scurried on the wall.

After Camilla's song ended, it was time for the Circle of Loss where the latest family tragedies were recounted. Then came the recurring reports that the kingdom's midwives had once again only ushered stillborn corpses into the world last night. And of course there was Aladar's long expected wrist slitting, which Prince Yoht had to cover up, less the approaching festivities be ruined.

Then, at long last, the time of the Grand Masque was at hand.

The beginning of the Final Act was announced when the scenery upon the bullet-scarred walls that surrounded the Royal Court in shadow black and blood red began to shift. They swirled and shimmered like a greasy oil rainbow floating on a mud puddle, until the Great Hall became the Grand Ballroom. The unseen orchestra stopped their dirges and requiems and began to play merry waltzes that wafted up from the rubble strewn floorboards. Through empty archways came the sounds of laughter, friendly conversation, and the clinking of long stemmed crystal glasses.

When far off trumpets sounded, the Royal Court held their breath, for they knew the King in Yellow had arrived at last.

Sweeping majestically into the ballroom, the Lord of Carcosa came. He was resplendent in his long, flowing, tattered robes of bright yellow. He was as silent as the grave behind his chipped and cracked pallid mask. He twirled about, causing the ends of his yellow tatters to leave fresh gouges in the stone and wood of the floor and walls in his wake. His amber eyes beneath the featureless pale mask marked each member of the Court in turn.

It was Queen Cassilda that first broke the silent spell when she rose from her throne and called out, "Hail, King in Yellow, Scion of Lake Hali and Wise Monarch of Carcosa. You do my kingdom a great honor by gracing us with your presence this night."

The Tattered Lord glided toward Cassilda and extended a dripping hand swaddled in tawny bandages and wearing a signet ring of his shifting Yellow Sign. The queen took the hand hesitantly and brought it to her trembling lips to give the twitching ring the briefest of kisses.

It was then that the Yellow King spoke in a rough whisper of razors and flesh, creaking hangmen's ropes, buzzing flies, and of stone sepulcher doors sliding closed. "My dear Queen Cassilda, I have been gracing your kingdom for so long, why only now do you greet me?"

The Queen responded with a confused, silent stare, so the Yellow King continued.

"In yon Fields of Sorrow when your Royal Lancers were cut down to the last man by the barbarian hoard, was I not there? When the father of the curiously absent Aladar tore through sixteen young girls before turning his knife upon his wife and then himself, was it not I who placed the blade in his hand?"

The king then turned and faced Princess Camilla and said in a voice of rusted coffin nails being pulled free and of misery coils unsheathing, "And I could not have made my presence anymore marked then when the Yellow Death swept through your land, snuffing the life from your children and rotting the wombs of your women. Yet with all that, never once did you hail me. Only now, with the last rays of day long gone and the deepest dark of night welling up, do you bid me 'well met' in an attempt to hold on to something that has abandoned all of you so long ago."

"What?" Camilla squeaked out.

"Why hope, my dear princess. You still cling to hope when you know it to be folly."

The king then turned back to the queen who was now slumped in her throne with her head buried in her hands. The Tattered One leaned close to Queen Cassilda as his yellow robes began to billow and stir without the aid of wind. He said, "But fear not, lovely Cassilda. As King of Carcosa, I am not without pity. The wisest among you have already left this dying world by their own hand. As for the rest of you, I shall now relieve you of your meaninglessness."

With that, the King in Yellow began to twirl about, causing his countless tatters to splay out around him. As the yellow shreds caressed the woman sitting next to him they left deep red furrows in her flesh. So quick and clean were the cuts that the white gleam of bone could be seen at the bottom of the red trenches for a few brief moments before they overflowed with crimson. Queen Cassilda tried to scream while this was happening, but by the time she thought of doing so her throat had been gashed and only red bubbles escaped.

The rest of the Royal Court began to scream and run, or they just fell to the ground awaiting the inevitable. Whatever actions they took, the King in Yellow took turns dancing with each and every one, leaving only bloody, twitching heaps of flayed meat in his wake.

Yoht was the last member of the Court left standing when the Tattered King stopped twirling an arm's reach from him. The lord stood facing the prince, pondering the trembling man with his amber eyes as his yellow robe again came to rest about him without a single drop of blood to mar its brilliance.

With a whisper full of unbearable misery the King said, "As for you, Messenger Prince, I have a message for you to deliver. When this grand horror that now holds sway over these lands at last ends, tell my tale to others so they can know the truth. So they can understand the meaning of mortality."

Then the King reached up and scraped off in steaming, dripping shreds the mask Paul had been wearing all his life.

***

"Uh…yes sir, can I help you?"

Paul snapped out of his reverie at the sound of that voice and was surprised to see that he was standing at the pickup counter of the post office in London. His body had acted on its own while his mind had been entertaining itself and following the line in front of it. Of the fat mother and little inquisitive Gilbert, there was no sign. Instead Paul was looking at an aged man with missing teeth in a tan uniform. Like so many others, the old man couldn't bring himself to look at Paul's new mask. He was about to give the postman the slurred speech treatment, when Paul's impatience overcame him. Instead he just handed the clerk his identification and whispered, "I have a package from France."

The postal worker looked at the ID, nodded, and told Paul to wait a moment before disappearing into the back room of the building. Several minutes later he returned with a sizable package wrapped in brown paper and bound in twine. Without another word between them, Paul took the parcel and his identification card back and left the crowded post office.

Outside in a light gray drizzle Paul sat down at a curbside bench to inspect his package. Peeling away the brown paper revealed the yellow robes within. They were the first bright colors Paul had seen in months. Wrapped within the center of the robe's tatters were two hard items. The first was a thin, leather-bound book that had seen better days. The cover was creased and worn with one corner blacked as if exposed to fire. The title, *Le Roi en Jaune*, was French for *The King in Yellow*, not that Paul

read French. He didn't have to: the twirling, twitching Yellow Sign was pressed into the book's cover right beneath the title.

He had spent weeks searching for this book. It was a two act play written by an unknown hand in 1895. By 1896 most copies of this book had been reduced to ashes after being labeled immoral and seditious by the French government. This caused what few copies remained to become coveted collectors' items. Paul had to go to five rare book dealers in Britain, not to mention murder and rob, before he found one with connections to a Frenchman with a copy he was willing to sell. After a few more deaths, Paul acquired the money necessary to pay for it and the other items he required.

It was a lot of effort for a play that Paul already knew well, one that he had already been a part of even, but he needed the book. Before, Paul was but one of many, but this time he would be the star of the show. As such, he had to know the play intimately. Now that he had the book, Paul would consume it line by line and it would become a part of him.

The bundle concealed one more item. Cold to the touch, with a cracked and pitted surface, was a pallid mask. Paul's *new* mask. The one to replace all the false masks he had ever worn. Gone was the frailty of flesh and soon the cruel tin joke would be cast aside as well. Paul would be made whole again, if only for one grand performance.

He looked about the crowded London streets with his amber eyes hidden behind his temporary tin face. What was beneath Paul's mask twitched and formed a rictus grin, as he glared at the witless fools jostling around him. *They think they know horror, they think they know pain and loss and hopelessness. They think they see all of that summed up in my shattered visage, but they don't know anything.*

Then the soon-to-be new Yellow King thought, *But they'll learn. Soon the show will begin again and I will gather a cast of familiar strangers. Only then will they be privileged to know the futility of life. They will all gape at the face of truth when I take the stage in my yellow tatters and brand new mask.*

A familiar pair of faces in the crowd caught Paul's yellow eyes and drew his attention. He looked across the street and saw little Gilbert and his blubbery mother entering a narrow two story walkup. Paul then did something that he had not done since he went over the top of a trench in some forsaken part of France years ago—he laughed. The simple act of laughing caused pain around his tight mouth, but he continued through the agony. Paul knew that he had found his theater. Not only that, but Queen Cassilda and a new Messenger Prince Yoht as well.

Soon, so very soon, young inquisitive Gilbert would have all of his questions answered.

⚜ ⚜ ⚜

WHAT THE HELL EVER HAPPENED TO…?

An interview with Frank De Felitta

By Robert Morrish

Often, the authors profiled in this column are individuals whose disappearance from the genre can be traced back to a simple fact: their popularity waned, and their publishers chose to move forward without them. This issue's profile subject, however, chose to semi-retire near the top of his game, after a highly successful career both in print and on screen.

Frank De Felitta penned multiple best-selling novels, several film scripts and teleplays, and was an accomplished director as well—helming four made-for-television movies, the feature film *Scissors* (1991), which starred Sharon Stone and Steve Railsback, and countless documentaries, with an Emmy nomination for his work in the latter field.

De Felitta's nine novels include highlights such as:

- *Audrey Rose* (1975), in which a picture-perfect couple discover that their daughter is seemingly possessed by the reincarnation of a dead girl, namely the titular Audrey Rose. Later followed by the sequel *For Love of Audrey Rose* (1982).
- *The Entity* (1978), centering on a single mother, who's supposedly the victim of repeated rapes by an invisible creature, and the team of scientists investigating the case.
- *Golgotha Falls* (1984), also involving a team of scientists, this time investigating a haunted church.
- *Sea Trial* (1980), a tense survival tale featuring an adulterous couple on a fantasy holiday cruise, where they encounter another couple who are not exactly who they appear to be.
- *Funeral March of the Marionettes* (1990), a Hitchcock homage in which an expert on thriller films investigates a series of murders.

Both *Audrey Rose* and *The Entity* were made into well-received feature films.

Although he's now 92 years of age, De Felitta remains active, having published a memoir of his father, *L'OperaItaliano,* in 2012. In the following interview, he talks about accomplishments from various stages of his lengthy career.

RM: Your first writing credits were for the science fiction TV series *Tales of Tomorrow* in the early 1950s… how did you first begin writing for that series? Any particularly fond memories of the seven episodes that you wrote for that series?

FD: After I saw this film *The Thing*, I was so impressed that I decided then and there to do a 'Thing' of my own. So I quickly wrote a script, which I called *The Fury of the Cocoon*. I brought it to my friend Mort Abrahams, the producer of *Tales of Tomorrow*, at ABC, and after reading a few pages, he smiled and said he loved the concept, but he felt it would be too expensive for their budget. He liked it enough to give it to his art director, who finally agreed to do a budget. The next day *The Fury of the Cocoon* was put on the board for action. *The Fury of the Cocoon* was a smash, and the sponsor asked for more of the same. With Mort's help, I wrote about ten more scripts—a couple of which made me something of a golden boy at ABC.

RM: Between 1955 and 1968, I see only one film/TV credit for you (albeit one for which you were nominated for an Emmy)—what were you doing during that period?

FD: That period was when I left fiction and turned to documentary programming. For close to twenty years I was the co-producer of *Adventure*, a series that originated each week from the museum of natural history.

RM: One of the four made-for-TV movies that you directed was the cult favorite *Dark Night of the Scarecrow*. What are your memories from working on that film?

FD: My memories from working on that film are mostly to do with the weather, which was a steaming cauldron of heat. We had the fire department on our backs, wanting us to quit using the electricity for our lighting. They feared fires and at their discretion would serve us threatening notices.

RM: You co-wrote two screenplays—*ZPG* and *The Savage is Loose*—with Max Ehrlich, who was also known in the horror genre for penning *The Reincarnation of Peter Proud*. What led the two of you to become co-writers?

FD: At the time I was working for Universal as a producer when he decided to pay me a visit. I didn't know the man but had known of him. He came into my office and presented me

with a screenplay he had written, which was actually two screenplays, both of which I liked. We worked together for about a month co-writing the screenplays. Both screenplays sold to individual directors and that's when I found that Ehrlich could be something of a villain since he demanded that I allow him to have a larger credit. I reacted negatively and he threatened me with guild action. From that point on, we were not talking at all. At the time, Random House was in need of material. They sent a man around to collect viable screenplays and turn them into books. Since Ehrlich had written books before, naturally they seized upon him and he offered them both our screenplays.

They were delighted to have him aboard and gave him publishing orders. At which time I said, "What about me? I'm not a writer of books." He said, "Right, you get nothing." Nice guy.

Of course I objected and threatened to never allow him to never make anything, as I would fight it. This extended into several months of bad feelings. I wound up with Ehrlich offering to give me five percent of what he made. I asked for fifty percent because we were equal partners on the screenplays. He laughed and turned me down and from then on we were enemies. I didn't know how a man could be so lacking in consideration of other people but I was to learn, as he then went to the guild and sought to have me blacklisted for interfering with his ability to earn a living. When I spoke my piece at the guild, they saw that he was wrong. It all resulted in my receiving 25% of his take, which was better than what he offered. We never spoke again.

RM: What led you from your earlier experiences with screenwriting to try your hand at novel-writing?

FD: I had a screenplay called *Day of the Damned*, which turned out to be a very good book called *Oktoberfest*. It was the same story - which I used in the screenplay—and had never been able to sell. After three months of trying, there was no picking up of the novel by any of the companies until a new company was formed and Seldes, the man who owned it, loved the book and bought it for $1500. It later sold to a paperback house, who paid me $100,000 for the rights. I realized then that there was gold in books.

FD: My next book *Audrey Rose* was in the works and after a year of work was finished. Because of my first book, several companies were interested in reading *Audrey Rose*. I was glad to send it to them. But horror of horrors, none of them liked it. At that point I turned to Seldes again and he loved it and it sold to Putnam for several hundred thousand dollars. Because of the success of *The Exorcist*, this quickly sold to Metro Goldwyn Mayer.

RM: So, was the success of the book and film versions of *The Exorcist* a catalyst that led to you writing *Audrey Rose?*

FD: The reason I wanted to write Audrey Rose was I wanted to write a better book than Ehrlich's book (*The Reincarnation of Peter Proud*).

RM: One reviewer described *Audrey Rose* as a "horror novel for people who don't like horror," saying that the "horror in the work is relegated to an almost secondary status."What're your thoughts on those statements?Did you intentionally try to tone down the horror element, or were you simply telling the story as it came to you?

FD: *Audrey Rose* was in my opinion not a horror novel for people, but a religious novel. I believed that the reviewer who said Audrey Rose was a horror novel for people who don't like horror was exactly right, but I will go on to say that people who bought it – mostly teenage girls—made it a major bestseller.

RM: Your novel, *The Entity* (1978), regarding the repeated rapes suffered by a woman at the hands of an invisible creature, was purportedly based on a true story.What can you tell us about the basis for that novel, and how did you learn of the experiences on which you based the novel?

FD: I was begged by publisher to consider a sequel to Audrey Rose because of the resounding success of the first novel. If I wouldn't consider it, he wanted to be allowed to hire a writer to write the sequel. That was entirely wrong, I thought, and he propelled me into spending another year on the sequel.

During the writing of the sequel, I was approached by Barry Taff, a student of parapsychology at UCLA who was a part of Thelma Moss's Neuropsychiatric Institute. Barry came to see me and spoke very convincingly of a woman named Doris Bither he'd discovered, who was being abused sexually by an invisible being. She had devastating marks on her body and he thought it could make for a compelling story. I didn't believe the woman was sincere. I thought she was just looking for attention. Taff came back to me several times and claimed that they had actually seen evidence of some kind of a creature. He said that they were meeting with a noted parapsychologist from London, who believed entirely that this woman was being beset by a creature and wanted to work out a system to trap it in her home. Well, I felt it was all foolishness but something told me to honor it with at least a visit. Maybe I could bring a friend who has camera equipment that is able to record experiences.

The night we went to the small house in Culver City. Doris was eminently cooperative and wanted to catch this creature and get it out of her life. She didn't seem to be a woman who would make this all up. She was obviously telling a truth as she knew it. I still didn't believe it but I stayed to witness what happened that night. There were 23 people gathered in a tiny room and the party got off to a very dull start. Everyone was laughing. It seemed we were there just to crack jokes. A time of great silence followed as everyone sensed something was about to happen. And it did. Thelma Moss was sitting on the floor and she gave a signal by yelling, "Show yourself! Show yourself!" Immediately, a flare of lights started shooting around the room, which led Thelma to say, "We don't want to see your lights, we want to see you! Show yourself!" To everyone's amazement and horror, a grayish substance became visible and started to develop a musculature. It seemed like pieces of a human being separated but never developed any vision of a human being. At this point, Doris took over and started screaming at him and saying, "You're ugly, you're ugly!"

The next thing that happened, we were all

terrified by the sound of an explosion and we saw that some of the lights outside the house were exploding. We knew that this was not a normal occurrence; that something very important was happening. Someone put the lights on and we all sighed and laughed but everyone was very much impressed and touched by everything they had seen. This really happened. The pictures didn't come out. No one got any record of it. I had seen enough to know that there was a woman who was being brutalized not by her own imagination but by some invisible creature. I decided to spend the next year writing a book, which I did with her help. She had moved to San Bernardino and was suffering great pains because the creature had followed her there. I spent a year taping her and writing *The Entity*. When it was finished it sold immediately and became a best-selling novel. A very impressive movie was made by Sydney Furie, the director. Needless to say I was very happy with how the movie had come out and thought Sydney had done a wonderful job.

There isn't a week that goes by that I don't get somebody contacting me about *The Entity* and wanting to know who the lady really was and whether I believed her. Of course I believed her. I wouldn't spend my time with a kook. I didn't believe her at first—and then I did. I wrote the book in a year, at her home, taking notes. She had a doctor who was really her soothsayer and he did everything until she realized that he was falling in love with her, which she didn't want. He sought her out and brought her to their clinic. They had a hospice that took care of people who were in terrible trouble. She had seizures every night. He would peek in and see her, he would time the seizures and see that they were lessening in intensity. At that point she left—she was escaping life. The doctor saw her being manipulated by nobody and it drove him absolutely stark raving mad. He started punching the air, and picked up a guitar and smashed it over her head. She ended up in the hospital.

She didn't like the book. She didn't want to be a part of any of it. The whole thing was a sad story, left a dirty taste in my mouth. I felt sorry for her but I was eager to do a book that would be honest. It was a seamy, horrible situation and I made a job of reporting about a woman under tremendous stress. She was interesting—one of the most interesting people that I ever knew. I wanted to create a character that we could all respect. It's interesting to know that I supplied her with five to ten percent of the money I received for the book and movie. And that was our only form of contact after a while. She was very objective about getting money because she needed it. But as I say, to this day I believe her. One day I got one of the checks back and a note that said she was no longer alive. She always said that creature would kill her and I believe that it did.

RM: From 1991 until now, you've published only three books, and have not had any involvement in films, as far as I can tell. What have you been up to during these last couple of decades?

FD: Last year I wrote *L'OperaItaliano* as an e-book, which is a memory of my father–a man who was at odds with the world. A man whose personal life followed in the tradition of Bacchus, much to the horror of my mother, who tried to ameliorate his life and was a very potent force in his artistic development. He paid her back in a niggardly fashion with every opportunity to disregard her. She didn't mind. She developed an understanding of him, but nevertheless it must have hurt her.

Most of the book was conceived after I returned from World War II and lived with my mother, who took the opportunity to fill me in on all my father's horrible ways of life. My mother was extremely patient and understanding of his ways and needs, which were far beyond what she could provide. I demanded that she tell me everything and she hated to go back to that time. When he died, we both cried and we went to the funeral. I always said I was one day going to tell the story. His true love also died at the same time practically that he did. Imagine living with a man who was in love with someone else. In those days, you couldn't get a divorce.

My mother died soon after, too.

❦ ❦ ❦

"Hello, Duffy's Tavern, where the elite meet to eat. Archie the manager speakin'... Duffy ain't here"

DOUBLE X CHROMOSONE:

By Yvonne Navarro

Life by a Thousand Annoyances

Have you heard of the ancient Chinese torture method, "Death by a Thousand Cuts?" I'm betting you're already seeing the correlation here.

Let me see if I can relate how part of my typical last month or so has been, not necessarily in as-it-happened order:

Dad falls outside his apartment complex and ends up with 17 staples in his head, 7 stitches above one eye, and one ribboned ear sewn back together; go to closest bank to get a document notarized, no one available, end up going to farther bank anyway; the guy I get the notarized document for doesn't show up, doesn't call (rude much?); youngest dog inexplicably starts snarling and lunging at random people on the street; bank password stops working; I have a nightmare about grasshoppers (don't ask); it takes a week and three telephone calls to get the Sirius account number so I can cancel The Husband's account, only to find out I never needed it—a delay that costs us a chunk of our refund; I'm late mailing our daughter's anniversary card; $9.00 light bulb broken inside package; eight-month-old car radio dies, installer offers to send it for repair, will take four to six weeks, I make them reset it instead; I take the car through a carwash and the moon roof leaks; my Dad forgets my birthday; The Husband's credit card is frozen because of fraudulent charges; dog pees in the kitchen; despite medication that knocks me practically flat, I manage to proofread a retyped story one night before bed but save it somewhere in The Twilight Zone and never find it again; Dad falls in his bathroom, ends up in ER for the second time in 2 ½ weeks; different dog eats all the tomatoes off one of the plants outside; living room lamp dies for no reason; I realize dog has also peed on the carpeted stair landing because I go downstairs barefoot; car radio dies again (two days later)…

And the list goes on to be much bigger than what you read up there. Now, contrary to what you're thinking, the purpose of my rant in this column is not to vent or whine ("Hey, want some cheese with that whine?"). I can torment my coworkers, who have the dubious luck of also being really

good friends, by subjecting them to my grand adventures five days a week. No, it's to illustrate the kind of shit (expletive intentional) that a woman who writes horror, a *single* woman, might go through. I know there are hundreds, maybe thousands, of woman out there who would say "Don't get me started!" if

I were to add *with kids* to that. I sort of have kids because I have three Great Danes; dogs are like happy toddlers who never grow up, except that these three weigh 140, 145, and 165 pounds and when they want attention, food, or need to potty, pretending you don't hear them is not an option.

But I digress. I'm sure I'm going to get a lot of cheese and whine from the guys for this, but it's just not the same. I know this because my husband, Weston Ochse, is also a writer. He's very good about offering me encouragement: "Just ignore [fill in the blank] and get some writing done." Awesome. Let me ignore the dishes (he won't do them until they're stacked as high as Mt. Everest), the dust on the furniture (because I *want* the house to look like a haunted old mansion), the dog hair (don'tcha love that dog groomer shop look?), the weeds in the yard (goes back to the haunted house look), and the dog poop in the yard (nothing at all attractive about that). He seems to be remarkably adept at ignoring that [fill in the blank] item and tuning out the world. It's like he can just flip that internal switch to OFF and I can't even find my damned switch to begin with.

My point here is that as a woman writer, you'd *better* find that internal switch. If you don't, you have no hope of accomplishing anything in today's world unless you have a nanny for those rug rats and/or a 24/7 housekeeper. Your writing will die due to a *Life by a Thousand Annoyances*. This isn't about disregarding stuff that's important—I guess I *will* feed the dogs now, instead of waiting until next month—and it's not even about prioritizing. If it was, the house would be filthy, the UPS guy would have to machete his way through the weeds to get to the front door, and a cloud of dust and flies would poof up every time I plop onto the couch. It's about making sure that somehow you squeeze in that thing that you love so much—writing—come hell or high water, even if it's jotting down a sentence or a paragraph on a piece of scrap paper in your purse or on the Notepad program in your

phone. If you're actively working on something longer, like a story or a novel, get yourself a little recorder so you can continue the story or the chapter while you're driving, then transcribe it when you get home. Doing that may seem like an extra step but it gives you the chance for an immediate quick edit, and that, in turn, gives you a more finished first draft. As The Husband likes to say, writing is a muscle and it needs to be used daily. That "use it or lose it" saying really applies here. Like to watch TV? It's your choice: type up a draft of that really great story idea, or sit on your ass for an hour and watch *Honey BooBoo*. By the way, if a woman sits for more than four hours a day, it shortens her lifespan. Sit on *that* little factoid for awhile, babe. So if you're gonna die for something, it might as well be writing, right?

Uh oh—wait a second. The editor told me this issue has a movie theme and I'm supposed to tie that in. Hmmm. I've got it! Movie star Hedy Lamarr was also a mathematician who invented an early technique for spread spectrum communications and frequency hopping (for which she and her co-creator were granted a patent in 1942), which is necessary for wireless communication and is still used today. She did this *while* she was an actress, carving out time to work on these complex equations (the best I can do to describe something so far above my understanding that the concepts reside on Pluto). As an actress, she would have been memorizing scripts, rehearsing, shooting, dealing with costuming and makeup and any number of things that made up her *Life by a Thousand Annoyances*.

If Hedy could do it, so can you.

~~~~~~~~~~~~~~~~~~~~~~~~~~~~~

Comments? Questions? Suggestions? Yvonne Navarro can be reached via her website, Facebook page, or at her Dark Discoveries email: yvonne@ journalstone.com.

THINGS THAT BITE

Legends and Folklore of Supernatural Predators

By Jonathan Maberry and David F. Kramer
Bram Stoker Award-winning authors of THE CRYPTOPEDIA

(NOTE TO READERS: *THINGS THAT BITE* is a new regular nonfiction feature here in Dark Discoveries. In each installment, my co-author, David F. Kramer, and I will shine a light on a different aspect of the supernatural or paranormal. We'll explore myths and legends, theories on the origins of these monsters, and explore the impact that monsters have had on everything from religion to pop culture).

#1: VAMPIRES IN ALL THEIR GUISES

No supernatural predator has gotten as much press or inspired as many stories as the vampire. In folklore, pop culture and (in some cases) actual belief, they are the quintessential supernatural predator because they are practiced and deliberate.

Sure, there are some fangy dimwits, but most vampires are thinking monsters who used their longevity to acquire insight, improve hunting skills, gain practical experience, hone their self-control, and cultivate their appetites. Their long lives gives them time to refine their cruelties so that they not only hunt for sustenance, but feed off of the pain and misery they cause.

Vampire legends can be found in the myths and religions of all nations. Vampire talesappear among the earliest stories of the Assyrians, Hebrews, Romans and ancient Greeks. And the vampires exists in hundreds of variations, some of which are quite human in appearance while others are so bizarre that they are entirely monstrous. This difference extends to their feeding habits, diet, sexual proclivities, nature, powers, weaknesses and even the ways in which they are created. Some of the vampire species overlap our contemporary views of ghosts, witches, werewolves and even zombies.

These monsters have a great many aspects, ranging from rotting ambulatory corpse to seductive temptress; however the stereotypical image of an Eastern European nobleman in a tuxedo and opera cloak generally doesn't fit any of the world's folkloric bloodsuckers.

Some vampires are human, some are not. Some vampires drink blood, many do not. Some vampires are shapeshifters; others appear in a single form. They may have become vampires as the result of a curse, a bite, damnation, bad luck, unfortunate deaths, or any of a hundred paths to darkness. And, not all of them are evil.

What most people know about vampires comes from pop culture —movies, comics, novels, TV. The vampires of folklore and ancient myth are often quite different from the popular versions with which we're all so familiar; they're so different that even labeling them all as 'vampire' gets tricky. It's tough to even make a short list of '*Things We Know About Vampires*' because most of what we know has been filtered through storytelling and embellished by screenwriters and novelists. It's okay that they did that —storytellers are supposed to keep things fresh and interesting; but if the story is based on folklore then it tends to muddy the view of the source material.

Bram Stoker created much of what most people 'know' about vampires; and although *Dracula* does have some basis in vampire folklore, Stoker takes great license in his presentation of vampire powers and defenses. But Stoker was a novelist not an historian or cultural anthropologist. He took bits and pieces of lore, picked what he thought sounded most interesting and

Desolation by Fran Kirsch, Courtesy of Jonathan Maberry

Nosferatu -Max Schreck as Count Orlock

made up the rest; and even with the folklore he used he was often mistaken.

Case in point is the word *nosferatu*, which has always been linked with vampirism but Stoker either misunderstood its meaning or simply didn't know it and gave a new one for his novel. He translated the word to mean either "undead" or "not dead"; but the term is a relatively modern word derived from an old Slavonic expression, *nosufur-atu*, which in turn was drawn from the Greek term *nosophoros*, or "plague carrier." Historically, the *nosferatu* was an invisible evil presence that spread disease, and was widely believed to be an intelligent and malevolent driving force behind the great plagues of Europe.

Stoker's error may come from the fact that many of the world's most dangerous vampires do not take a physical form, but instead exist as a presence of evil that brings sickness, misery and death. Like vampires that take blood, the *nosferatu* take health and vitality; and in both cases death ensues. These two supernatural predators have become inextricably linked, their crimes overlapping so that it became common to believe that vampires, apart from drinking blood, also have the ability to spread disease, and in a number of the cases we'll discuss they actually are capable of both. A number of films and movies have run with this theme, notably Werner Herzog's under-appreciated 1988 *Nosferatu the Vampyre*, which is a remake of F. W. Murnau's 1922 silent film, *Nosferatu: A Symphony of Horror*.

Ask the next hundred random people you meet to describe a vampire's powers and limitations and they'll pretty much say the same thing: vampires are pale, non-breathing corpses who cast no reflection, cannot enter a house without being invited, cannot cross running water; they can be warded off by holy objects and garlic, and can only be killed by a stake through the heart. This is canon law as far as vampires go...except

that it *isn't*. Most of this so-called common knowledge is actually faulty because it's been run through the filter of pop culture which changed it substantially from its older folkloric roots. From an entertainment standpoint this is great because it keeps monster storytelling from getting stale; but for a vampire slayer researching ways of destroying the undead this is misinformation that will get him (or her) killed.

We can probably make a solid argument that virtually all beliefs have been similarly filtered. Granted in centuries past we didn't have horror bestsellers like Bram Stoker or Stephen King retelling the old vampire tales. Or where there? We've had storytellers throughout history who told classic tales of monsters and perhaps embellished them for effect or edited them to fit local beliefs or current doctrine. This is what storytellers do, and this is why stories endure. The Scottish fairy story of Tam Lin, for example, exists in hundreds of forms in folktale, song, story, novel and film. When dealing with the fantastical the very nature of the material provides a marvelous elasticity. So, novelists, poets, and screenwriters have taken a lot of perfectly acceptable liberties with the vampire over the years by changing this, modifying that, completely fabricating the other—all in an attempt to create a fresh slant or a novel twist.

When writers began telling tales of vampirism in a way that was purely fictional as opposed to recounting folktales that were intended to be believed as true, they took the position that these monsters were in direct opposition to the church and established new 'traditions' to retell the stories of vampires in relation to purely Christian concepts. Once a concept was established through a popular piece of fiction or a landmark film there was often a pretty quick transfer to our shared body of vampire knowledge. We see something in a vampire flick and we accept that it's so because the writer did his homework.

For example, the inability to face a crucifix was invented for fiction but was presented with such deftness that it appeared as if the writers were using established folklore practices as back-story in much the same way that Michael Crichton used established genetic science as back-story for his fictional dinosaur novels. When other writers played off of the same concept it served to reinforce the belief. This has continued since the publication of *Dracula* and it's clear that the general populace was accepting the newly-created methods, powers, and limitations of the vampire as a new kind of gospel.

On the other hand, many of these new paradigms

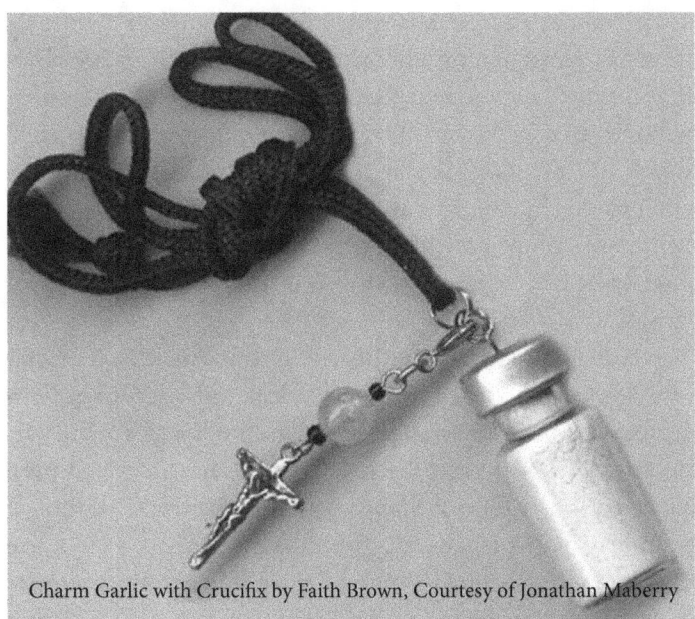
Charm Garlic with Crucifix by Faith Brown, Courtesy of Jonathan Maberry

do have ties, however tenuous, to folklore. Take the use of the crucifix in vampire fiction. Stoker wrote that vampires cannot bear the sight or touch of consecrated items such as Holy Water, the Crucifix, the Eucharist and similar apotropes (any object that wards off evil). In movies the cross itself is not just a protection but also an actual method of destruction, as shown in the Hammer Films' 1960 classic, *The Brides of Dracula,* in which a real holy cross isn't even used—Van Helsing turns the vanes of a windmill so that their shadow falls across a fleeing vampire and that alone destroys him. In 1958's *Horror of Dracula,* candlesticks are used to form a cross and, combined with the rays of the sun, turn the Count to dust. This suggests that any 'cross' was fatal to vampires. If you don't think too carefully about that it seems reasonable; but stop for a moment and look around you and see how many times lines intersect at right angles. By that reasoning a man in checkered suit would be a mass-slaughterer of vampires. And don't even get us started on hot cross buns.

In folklore the best weapons aren't religious symbols but charms made specifically for the purpose of protection. Local tradition and ritual are often crucial in these matters.

Stoker also states that vampires can't enter a church or sacred ground. Um…most of them are buried in cemeteries, many of which are part of church grounds, which makes the ground sacred by definition. And during most burials a cleric of some kind prays over the deceased. That further consecrates the ground. And, as we'll discover in this chapter, there are vampires who even attend church.

Nearly all vampire movies and books use a vampire's inability to cast a reflection as a nice trick for establishing that a person is actually a vampire. But this is another bit of information that isn't found in vampire folktales…except in China. Oddly, the Chiang-Shih of China *does* possess most of the qualities ascribed to the vampires in Dracula. Running water, garlic, mirrors, shapeshifting; all of it affects them. But this vampire is an anomaly and by no means the standard.

As for a vampire's inability to cross running water, few vampires have that restriction, and there are several vampires who actually live in water. If that was the case then Dracula would not have been able to take ship to England. In the 1966 Hammer Films flick *Dracula Prince of Darkness,* the titular count falls through a break in a patch of ice and the rushing water beneath kills him. However, that would not have worked against any of the European vampires who could easily cross bodies of water. Besides, there is running water everywhere, from rainwater run-off to sewers, indoor plumbing and underground streams. The Kappa of Japan and the Animalitos of Spain are water-dwelling demon-vampires, as are the Green Ogresses of France.

Sunlight has little actual power against true vampires (again with the exception of the Chiang-Shih). Even in the novel *Dracula* the count was able to move around in sunlight, though his powers were diminished. The idea that sunlight is fatal to vampires was concocted by film director Friedrich Wilhelm Murnau as a way of disposing of his Dracula-pastiche vampire, Count Orlock, in the 1922 silent classic *Nosferatu.* Since then it has been accepted as gospel in vampire stories, but in folklore most vampires can exist during daylight hours. The Upierczi of Poland, for example, rises at noon and hunts until midnight. The Bruja of Spain lives a normal life by day and only becomes a vampire at night, as do the Soucouyan of Dominica and the Loogaroo of Haiti, along with many others.

In most vampire fiction the monsters don't cast shadows, won't have a reflection in a mirror, and

Vampire by Edvard Munch

Hollywood Vampire -Long Chaney in London After Midnight
Courtesy Warner Bros and Jonathan Maberry

won't appear on film. This varies, but for the most part the lack of a shadow or reflection does not appear in folklore. Bram Stoker is also responsible for this.

In almost every vampire story the creatures have exaggerated canines. Folkloric vampires seldom have fangs of any kind beyond ordinary human teeth. In fact most of them use their normal teeth to tear through flesh. Their teeth are not hollow like soda straws (an element that pops up every now and then in movies). Once the flesh is torn they suck blood the way you'd slurp barbecue sauce off hot wings.

Vampire fiction also insists that no vampire can enter a house uninvited, however this is not something found in legend. That's Stoker again...otherwise Dracula would have slaughtered the Harkers and everyone else ten minutes after he landed in England. In folklore special precautions usually have to be taken to keep a vampire out. Various rites, spells, or herbs are employed by different cultures to bar a vampire from entering. In the absence of those protections, the vampire can enter freely and of his own will.

Their hearts don't beat, nor do they breathe, right? This varies. Some vampires are corpses that rise to attack the living, so there's no organic function of any kind happening. However, most of the world's vampires are alive to some degree, so circulation and respiration are probably happening even if at a reduced level. Also, vampires talk and speech requires exhaled air causing the vocal chords to vibrate.

In movies vampires shy away from garlic, but in folklore the vampires actually fear it; and this is something seem in virtually all of the world's vampire legends. Garlic is a blood purifier and is believed to cleanse the blood of supernatural impurities. Throughout Europe garlic plays a big role in the Ritual of Exorcism, which is the standard method of vampire disposal. In this Ritual, after a vampire's grave has been opened garlic stuffed into the monster's mouth, then its head it cut off and turned backward so that it looks downward to Hell. The body is then tied or pinned and reburied. Or, if there's some doubt as to whether the vampire is truly destroyed the vampire slayers might douse it with water and flick a Bic. Garlic can also be used to bar entry to a house by making a paste out of it and smearing window frames and door jambs.

The stake through the heart business is a tricky one because it does appear in folk tales of vampires from all over the world, but it is not used to kill the undead. Despite the quick, clean "dustings" shown *on Buffy the Vampire Slayer*, or the bloody stakings in so many vampire films, the stake was not a weapon used to actually destroy a vampire but a tool in a more elaborate exorcism. In the Ritual of Exorcism a long stake of wood or metal was driven through the body (chest, stomach, wherever) of a resting vampire; not to end the vampire's life (or un-life) but to pin it down to prevent it from rising while the other vampire slayers do their work. Only the Kozlak of Dalmatia will perish from a staking.

Fictional accounts of vampires shapeshifting into animals are a bit closer to the mark than most information found in books and movies, though there are very few legends that say anything about bats. Only about a third of the world's vampires possess shapeshifting powers at all, and out of the hundreds of vampire species around the world, only a handful (the South African Azeman, the Jaracacas of Brazil, the Croatian Kudlak, the Dalmatian Kozlak and the Bhuta of India) can transform into bats. So, despite the fact that the root word for vampire can be translated as 'bat', bats are in fact not that commonly connected to vampires. The most common creature for a vampire to morph into is a bird. Owls, crows, ravens, hens, and turkeys are also common shapes. Cats are another popular beast-shape for vampires, as recounted in the Japanese legend of Ō Toyo and Prince Hizen, the Chordewa of Bengal, and the Jaracacas of Brazil. Other shapes seen in vampire folklore include such diverse creatures as the moth, snake, wolf (again, not as common as the movies suggest), fly, dog, tick, flea, mouse, rat, or bee.

Several vampires also take the form of fireballs or something resembling a will-o'-the-wisp. These include the Soucouyan of Dominica, the Hungarian Lidérc Nadaly, the Zmeu of Moldavia, the Obayifo of Africa's Gold Coast, the Loogaroo of Haiti, the Asema of Surinam, and the Vjestitiza of Montenegro.

On the subject of vampiric strength, all of the sources—from folklore to the most current direct-to-video fang flick—seem to agree: they are very, very strong. The Draugr of Scandinavia, for example, is a vampiric ghost that inhabits and reanimates the bodies of dead Viking warriors, creating a monster so strong that no weapon can harm it. The Chiang-Shih of China actually entertain themselves by ripping their victims limb from limb with their bare hands, as do the Callicantzaros of Greece and the Czechoslovakian Nelapsi. Since the vampire is so powerful, getting close enough to one to fight it is generally a fatal gambit.

Some vampires do not require physical strength to kill their victims; some can do it merely by the intensity of their gaze. The Jigarkhwar of India and the Russian Eretica both possess lethal stares. Strangely, the Asuang vampire of the Philippines is best defeated by engaging it in a staring contest and waiting until it backs down and slinks away. Kind of makes him the schoolyard punk of the vampire world.

Decapitation is also a handy tool against vampires, whether in the movies or in real life. Sadly, popular fiction doesn't use this method enough, perhaps because it is too quick and simple a solution. A skilled swordsman, a woodsman with an axe, or a reaper with a scythe would each be ideal as a vampire slayer or slayer's assistant. The downside of this method of disposal is that one has to identify and locate the vampire, then get close enough to swing the weapon. Vampires are secretive by nature, and being unnaturally fast and powerful, they generally offer a strong resistance.

One thing on which pop culture and fiction agree is that fire destroys vampires, just as it destroys everything else. It is often called "the great purifier," and in the battle against undead evil it certainly lives up to that claim.

A major rift between fiction and folklore is how a person becomes a vampire. In pop culture a person is bitten by a vampire then has to drink some of the vampire's blood, and this exchange brings a person from life to unlife. Following death the new vampire rises from the grave after three days. But that process is another of Stoker's inventions. It's also another link to his personal beliefs. The process of exchanging blood and then resurrection after three days was his way of showing the vampire's mockery of the process of Jesus shedding –and symbolically sharing—His blood then rising from the tomb after three days.

The fact that vampires exist in so many forms, have such a changeable nature, and have such rich backstories has a couple of important effects. The first and most obvious that they scare the bejeezus out of us, even when we know that they're not real. Or, when we're pretty sure they're not real. Opinions genuinely vary on that.

And second, they offer the greatest opportunity for storytellers to continue to scare the bejeezus out of our readers. Or to make them laugh. Or to bring tears to the eye. Or to make us ponder the darkness without and within. They are elastic monsters, and as such they allow authors to tell an infinite number of tales. Look at how many vampire stories there already are. The genre endures and is frequently refreshed and renewed because the vampire allows, even invites, new interpretation.

Vampires are immortal.

Even when the mass market interest wans and the genre crumbles to dust, it won't stay dead. All it requires is some fresh thought –or, let's face it, fresh blood—and the vampire rises again. We see the proof of this with Sheridan Le Fanu and Bram Stoker, with Universal and Hammer pictures, with Stephen King and Anne Rice, with Buffy the Vampire Slayer and True Blood, with Twilight and The Strain.

Hard to predict what's next…but it's absolutely certain that the vampire will rise again.

While we wait, we'll sharpen our stakes, lock our doors and polish our crucifixes.

--Jonathan Maberry and David F. Kramer

⚘ ⚘ ⚘

Places of the Dead by Fran Kirsch, Courtesy of Jonathan Maberry

On Ghost Stories

Michael R. Collings

I HEARTILY ENJOY A GOOD GHOST STORY—one that is taut, thrilling, suspenseful; one that leads inevitably to a convincing yet unanticipated conclusion. Peter N. Dudar's *A Requiem for Dead Flies* succeeded perfectly, as far as I was concerned, as did my son Michaelbrent's *The Haunted* (soon to be available as an audio book)—yet it would be difficult to name to more diverse treatments of a theme. And, if I may include my own works among those I enjoy, *Shadow Valley* succeeds, I think…and yet again, for entirely different reasons. Each book comes from entirely different angles, yet work as ghost stories.

On the other hand, I do not enjoy an ineffective ghost story—one that is the literary equivalent of a malevolent teenager creeping through a dark house, dressed in a white sheet, rattling superfluous chains, and hollering "Boo" from the corners. Such things are trite, stereotypic, and ultimately laughable.

Wherein lies the difference between the two sorts? Well, when I assess ghost stories for their effectiveness, I concentrate on three elements:

GHOSTS: It would seem that this element should go without saying. After all, we're talking about "ghost" stories. The word itself comes from an ancient root meaning "horrible" or "frightful"; modern cognates include *aghast*, with its suggestion of sudden fright or horror; and *ghastly*, something both shocking and frightful.

Somewhere along the way (that is, a millennium or so ago), *ghosts* assumed overtones of "spirit" or "breath," at which time a segment of the word's meaning branched off into the realms of theology, with "Holy Ghost," usually accepted as synonymous with "Holy Spirit."

But when talking about literary ghosts, we enter instead into the dimensions of the metaphysical and the supernatural, of uncanny and inexplicable intrusions of something ethereal, disembodied, ectoplasmic into 'real' life. And, in general, we almost automatically think of a ghost as little more than the spirit of the dead, whether frightening or not.

But just as with so many other monsters in horror, there are ghosts and there are ghosts. Synonyms for the word include *apparition, daemon, haunt, phantasm, phantom, poltergeist, revenant, shade, specter, spook, wraith,* and others. Each of these differs subtly from the others, both in connotation and in denotation, and a successful ghost story clearly identifies which tradition is being followed…and, even while perhaps expanding or otherwise engaging it, nevertheless follows it. Ghosts are not omnipotent; they cannot simply do anything the writer wishes. An apparition may not act as if it were a specter.

Perhaps the best way to illustrate the fact that each of these words carries a specific meaning is to look, not at the stories themselves, but at a classic non-horror poem: "In a Station of the Metro," published a century ago by Ezra Pound. The poem runs as follows:

The apparition of these faces in the crowd;
Petals on a wet, black bough.

It is justly famous as one of the first haiku-like poems in English, but for my purposes, it demonstrates clearly that the many words we have for *ghost* are not mindlessly interchangeable. Notice what happens when we simply replace the key word in the first line, *apparition*, with supposed synonyms:

The ghosts of these faces in the crowd….
The daemons of these faces in the crowd….
The phantasms of these faces in the crowd….
The revenants of these faces in the crowd….
The specters of these faces in the crowd….

The spooks of these faces in the crowd....

Each change essentially forces the short poem to move in a new direction, not one of which is entirely compatible with the final line. Ghosts are ghosts; and apparitions are apparitions.

So an effective ghost story incorporates a tradition, identifying it at some crucial point, enhancing and amplifying it when needed, but ultimately remaining true to it. Because there are so many approaches to ghosts, there are an equal number of effective ways of treating them, from the sheerly horrific to the pratfallingly comedic (assuming a ghost can perform a pratfall). Writers may exploit the opportunities; and when they do so creatively, consistently, and purposefully, the story benefits.

ATMOSPHERE: Effective ghost stories gain almost as much from the proper atmosphere as from the ghost itself. I am not talking necessarily about haunted mansions, web-cloaked castles, or other low-budget props escaped from Hollywood B-films, although they might be made highly effective in the hands of a strong writer.

I am thinking more in terms of atmosphere as almost a character; and here all three of the stories I mentioned in the first paragraph share a single distinctive element: *isolation of the key characters*. The best example I can think of is again not from a ghost story but rather from another literary classic. The moor in *Wuthering Heights* is almost more important than the characters themselves, since it provides the backdrop, the emotional surroundings that mold and to a certain degree control the characters. Whether a ghoststory takes place in an ancient, crumbling pile in the depths of the Black Forest or in a modern, glass-faced high-rise in New York, certain elements must occur that allow for the appearance of the ghost...and that tingle the reader's spine even before the supernatural intrudes. And those elements almost *must* be preceded by the physical, mental, or emotional isolation of the character or characters.

In ghost stories, however, atmosphere is more than the sum total of successive adjectives and adverbs. Just as dropping the word *eldritch* into every other paragraph does not make for an effective piece of Lovecraftian horror, so dropping ghost-related words and situations does not create a ghost story. Cold spots, eerie creakings and half-heard mutterings, lights unaccountably flickering or going out—these and more may accompany a haunting, but they are never quite the same *thing* as the haunting itself.

Instead, the atmosphere develops through every detail of the surroundings, as in Dudar's *A Requiem for Dead Flies*, in which each event, each moment of characterization, each component of the story *as a whole* ultimately goes toward building the tone, the feeling, and almost smothering quality that defines the book.

Careful, incremental, organic creation of a context in which the ghost appears, then, can be as essential as the ghost itself.

SUGGESTIVITY AND AMBIGUITY: If a ghost appears to a large group of people in the first paragraphs of a story, unambiguously establishes itself as the spirit of one dead, and announces its intentions and desires, there is no story. If, on the other hand, a ghost appears to one or two terrified witnesses in the opening scene, speaks so elliptically that neither can truly say whether the experience is real or not, then disappears for much of the story, reappearing only to speak to a character who may or may not be wholly sane, then there is the potential for a story...or a play, such as *Hamlet.*

If readers know from the onset that there is a ghost, that it exists within the accepted reality of the tale, much of the required suspense and tension simply dissipates. If readers are not certain until the final pages—and perhaps not even then—that the ghost is 'real,' the story becomes more compelling, more disturbing, more effective. Here, the prime example is Henry James' classic, *The Turn of the Screw*; for decades, readers and critics have wondered whether the ghost of Peter Quint actually exists or whether the governess is simply insane.

In filmic terms, showing the spook in the opening frames would be disastrous; *suggesting* that something eerie is present through hints and possibilities keeps the audience interested and focused. This is the ultimate purpose of ubiquitous cold spots, slamming doors or windows, mysteriously motile objects, unaccountable sounds from attics and basements...but not specific appearances, at least until toward the end.

Taken together, these elements work toward an effective ghost story. They aren't intended as programmatic, of course; working on these three elements separately, then bluntly forcing them together will not create an effective story. But when used thoughtfully, creatively, and organically, the right kind of ghost, an unsettling atmosphere, and an essential ambiguity throughout much if not all of the story will usually enhance the final product.

※ ※ ※

ONCE UPON A NIGHTMARE YA HORROR

By Amy Shane

Movies have become the heartbeat of our lives. They are a pulse beating all their own, which creeps into our hearts, evolving into a way of life we almost depend on. We can attend a theater, or we can watch, stream, download, or insert a DVD at any time of the day. Movies are always within our grasp, available on every electronic device, ready at our disposal with one click of a button. Yet, most of us push that button without thinking about where the ideas come from.

Some of the most iconic horror movies, like Alfred Hitchcock's *Psycho* written by Robert Bloch, Stephen King's *The Shining*, to Mary Shelley's *Frankenstein,* startedout as spine-tingling novels. Capturing their readers with one of the most primary and primitive arts—that of pen and paper. Mesmerizing you, holding you, snaring you in their graspwith each turn of the page, and allowing your mind to becomethe story's illustrator.

As readers, we are usually not aware of this; we become the artistic means behind the characters thatlatch onto our hearts, slowly becoming pieces of who we are. Transforming us into part of the magic, we suddenly then have an investment, because a piece of it is now ours.

The author provides the canvas and places the art before us, although it is the readers who carry the magical ability to breathe life into the words. Without the reader, a book remains lifeless, waiting, wanting to find a place in which to come alive.

However, something else magical happens to our novels. We have found another way to awaken the beast.

Like Dr. Frankenstein, filmmakers create new vitality from an old form. They give life to the body of a novel through their own means of electrical current. Like mad scientists, filmmakers resurrect with fragments and pieces from the storyline, pulling images and bits of magic from the novel to create an amazingly brilliant masterpiece. Allhaving one common goal: to bring the novel to life by way of the silver screen, bringing us one step closer to the characters that we have carried in our hearts, putting pictures to both the faces and scenes that we have carried in our minds. Enchanting thousands and even millions with the story that originally captivated readers. Filmmakers bewitch audiences by pulling us under their spell.

However, with the merging of the two I often question, "How do the masterminds behind the novels feel once their creations have been given a new life? Do they love thecreation as much as they loved their original work, or is all that remains of the original masterpiece a mere resemblance?"

One such creation that has been recently brought to life is the gothic horror, *Beautiful Creatures*. Written by #1 *NYT* bestselling novelists Kami Garcia and Margaret Stohl. A series that holds a space in my heart and has been a favorite since its debut.

On a quest for answers, I was able to interview Kami Garcia, co-author of *Beautiful Creatures* and author of *Unbreakable,* and ask her some heartfelt questions about seeing the novel turned into a feature film.

Starting off: "What was the one thing that you feltthe movie captured perfectly from the book, and is there anything the film didn't capture as beautifully as you described?"

Kami:"Theactorswhoplayed Ethan and Lena, Alden Ehrenreich and Alice Englert really nailed the roles. I think Amma is a very different character in the book. She is also one of my favorites, because she is loosely based on my great-grandmother and Margie's grandmother—two of the strongest women in our lives."

"What was the best thing about seeing your book on the big screen?"

Kami: "It was amazing to see the town of Gatlin as a real place—to see our world literally come to life."

"With such a successful series and movie, do you feel stove-piped into the *Beautiful Creatures* label? Where do you go from here?"

Kami: "I don't think the *Beautiful Creatures* series limited me in any way. I am incredibly proud of the series (written with coauthor Margaret Stohl), and I don't think we will ever go our separate ways. We wrote *Beautiful Creatures* on a dare from seven teens, with no notion of publishing it. Now the book is in fifty countries, *Beautiful Creatures* made me a writer; I can only hope *Unbreakable* and the Legion Series will make me a better one, by forcing me to stretch and explore new territory. In this case ghost hunting, secret societies, and demonology."

"Do you feel the release of the movie increased interest in the book, and is there any added pressure with writing *Unbreakable* with your last series being such a huge success?"

Kami: "Movies always increase interest in the book upon which they are based, because, in our country, there are more moviegoers than readers. Anything that gets someone to pick up a book is a good thing. When I am writing, the pressure always comes from the same place; the fear of disappointing my reader."

Which brings me to ask, "In a few words how would you describe your new novel, and series, *Unbreakable*?"

Kami: "An ancient secret society of ghost hunters, gorgeous identical twin brothers, a girl who doesn't know the truth about her past, and an impossible choice."

After talking to Kami Garcia it allowed me the opportunity to peek inside the creative mind of an author, showing that it takes not only that author but also the filmmakers to bring a film to life.

❧❧❧

World Horror Wrap-Up

By Aaron J. French

Aaron J. French holding a copy of *Dreaming in Darkness*, Photo Courtesy of Aaron J. French

The Bram Stoker Awards™ Weekend 2013 incorporating the World Horror Convention is over! And what an excellent convention it was. Held in the rousing old city of New Orleans, Louisiana, where the voodoo influence shines through on every street corner, the graves are situated above ground (providing easier escape access for living dead), and Bourbon Street is as lively and crazy as the Las Vegas Strip. The convention and the Bram Stoker Awards banquet were both held in the historic French Quarter at the Hotel Monteleone.

This year's guests included John Joseph Adams, Amber Benson, Bruce Boston, Ramsey Campbell, Glenn Chadbourne, Caitlin R. Kiernan, Jonathan Maberry, and Robert McCammon. There were interesting panels held on various subjects ranging from "Lovecraft's Eternal Fascination" moderated by S.T. Joshi to "Are You Ready For An Agent?" moderated Tim Waggoner. Also there were the pitch sessions, which matched writers up with publishers; the Kaffeeklatsch events, where small groups got to meet in private with some of the biggest names at the convention; and a dealer's room chalk full of new horror titles and coveted rarities. All in all, it was a fun and educational experience for writers, editors, seasoned veterans, newcomers, and fans alike.

Dark Discoveries magazine was well received and all attendees got a copy of issue #23 in their goody bag. That issue, you'll remember, featured a comprehensive list of every WHC convention ever held and its location, as well as all past Stoker Award recipients. Saturday night, June 15, saw the most recent Bram Stoker Awards ceremony, and I was fortunate enough to attend. So, we at DD thought we should include a quick rundown of what happened there, as well as a list of 2013's winners.

The Happy Hour Pre-Bram Stoker Awards Event was sponsored by our publisher JournalStone, and as everyone mingled and had their drink before the ceremony, our *Dark Discoveries* and JournalStone promotional video, created by Cyrus Wraith Walker, played up on the projection screen in the background.

The banquet itself was held in the Queen Anne Ballroom and featured a vast spread of New Orleans style food, and the awards ceremony was delivered in streaming video to all those horror fans unable to attend. The always funny Jeff Strand hosted the event, with various awards being presented by William F. Nolan, David Morrell, Tom Monteleone, Douglas Winter, Jonathan Maberry, Jason V Brock (DD's former Managing Editor), Chad Hensley, Lisa Morton, Bruce Boston, Rocky Wood, and a hilarious announcement for posterity delivered by the great Ramsey Campbell.

Robert R. McCammon was on hand to accept his Lifetime Achievement Award, and he gave a nice speech remembering the late Ray Bradbury. Other writers who passed away this last year, such as Dave Silva and Rick Hautala, were also remembered. Mark Miller accepted the Lifetime Achievement Award on behalf of Clive Barker, who told us that Barker was hard at work on *Abarat IV*. The Specialty Press Award went to the well-deserving Jerad Walters of Centipede Press. The Silver Hammer Award for outstanding service to the HWA went to Charles Day, and the Richard Laymon Service Award was given to James Chambers.

But without any further ado, below is the list of all the winners, and DD would like to extend a big congratulations to them. Next year's World Horror Convention will be held in Portland, Oregon, May 8-11, 2014, and the HWA will again be holding the Bram Stoker Awards™ presentation in conjunction with the convention. Guests include Nancy Holder, Jack Ketchum, Norman Partridge, Greg Staples and Paula Guran. Hope to see you there!

Awards

Superior Achievement in a NOVEL
The Drowning Girl by Caitlín R. Kiernan (Roc)

Superior Achievement in a FIRST NOVEL
Life Rage by L.L. Soares (Nightscape Press)

Superior Achievement in a YOUNG ADULT NOVEL
Flesh & Bone by Jonathan Maberry (Simon & Schuster)

Superior Achievement in a GRAPHIC NOVEL
Witch Hunts: A Graphic History of the Burning Times by Rocky Wood and Lisa Morton
(McFarland and Co., Inc.)

Superior Achievement in LONG FICTION
The Blue Heron by Gene O'Neill (Dark Regions Press)

Superior Achievement in SHORT FICTION
"Magdala Amygdala" by Lucy Snyder (*Dark Faith: Invocations*, Apex Book Company)

Superior Achievement in a SCREENPLAY
The Cabin in the Woods by Joss Whedon and Drew Goddard
(Mutant Enemy
Productions, Lionsgate)

Superior Achievement in an ANTHOLOGY
Shadow Show edited by Mort Castle and Sam Weller
(HarperCollins)

Superior Achievement in a FICTION COLLECTION (tie)
New Moon on the Water by Mort Castle (Dark Regions Press)
Black Dahlia and White Rose: Stories by Joyce Carol Oates
(Ecco Press)

Superior Achievement in NON-FICTION
Trick or Treat: A History of Halloween by Lisa Morton
(Reaktion Books)

Superior Achievement in a POETRY COLLECTION
Vampires, Zombies & Wanton Souls by Marge Simon (Elektrik Milk Bath Press)

Brian Matthews & Christopher Payne at the Happy Hour, Photo Courtesy of Douglas Wynne and Jen Salt

Dark Discoveries Invades JournalStone Video, Photo Courtesy of Cyrus Wraith Walker

Brian Matthews at the Mass Signing, Photo Courtesy of Douglas Wynne and Jen Salt

Rena Mason at the Mass Signing, Photo Courtesy of Douglas Wynne and Jen Salt

Christopher Payne, Hank Schwaeble, and Douglas Wynne at the Happy Hour Photo Courtesy of Douglas Wynne and Jen Salt

Jonathan Maberry, Ramsey Campbell, and Robert McCammon at the Mass Signing , Photo Courtesy of Douglas Wynne and Jen Salt

Douglas Wynne, Patrick Freivald, Jeffrey Wilson & Brian Matthews at the JournalStone table , Photo Courtesy of Douglas Wynne and Jen Salt

Benjamin Kane Ethridge at the Mass Signing, Photo Courtesy of Douglas Wynne and Jen Salt

Brian Matthews and Brad Hodson at the mass signing, Photo Courtesy of Brian Matthews

Patrick Freivald at the Mass Signing, Photo Courtesy of Douglas Wynne and Jen Salt

Brett Talley and friend talking with Douglas Wynne, (center), Photo Courtesy of Douglas Wynne and Jen Salt

Douglas Wynne & Ed Kurtz at the Mass Signing, Photo Courtesy of Douglas Wynne and Jen Salt

Aaron J. French with Jason and Sunni Brock and living legend William F. Nolan at the Cycatrix Press table, Photo Courtesy of Aaron J. French

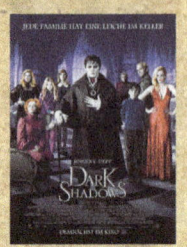

Dark Shadows – Film Review
Directed by Tim Burton
Warner Brothers, 2012
Cast: Johnny Depp, Michelle Pfiefer,
Helena Bonham Carter.

Dark Shadows is director Tim Burton's latest film production, loosely based upon the soap-opera from the late 60's/early 70's. Burton has created his own interpretation of the series as a horror comedy. However, the movie just touches on each of these genres. Sure, the main character is a vampire, and there are ghosts, a werewolf and a pumpkin patch – but I would hardly call it a horror film. The sets were beautiful and dark, but in the end there was not much to be frightened of. The main comedic elements were with Johnny Depp's character, Barnabas Collins, as a vampire who was locked away in a coffin for 200 years and then released in the 1970's hippie culture movement. Those jokes revolved around his reactions to a new world full of electricity, paved roads, short skirts and female doctors. Although being very funny, they grew short after the movie played on.

I have only watched the first three or four episode of the original soap opera (there are 1,225 episodes!) so I cannot give much of a comparison of that to Tim Burton's new vision. I can tell however, that the two cannot compare to each other. The original took a very serious and dark tone to it, where as the new version has been updated to a more upbeat feel. To me, Burton's *Dark Shadows* felt like a combination of the colors, angle and cinematography of his Sleepy Hollow coupled with the feeling of disconnection, isolation and awkwardness of *Edward Scissorhands*. I don't want to say that Tim Burton is simply utilizing the same formula time and time again to solve a different equation – but I find it difficult to believe that when you have the same director with the same composer, same cast (many of which are duplicating characters in a sense) and same cinematographers, that you will achieve a different film. Now perhaps this isn't something to hold against Burton – he's making his films the way he wants doing whatever he wants and has no desire to make a movie that is different from what he has done. This is what he likes and this is what he does. I for one would like to see him expand.

But this is a review of *Dark Shadows*, not Tim Burton. So what do I think of the movie? Overall, I liked it. But I did not love it. I would watch it again because I did enjoy many of the visuals and found most of the jokes funny. The storyline and ending didn't particularly grab me though, relying on the beautiful visions and sets to propel the movie. The special effects primarily relied on CG rather than practical effects and it showed. If you are in the mood for a light-hearted dark comedy and love the style of Tim Burton, then this film is a must-see. If you are looking for anything more than that, this will most likely disappoint.

- Reviewed by Anthony Dluzak

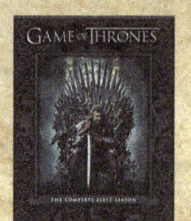

Game of Thrones
Seasons 1 & 2 – Blu-ray review
Creators: David Benioff, D.B. Weiss
Cast: Sean Bean, Lena Headey,
Peter Dinklage

This ongoing HBO series is based on the Song of Fire and Ice series of books by George R. R. Martin. The story takes place in what I would call a "low fantasy" setting. There are no elves or fairies and magic and wizards are in very short supply. At least that's how Season One starts. As Season Two progresses you can see the slow and gradual return of magic to the world of Westeros where this show is set. Still, even then the magical and supernatural elements are used sparingly but effectively, such as the mysterious and creepy white walkers, not to mention everyone's favorite beast of fantasy: dragons.

At its heart, *Game of Thrones* is a story about men and woman and all the various political intrigues, backstabbings, and dirty deals that revolved around a collection of noble houses tenuously united underneath the banner of a usurper king. The king sits upon an iron throne created from all the melted swords of the previous dynasty's enemies that everyone wants for their own. There are enemies within the kingdom that plot and scheme, not to mention the deposed heir of the last mad king, now in exile across the sea with the barbarians and powerful, albeit young, allies. Then there is the largely forgotten threat of the undead hoard from the north that is just waiting for winter to come.

In Westeros the weather seasons don't act like they do in our world. When this story begins, the lands have enjoyed a many-years-long summer, but all the signs point to the fact that winter is coming and that it's going to be a particularly long and harsh winter. And in addition to all the hardships that a mini ice age would cause, it looks like the undying white walkers shall return this winter after a thousand-year-long slumber.

Things start to fall apart for the kingdom in record time and on all fronts. There are battles to be fought of a personal nature, and those that will leave hundreds dead on the field. There are enemies on distant shores, those that share the same bed, and even those that mock death. Once the Iron Throne comes up for grabs, no less than five kings will via for it and are willing to lead thousands to slaughter to get the crown. With all that conflict, it is only natural that some die, however who dies may surprise. Know that in this world no one is safe and many times very bad things happen to good people.

Combine that rich, incredibly detailed story with beautiful settings, well done special effects, competent direction, and amazing acting (some of the best I've seen in any TV show or movie) and you have one hell of a must watch show. On that last bit, the acting, while all involved do a superb job to the last man, woman, and even child (and I usually hate watching kids trying to act), I feel special praise must go to Peter Dinklage, a little person who plays Tyrion "the imp" Lannister, a dwarf who is remarkably intelligent, pragmatic, charismatic, and just plain fun to watch every second he's on the screen. Mr. Dinklage is the break out star of the show and he richly deserved the Golden Globe and Emmy he won playing "The Imp" in season one. In a show with a cast this huge, and with as many great and memorable characters, that he should so clearly be my favorite speaks volumes to his acting chops.

As good as this TV show is, the two Blu-ray collections for Season One and Two are just as good. Not only does everything look amazing in High-def, but these discs are jammed packed to over flowing with extras. So much so that I shall save us both a lot of time and not try to list them all here. I will just say three things here about them. First, wow. Second, this is how a flagship show for a premium cable channel should be released: with tons and tons of extra features. This is a lesion Showtime needs to desperately learn, as all their seasons of *Dexter* have so far only had a pitiful amount of extras between all their seasons. And third, these Blu-rays come with a very detailed, illustrated and acted out compilation of histories all about the lands, people, religions, and past events of the world this show is set in. These were entertaining, informative, and a great way for someone like me, who had never read the books, to learn more about all the behind the scenes bits. I loved it.

Both seasons of *Game of Thrones* are winners. You will find no sophomore slump here. It is simply a great show that looks great on Blu-ray and comes packed with a bunch of cool extras. This one is a no-brainer, you need to get these Blu-rays. Consider both seasons very highly recommended.

- Reviewed By Brian M. Sammons

Don't Stand So Close
Eric Red
Short, Scary Tales Publications
Trade Paperback, 2012, $14.95, 277pp

Have you ever had a crush on your junior high school teacher, or a high school teacher, or even a professor in college? This question is directed as much to the ladies as to the men. I know I did when growing up. My first crush goes as far back as the sixth grade when I had a total crush on the teacher in the next room. I couldn't get my mind off of her. I even used to ride my bicycle past her house on occasion. Today, that would be called stalking.

In college, I had a hot obsession with my psychology professor, who also taught German. I took German so I could be close to her and ended up barely passing the course. It screwed up my GPA. Needless to say, I didn't sign up for German 102, no matter how beautiful the blond professor was. Ah, the good old days of youth and sexual obsession. Yes, sexual obsession because that's exactly what it was.

Well, *Don't Stand So Close* by Eric Red raises it up a notch and increases the stakes as this dark novel delves into obsession, perverted sex, and murder in the first degree.

This is definitely my kind of story.

The story centers on seventeen-year-old Matt Poe, who has just moved from California to a small town in Iowa, and it's not near Field of Dreams, either. Matt's mother is a teacher, and this is where her new job has taken her. I come from a southern town where everybody knows you and your business. I therefore understood the culture shock Matt goes through at being the new kid on the block in a small mid-western community. Since Matt is a good-looking California teenager, it isn't long before he makes friends with Rusty and Grace. Rusty is a strange kid, who stays by himself, but is smart with a high IQ. Grace is also smart, a cheerleader, the girlfriend of the football captain, and the daughter of the local sheriff. Matt, however, only eyes for his teacher, Linda Hayden. Naturally, she's older, great looking, sexual in every sense of the word, and seems to have an eye for the new kid in school.

It isn't long before Ms. Hayden offers to tutor Matt after school, and it isn't long before one thing leads to another and the two are doing the hanky-panky. In fact, Matt quickly becomes obsessed with the teacher and the hot sex they have. Things, however, aren't what they seem. Within a short span of time, other kids start dying in ways which seem like accidents but aren't. Matt soon grows leery of Ms. Hayden, especially when he finds himself developing feelings for Grace in an unexpected way.

The teacher is certainly steadfast in what she wants. She refuses to let Matt go. You see Ms. Hayden has plans for Matt … plans that will destroy his life in ways he could never dream of suspect. Ms. Hayden is a sexual predator of the worse kind and Matt isn't her first victim. What started out as a fantasy fulfilled quickly turns into a nightmare that simply won't end.

As the old saying goes, "Be careful what you wish for. You might get it."

Eric Red, the author, is generally known for his screenplay writing and directing. He wrote the great cult films *The Hitcher* (1986) and *Near Dark* (1987) and *Blue Steel* (1989), plus the revised version of *The Hitcher* (2007) with two other screenwriters. Though he's also written a number of short stories in the suspense genre, *Don't Stand So Close* is his first novel. My only question is what took him so long to finally write a book?

Mr. Red is clearly a very talented author who sees descriptive imagery with the eyes of a screenwriter and director. He captures everything perfectly in his novel from the personalities of the characters, the hunger a student has for his teacher, the atmosphere of small-town life, and the edge-of-your-seat suspense that keeps you wondering what will happen next. I not only hope *Don't Stand So Close* won't be Eric Red's only novel, but that it will be turned into a feature film in the near future. Though this actress is older than I imagined Linda Hayden to be, I kept seeing her face in the role of the teacher – Lena Olin. She would be the perfect Linda Hayden.

All in all, *Don't Stand So Close* was a pleasant surprise I greatly enjoyed. I'm now happy my sexual fantasy about my college professor remained a fantasy and nothing else. This novel does for high school students what the movie, *Fatal Attraction*, did for married men back during the late eighties. Keep the fantasy in your mind and your zipper pulled up no matter how strong the allure. That's how you stay sane and alive.

- Reviewed by Wayne C. Rogers

Holes for Faces
By Ramsey Campbell
Dark Regions Press
ISBN: 781937128449
2013; $15.99

It's important to place the short story output of vastly important and influential authors into short story collections every decade or so. Although that doesn't mean that those collections are going to be masterworks themselves. One can hardly predict how those short stories might fit together when it comes time to collect them, or even gauge the quality from decade-to-decade.

Holes for Faces is one such book, as it collects the short story output of Ramsey Campbell from the last decade or so in one place. Easily one of the most influential writers in the horror genre, Campbell has not only redefined the contemporary ghost story, but has also managed to find both critical and popular appeal in the genre for at minimum, the past thirty years. So it's an important book based on Campbell's vast influence and output, but is it a good book?

This is a book of short story reprints with the exception of the titular story, which doesn't appear to have been published before. There are some odd selections in here too, such as 'With the Angels'. Based on my internet research, 'With the Angels' was only released as a printed chapbook. The online listing I found for its original printing suggests it is 300 pages in length, and its Amazon page suggests the chapbook itself doesn't actually exist when you try to purchase it.

This book focuses heavily on Campbell's work in the ghost story sub-genre and less on his very particular "urban grotesque" work. While the author is often very good at blending both of these things together, many of these short stories are very traditional ghost stories. That said, this is definitely a distinctive Ramsey Campbell collection, as all his usual elements are still evident here: children, Christmas, vacations, telephone/internet communication, film, and madness.

With the exceptions of 'Peep' and 'Chucky Comes to Liverpool', and my personal favorites from the selections, 'Getting It Wrong' and 'The Decorations', a lot of these stories feel like they are rehashing old territory. 'Holes for Faces'leans towards the more literary side of things in the most clichéd sense of the label 'contemporary literature'. And while it's an interesting experiment, it is upon its conclusion, a straightforward ghost story. And that renders the rest of the unique narrative pointless.

I did find some interesting minor changes in the work. I found a lot of crime fiction elements in many of these stories, and some political commentary as well, which struck me as unique to Campbell's usual techniques.

Overall however, this is probably not a good introductory book to Campbell's work, and I suspect those interested in the authors output from a critical standpoint might find this largely rehashing his previously covered ground. I would recommend this to readers who have enjoyed what they've read of Campbell's fiction in the past, but aren't overly studious of technique or particularly interested in the scholarly aspects of the authors work. Of course, all of my opinions are void if a reader is simply looking to read some quality ghost stories – as this may be a definitive work of that particular sub-genre.

- Reviewed by Michael Colangelo

Midnight Echo, the Magazine of the Australian Horror Writers Association
Issue #9: Myths and Legends, May 2013
By Various Contributors
Pages: 149

"Horror is its own mythology…"

Geoff Brown, editor of Midnight Echo's Myths and Legend issue, speaks to the core of what horror is.

It is tales that created some of the deepest fears we still live with. We begged to hear them, even though we knew sleep would elude us.

We grew up with fairy tales intended to make us dream of magic, beauty, or heroic deeds.

Those are not here.

This issue focuses on the ancestors of those tales; the ones told in hushed tones in an attempt to warn us and make us stay inside when night falls. Midnight Echo's Issue 9 has removed the happily-ever-afters from these stories and replaced them with something more cringe-worthy.

The characters you know are still here: the old crone in the woods, the elusive fae, even merfolk. But their masks have been stripped away, leaving only the undisguised horror of truly legendary creatures. These tales go beyond the façade of goodness to a place where evil is done for sport or because… well, one just can't help it.

Even Mel Gannon's cover artwork speaks to the evil disturbia in these pages. Even as I write this, I'm staring at the art, expecting the little girl thing on the cover to lift its head and reach for me.

But Midnight Echo isn't only fiction.

There's an article by Robin Furth on the legends used in Stephen King's Dark Tower series. A non-fiction article by Tony Vilgotsky on Russian folklore, which I admit to knowing precious little about, was fascinating. Before this read, I hadn't known that some of the symbolism from Russian legends bled into the Native American stories I grew up with.

This magazine the covers the entire horror genre: film, comics, poetry, and in this issue includes interviews with award-winning authors Jonathan Maberry and James A. Moore.

It's good to see a horror magazine gaining a foothold in the speculative fiction market.

- Reviewed by Eden Royce

The Evolutionist
By: Rena Mason
Nightscape Press
256 Pages

When Stacy Troy begins to endure one vivid, frightful nightmare after the next, she comes to the conclusion something has to give. A lady of many hats, upper middle class suburban housewife, mother, fundraiser coordinator and socialite, her hectic schedule begins to suffer as a result of increasing insomnia and night terror. Reluctantly she agrees to see a therapist. Dr. Light's techniques seem conventional enough, yet there's something a little off about the good doctor. As his eccentric demeanor becomes more prevalent, so do the frequency of Stacy's appointments. Gradually she loses an ongoing battle with distinguishing between fantasy and reality. Will Stacy be able to overcome the grisly symbolism within her dreams or will reality prevail as she adapts the persona of Evolutionist?

Author Rena Mason's debut novel is a highly imaginative, ambitious tale of supernatural themes. Her use of dreams and the subconscious to showcase the gory macabre is nothing shy of brilliant. We virtually feel the melancholy and despair within her character as she suffers a loss of intimacy with her friends, her absent husband, and her increasingly estranged teenage son. Her dreams depict a ghastly slaughter with an apocalyptic back drop as each of her neighbors and loved ones are dismembered and rendered helpless.

The portrayal of upper middle class/socialite America is illustrated so flawlessly it's comical. Everything from empty gestures such as air kissing, infatuation with Starbucks, shopping, book clubs and Pilates are reflective of a submissive, shallow society. Mason showcases Stacy and her friends' activities with pinpoint precision, giving average readers a look into a way of life otherwise unknown. They become our guilty pleasure comparable to the reality television shows that flood the cable networks today.

Adapting Stacy's first person point of view is executed with finesse and ease. A tremendous degree of emotion is captured while refraining on the repetitive or mundane. We feel Ms. Troy's plight and subconsciously cheer her on in hopes of overcoming her inner turmoil. The interpersonal relationships that exist with her husband, parents, son and friends are created to effectively enhance the very realistic, human qualities of Stacy. Within our own psyche we find ourselves comparing our own relationships, with nostalgia and reminiscence, Mason's prose often evokes a certain sense of living vicariously through one Stacy Troy.

The descriptions of Stacy's visions and dreams are so vivid we sense a virtual kaleidoscope of living Technicolor spiraling before us. This novel would make an excellent translation unto the big screen if directed properly. The surrealistic feel and unexpected plot twists within the final act are reminiscent of a veteran author, most comfortable on the New York Times best sellers list. Make way for a new Madam of Macabre, for Rena Mason has arrived.

- Reviewed by Rick Amortis

Deep Cuts: 19 Tales of Mayhem, Menace, and Misery
Edited by Angel Leigh McCoy,
E.S. Magill, and Chris Marrs
Evil Jester Press
ISBN: 978-0615750897
February, 2013; $14.95 PB

Deep Cuts is a celebration of the influence of female horror writers, released for Women in Horror Month, 2013. The title refers to "deep cuts" in music – those great tracks on an album that do not get commercial airtime or are overshadowed by the popular hits. In a clever move, the editors required each submission to come with a short recommendation for a story by a woman writer, a deep cut from the history of horror fiction. The result is an anthology that reflects the strength of the female voice in horror today, and reminds us that it has always been present. It was a smart choice, and one that elevates the anthology by giving historical context and providing intriguing suggestions for additional reading – an added value most anthologies don't provide. The other smart editorial decision was to open the anthology to submissions by men and women. Despite honorable intentions, I am not sure how effectively we promote diversity in writing through exclusionary practices. If women horror writers are every bit as capable as the men they can hold their own in a fair competition just fine. And *Deep Cuts* is a wonderful demonstration that they can, and always have been able to. The inclusion of male authors also reminds us that it is not only female readers and writers that have been shaped by the great women of horror fiction. The anthology is a great celebration of Women in Horror Month in ways that a simple collection from women authors would not have been.

The stories within come from a diverse group of authors, including many award-winning writers whose work has appeared in top publications. And, by and large, these stories cut quite deep. These are stories filled with fear and pain. Character after character is filled with toxic rage, perverse obsession, or unrelenting need. Horrific sexual violence is frequently present or at least threatened. We see terrible crimes and their lingering aftermath. Relationships are irreparably torn and spirits crushed in a world with little justice or redemption. The monsters within are, at times, demonic or ghostly, and at others merely human. In some cases, it is not possible to say whether the events described are the result of the supernatural or delusion. The prose and narrative voice is generally strong across the board. There is, at most, one story that struck me as relatively undeveloped and unpolished, so that it stood out poorly against the rest of the material. A second, while well-written, seemed thematically inconsistent with the overall bleak worldview of the rest, introducing a discordant element of ultimate light into the universe despite the darkness of the events described. But, as a group, the stories are quite disturbing and compelling, and most mature horror fans should be able to find multiple pieces that they enjoy; more than enough to justify getting a copy. Evaluated as a horror anthology, *Deep Cuts* is a clear success, and I would not be surprised to see it get some attention at year's end when award nominations begin to circulate.

As for the deep cuts themselves, the story recommendations reflect a nice mix of historic and contemporary writers, and the editors included an appendix containing the suggestions attached to many submissions that did not make the anthology itself, yielding sixty pieces for the reader's consideration. The stories described are an intriguing archeology of horror written by women. Even a seasoned horror fan will likely discover something she or he has not read, and will at least be reminded of gems perhaps forgotten from years past. You could argue that a few of these are more chart-toppers than deep cuts (who has

not read *The Lottery*?) but that is a quibble. As a celebration of the female horror writer, this effort has made a unique contribution and is a great achievement.

- Reviewed by K. H. Vaughan

Evil Dead – film review
Ghosthouse Pictures
Directed by Fede Alvarez

Sam Raimi's 1981 classic splatter fest, *The Evil Dead*, is my fifth favorite horror film of all time and is a much beloved genre classic. Working with almost no budget, Raimi gave us a truly funny, sickeningly twisted, scary, and original film. It is one of only a handful of horror films since the forties and fifties that we can call a masterpiece.

When word spread that there was to be a remake, fans of the original film were in an uproar, me included. As I have stated before, do not remake the great films! Remake a film that was flawed and could have been better. We do not need new versions of *Halloween*, *Carrie*, *Suspiria*, *A Nightmare on Elm Street*, and *TheThing*. Be original and write something new and pepper your film with nods to your favorite films.

I was ready to write off this new version until I heard that Sam Raimi and Bruce Campbell endorsed it. They did not just produce the film to add cred to the proceedings, they handpicked the director and, after seeing the finished film, came out publically in support of it. I was a bit more interested after knowing this but I was still leery of remaking such a classic.

I am here to tell you that, while not a classic itself and suffering from quite a few problems, the remake of *Evil Dead* is a fun, bloody, at times spooky, good time.

The spirit of the 1981 original is there at almost every moment. The buildup takes a bit longer than the original but, thankfully, we follow a few interesting characters until the events get going.

The story is basically the same. Five twentysomethings go deep into the woods, stay at a cabin, discover a Book of the Dead, and unleash violent and demonic forces. A new development works nicely, as their reason for being there is to help Mia, played by Jane Levy, go cold turkey and attempt to kick her life threatening heroin habit. It is a good touch and adds some drama to the proceedings.

She is joined by her brother David, played by Shiloh Fernandez, and three of their friends played by Jessica Lucas, Elizabeth Blackmore, and indie film mainstay Lou Taylor Pucci, whose Eric is the one that opens the book and reads the passage that unleashes the demons in the woods. Lucas plays Olivia and Blackmore plays Natalie. If you put the first letters of all five main character's names together they spell Demon; a nice in joke for us fans.

The performances are better than a movie like this deserves but that is not why we are here. We are horror fans and we crave blood and scares. *Evil Dead* gives us some scares and even more blood... lots and lots of blood. There is more blood in this film than any film of the past 25 or 30 years and I am shocked that the film got away with an R rating from the ever skittish ratings board. I liked the gore in this film and how they handled it. There is very little CGI and the director has stated that he wanted to go "old school" in creating the gore. I am glad he chose to do it this way, as it gives the film its proper grotesqueness; one of the standouts being the scene where a possessed character runs her tongue up the sharp end of a box cutter and splits it in two. Then she French kisses another character that writhes in horror. Great stuff! Of course the whole film is a nod to Raimi, but the final 30 minutes are a true love letter to the master director's love of outrageous gore as they fill the screen with buckets and buckets of blood.

Director Alvarez floods the film with nods to some great horror films while making it his own. The opening credits play over an askew aerial shot of a car driving through the wooded hills. This is an obvious reference to the opening titles of Kubrick's *The Shining*. There are a couple of references to *The Exorcist* by way of the make-up and sound effects when characters become possessed. Of course there are many nods to the original film but they are handled subtly and with restraint. We get our first one at the opening when Mia's brother walks over to greet her. Mia is sitting on the car from the original film. We are also treated to the sawed off shotgun, the machete, the chainsaw, and more. The references are a large part of the fun.

The look of the film is appropriately grimy. You can almost smell the rotting flesh as we snake through shots littered with hanging cat carcasses and floors covered in blood and god knows what else. I was taken back to the uneasy feelings I had watching Raimi's original film and the brilliantly disgusting set design for Tobe Hooper's *The Texas Chainsaw Massacre*. Those two films created, in a good way, a sickening atmosphere that stayed with you. This film does just that in its design.

There are some problems with the film as there would be with any remake of a beloved classic. One major problem for me is the "fits and starts" approach to the attacks by the demons. In Raimi's original, once it started it didn't stop and the audience was taken on a frightening roller coaster ride. By the end of his film we couldn't catch our breath. In the remake, things begin and our blood pressures rise but then they let up, almost allowing us a breather to ready our senses for the next attack. If the original taught us anything, just let it roll. Once it gets going don't give us a break. Force us to be terrorized until you tell us it is over. The last 10 minutes do go nonstop but that is how it should have been as soon as the demons were unleashed. It is as Russell Crowe spoke in his most famous line from the film *Gladiator*, "Unleash Hell!" Yeah, do it!

Another problem I have is the trusty audience pleasing, cheer baiting, and gotcha line made famous and used to annoyance since, by Sigourney Weaver in James Cameron's *Aliens* when she told the mother alien to "Get away from her you bitch!" Here there are more than a few and they always seem to end in "bitch" or "mother fucker" to show us how evil or tough someone/thing may be. One of those kinds of lines is bad enough but we are treated to at least five or more of them with most of them spoken by the possessed. That kind of dialogue is passé and silly.

The sequence of the possessed girl trapped under the floor is not near as good as the original film. Her make-up is good but her eyes have too much life in them. In the Raimi version the girl had white lifeless eyes and it made her character all the more frightening. Here the scene, while having its moments, falls a bit flat.

The demonic stuff in the film is fun but not nearly as scary as the original. Raimi gave us brutally frightening demons and the distorted voices were terrifying. Here, the voices are barely distorted so when the possessed females say lines such as "I will eat your soul" and "you will all die tonight" it comes across as silly but not scary.

A large problem for me was the film's lack of humor. It is relentlessly grim from the first frame to the last. We smile at the clever film references but that is about it. There is no humor and a remake based on a film that was chock full of cleverly placed macabre humor should have plenty.

My final complaint about the film is not the film's fault at all. It is the inevitable comparison with the original. As I said, Sam Raimi's film is a masterpiece and one of the finest examples of true horror ever put to film. This film is no masterpiece but stands to be one of the more entertaining horror films in years.

I just feel that I do not need to own this film because, frankly, if I get in the mood to watch *Evil Dead*, I will just put in Raimi's original.

This is not to say I do not like this new film. I did enjoy *Evil Dead*; quite a bit actually and more than I thought I would. Despite its problems I had tons of fun with it. Director Alvarez knows how to craft a horror film and I am excited to see where his career takes him.

Despite its flaws, this is a good example of how to handle a remake. This film is fun from the start and gives horror audiences what is all too often lacking in the modern horror film; a blood splattered good time without being condescending to the filmgoer.

Fede Alvarez's *Evil Dead* is a profoundly violent and gruesome horror film that, once the backlash dies down, will be regarded as one of the better remakes of recent years.

- Reviewed by Anthony C. Francis

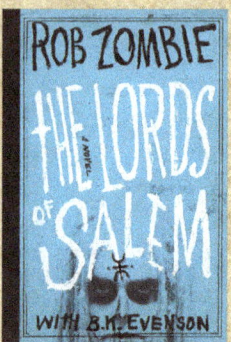

The Lords of Salem
Rob Zombie, with B.K. Evenson
Grand Central Publishing
March 2013

The plot of Rob Zombie's new novel is quite straightforward. A coven of witches is discovered in Salem, Massachusetts, in 1692. Two civic leaders, the Reverend John Hawthorne and Justice Samuel Mather, assisted by the Magnus brothers, take it upon themselves to capture, try and convict, and execute the coven, headed by Margaret Morgen. She and her followers are summarily tortured and condemned to excruciating — and lovingly described — torments before released by death. With her final words, Morgan curses the witchfinders, the town of Salem, and their progeny, declaring that their descendants will be used, willingly or not, to bring about the return of their Master.

Cut to Salem, present day. We are introduced to Heide Hawthorne, a descendent of John Hawthorne (apparently through her father). She is a DJ for the local rock station and, as part of her job, plays a mysterious black-metal recording sent to her office by a group that calls itself "The Lords of Salem." She unwittingly participates in fulfilling the long-forgotten curse as she plays the record on the air, triggering a clamorous and wildly positive feedback from female listeners (males uniformly hate the music) and — without her realizing it — truly horrific responses from several women ... not coincidentally descendants of Mather and the Magnuses.

At the same time, Heide's life takes a number of alarming turns, including dreams that may or may not be real; hideous experiences — or perhaps hallucinations — in an empty apartment down the hall; growing inability to control her need for drugs to help her make sense of what is happening; and a curiously ominous growing relationship with her landlady Lacy and Lacy's two sisters ... reminders, perhaps, of Shakespeare's three weird sisters at the beginning of Macbeth (a 17th-century response to the witchcraft scare), with just a touch of Ruth Gordon's Minnie Castevet from Rosemary's Baby.

The supporting cast — primarily Heide's co-workers at the radio station and an antiquarian expert on the original witchcraft trials — are either ciphers or innocents ... at least as far as the curse on Salem is concerned. They are essentially present to suggest how far removed from human community Heide becomes as a result of her experiences and how little anyone can do to forestall what is happening. As Lacy says when confronting the dying antiquarian, no matter what notes he or anyone else takes, what efforts he makes to connect the dots and discover the truth, he is, and has been from the beginning, powerless.

On a readerly level, *The Lords of Salem* is solidly written. I don't know how much B.K. Everson contributed to the actual text, but the result of the collaboration in general succeeds. There is a bit of an anachronistic moment on the first page when the witch's intended victim wonders fleeting if she were drunk, then remembers that she has been abstaining out of fear of alcohol's effects on her unborn baby — this, in 1692, when drinking was standard for almost everyone since the water was usually more immediately harmful than beer. Otherwise, there is nothing exceptionable in the text; readers coming to experience Rob Zombie's cinematic imagination reproduced in prose will find blood and gore aplenty, with generous helpings of mayhem and murder.

Which leads to one of two concerns about the novel, both conceptual rather than directly literary.

First, *The Lords of Salem* is a film tie-in; the movie will be released shortly after the book, but presumably it is in its near-final form. What results, a film-into-novel, is a mode of presentation that, particularly for horror, makes it difficult to recreate the suspense of film. The linear nature of written words gives advance warning of impending horrors, whereas a film can abruptly present them, sustained by lighting, music, camera angles, all perceived within a fraction of a second. The book must, as it were, stop the action and describe, in as much detail as possible. The first chapter is devoted to killing a pregnant woman (told from her point of view). The second spends even more time invoking the Dark Lord and, again in great detail, witnessing the destruction of the newborn. As a result, when the book tries to reproduce the same effects that readers anticipate in a film, it seems to drag.

Second, the novel falls into a logical trap almost endemic to horror tales concerning witches, vampires, and demons. In the late 17th-century, Sir Thomas Browne, one of the last supporters of witch hunting, defended his belief in witchcraft with what has become the apothegm "No witches, no God." That is, if there were no witches, the avatars of all things evil, then there would be no need for God. Since the former exist, he argued, so must the latter.

By removing half of Browne's equation — reducing it to simple "no God" — many contemporary horror writers inadvertently undercut the power of their stories. In *The Lords of Satan,* there is in fact no true opposition to the witches' plans, simple the incremental exploitation of evil. They recite cant phrasing from stereotypical Satan-worship, but without the existence (at least in the novel) of a God-figure, the words become meaningless. There is no threat to them for blaspheming; therefore there is neither strength nor courage in their apparent defiance. In the opening books of *Paradise Lost,* one of the most influential works of the latter 17th century, Satan's rebellion and his vaunting words challenging and repudiating God only work if readers believe that Satan believes in such a being and that He is capable of inflicting far worse that Satan already suffers. Remove God, and Satan's magnificent words epitomize empty rhetoric.

The Lords of Salem is well enough written and is probably faithful to the essence of the film to come. For me, however, it remains curiously flat and unconvincing.

- Review by Michael R. Collings

Shivers 7
Edited by Richard Chizmar
Cemetery Dance Publications
ISBN: 978-158767-225-5
July, 2013; $20.00 TPB

For the last twelve or thirteen years, Cemetery Dance has been putting out a regular horror anthology series called *Shivers*. This makes book number seven in the well-regarded line. Featuring mostly new stories, and a few choice reprints, this is another solid entry.

For the curious, the previously published tales are as follows: Stephen King's "The Weeds" (a mid-1970s Cavalier magazine publication later turned into a segment of the movie Creepshow), Clive Barker's "The Departed" (originally published as "Hermoine and the Moon" in 1992), Norman Partridge's " Red Rover, Red Rover" (from the short-lived online magazine The Spook), and Robert Morrish's "Memory Lane."

The rest of the stories are brand new by Graham Masterton, Rick Hautala, Bill Pronzini, Lisa Morton, Scott Nicholson, Norman Prentiss, Lisa Tuttle, Al Sarrantonio, Tim Waggoner, Del James, Brian James Freeman, Kaaron Warron, Bev Vincent, Roberta Lannes, Darren Speegle, Rio Youers, Joel Arnold, Don D'Ammassa and Travis Heernan. As usual, it is a diverse collection of dark stories without a unifying theme – much as their magazine usually is (themed issues notwithstanding).

I liked most of the stories and most were very solid. There's something for everyone in this book. If you're a collector or fan of King and/or Barker's work, you've got a couple of rare and uncollected stories there. If you're a fan of some of the CD regulars, there are plenty of those folks. And if you're looking to check out some newer writers, there's a few of them as well. It's nice to see a regular horror/dark fantasy anthology series that's maintained consistency and is coming out on a regular basis. Recommended.

- Reviewed by Trever Nordgren

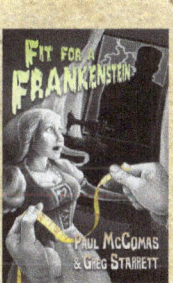

Fit for a Frankenstein
by Paul McComas and Greg Starrett
Walkabout Publishing
ISBN: 978-1-4826-2233-1
May 2013, $8.99

This is the first collaborative novella by Paul McComas, award-winning author and editor of six previous titles, and Greg Starrett, for whom this is a literary debut.

Fit for a Frankenstein is the solution to a mild inconsistency to be found in the fourth entry in Universal's classic Frankenstein series, released in 1942. Early in the film, Ygor and the monster leave the original village in a disheveled state, but shortly arrive in Vasaria cleaned up and sporting new threads. This novella fills in the gaps and explains where the monster got such an impressive suit from.

It is obvious that McComas and Starrett share a profound love for the glorious films that make up the Universal horror film back catalogue, and this shines through their effervescent writing laced with inside-jokes and subtle nods to the originals. Comparisons to the classic *Young Frankenstein* are unavoidable, but the authors take a different direction to Brooks, stitching together a grisly mass of groan-worthy puns and a smattering of Benny Hill-type bawdiness, resulting in a novella that can stand on its own size 14 feet.

Bela Lugosi's occasionally impenetrable accent is deftly

depicted with an excessive use of the letters 'v' and 'z' to wonderful effect and it requires just a few paragraphs to fully embrace the rhythm of his dialogue. Ygor is a hunchback of singular determination and devious thoughts, and the authors have fleshed him out perfectly, likewise with the supporting characters who sport a surprising amount of back story considering their scant appearances. Jammed full of literary easter eggs for horror fans, particular highlights include a confused conversation worthy of Abbot and Costello and a wonderful dream sequence wherein Ygor sees the past and future fates of the monster from the creature's point of view, predicting the brain transplant to come.

If I have one complaint it is that the story is over far too soon, and I would relish a full novelization of this and other Frankenstein films told from Ygor's point of view.

Recommended.

- Reviewed by Neil Baker

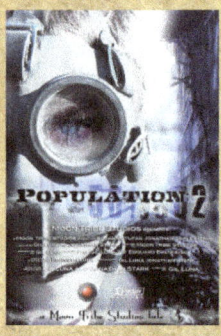

Population: 2
The Chaos of Unintended Consequences
– Film Review
Producers: Gil Luna and Jonathan Stark
Director: Gil Luna
Starring: Suzanne Tufan and
Jonathan Ashley Hall
Music: Edouard Brenneisen

Villainy abounds in this post-apocalyptic movie; but it is a vast, impersonal evil, that hinges more on humanity's inherent greed and stupidity than in eldritch terrors from other dimensions. There is no banishing the evil that animated the holocaust that has consumed all of humanity. Only Suzanne Tufan's Lilith remains.

We meet Lilith after humanity has been reduced to only her, alone with memories and artifacts of the defunct civilization. The somber mood is helped along by skillful use of Brenneisen's score, eerie and haunting at its best, still evocative at its worst. An excellent use of the score is its absence in the most emotional parts of the movie, leading the audience into the mindset that even the music has deserted Lilith.

A central theme of the movie is that the true evil is OmniCorp, which produces such miracles as the Solar Shield (which ends up working a little *too* well (judging from inference), and the Pandora Pill, billed as a discreet way to terminate a pregnancy. The males in this story are uniformly evil by act or omission, serving only the will of OmniCorp. The CEO of OmniCorp, Vincent Velo, never takes responsibility, and is only occupied with dodging the responsibility for his actions, and escaping the consequences. Lilith's husband, Simon Prime, is the CEO's mouthpiece, but not even his placement assures safe passage into a 'habitat' where the chosen people will live while the world burns.

In contrast, the women in the story are portrayed as being warm, sociable and caring, unless corrupted by contact with OmniCorp.

In order to improve their chances of being included on "The List", Simon drugs Lilith with the Pandora Pill. He has turned his traditional roles of husband and father on their collective head. Instead of protector and guardian, his role is merely as executor of OmniCorp's policies. In a fit of irony, Simon's acts avail him nothing, Vincent Velo telling him that the habitat will only support one person. Vincent Velo might well be considered 'the mouth of Sauron.', as he tells Simon that he doesn't have discretion on who or who will not be allowed into the habitat.

In terms of broad strokes, this movie illustrates deep unease with at least three modern developments: The rise of international corporations, the loss of appreciating a single life as unique and precious, and technology that outpaces any attempt to contain it.

The rise of corporations, billed as the 'new government', but accountable to no one, is a source of anxiety for many people, in and out of government. The rapid growth of technology feeds a depersonalization, in which it is no longer necessary to meet people in order to communicate. Lastly, technology has replaced magic as forbidden lore: once set forth on the world, it cannot be contained, unless by a greater magic.

The real lesson of the film seems to be that the real magic was in people, and that in wasting people, the world squandered its best chance for survival.

- Reviewed by Jim Smiley

The Dark Man
By Stephen King
Cemetery Dance Publications
ISBN: 978-1-58767-421-1; 978-1-58767-425-9
July, 2013; Trade HC $25.00, Slipcased HC $49.95

A special Limited Edition hardcover publication of an early poem by Stephen King from his college days, The Dark Man, is coming out soon from Cemetery Dance. Originally published in a college journal at University of Maine back in 1969, this is its first mass-market publication.

The Dark Man is significant to many Stephen King fans in that it features the first appearance of Randall Flagg, aka: The Walking Dude – later to be a major character in King's landmark novel The Stand. The moody, dark poem is interpreted by fellow Maine resident, artist Glenn Chadbourne, in 80+ pages of new black and white artwork. Collaboration in the true sense of the word, Glenn takes King's words and creates startling imagery to accompany it. (The poem follows in the back of the book sans artwork for those who want to read it straight through.)

The poem stands as one of King's strongest still and the added artwork is a treat. Although it's drawn out line by line with the art, it works very well and goes along with other illustrated short stories and single poems that have been published this way. The signed/numbered and signed/lettered editions sold out quickly pre-publication but you can still grab a copy of the unsigned one in either a nice slipcase with a bonus bookmark, or just the book itself. Recommended.

- Reviewed by Trever Nordgren

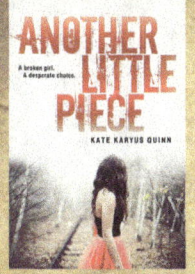

Another Little Piece
By Kate Karyus Quinn
Harper Teen
Hardcover, young adult, $17.99, 432 pages.

Stumbling out of the tree line screaming drenched in blood, Annaliese disappears, only to reappear a year later with no memories of who she is, or even who she was. Intertwining you into a story caught between the dangerous place that lurks in the midst of the past and future.

Annaliese is a girl who has lived many lives, displaying and taking advantage of the darkest part of the soul. Tempting those that will do anything and give everything for the allure of love. Annaliese holds a great power, one that grants the deepest wish, for a small price. For Annaliese, enticing the vulnerable ones is easy, those are the ones that that will give the ultimate sacrifice for the promise she can give them. Wielding the one thing that these girls would pay with their life for…perfect love.

When her memory gently starts to creep back, she begins to remember the horrific things that she has done. As her mind awakens to the paths that she has crossed, she realizes she has been a girl with too many names to remember, a monster in her own right. What she doesn't understand is that the past is coming for her, and the path of destruction she left behind leaves a wake of blood and tears. Taking with it, the girls who were willing to give the ultimate sacrifice for what they think is love.

Like from a film reel, scenes play in Annaliese's mind as she tries to piece together the horrors, making her re- live how she cut herself out of one girl, only to be eaten into another. Soon she realizes that the consequences of having such a strong power, it is like a hunger that will devour you. Bite by bite she disappears, and yet somehow it still isn't enough to feed what she really wanted.

Echoing back and forth between the past and the present, Annaleise falls into dark and dangerous waters. Once she is able to see with her eyes wide open, she realizes that they are tainted with the blood others.

A dark, intense, savage read, with shifting timelines, and lyrical interludes. With both horror and beauty, this harrowing tale comes to life. Like a snowflake scattered in the wind, it wasn't until the last page that the pieces fell into place, creating the most brilliant masterpiece.

Beautifully and eloquently written, Kate Karyus Quinn splays a horrifically dark and intense novel before us. She opens her heart for everyone to take a little piece. *Another Little Piece* rips your heart out and leaves you wanting for more.

- Reviewed by Amy Shane

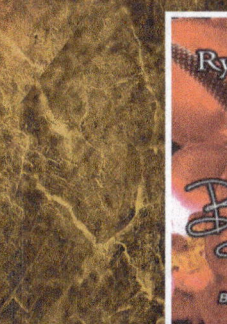
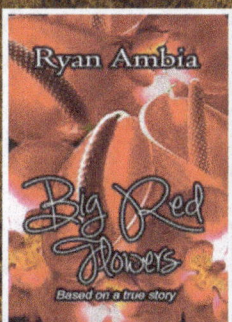

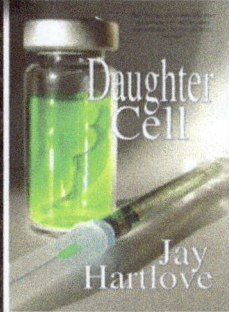

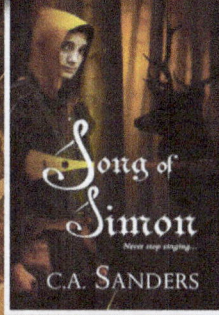
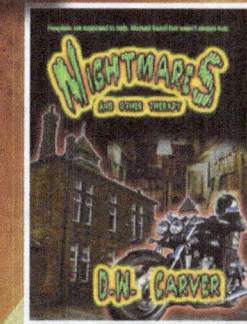

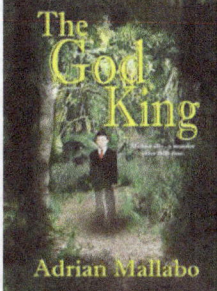

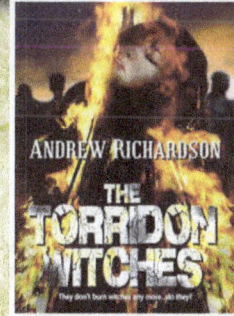

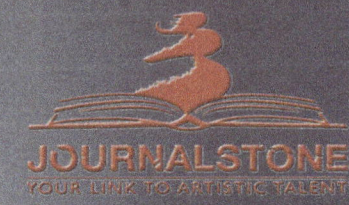